KNOCK ON THE SKY

A NOVEL

JAMES RANDALL MILLER

For my children, Jamie, Max, Patrick, and Jordan.
Each of you shines brightly in your own unique way.

Knock on the sky and listen to the sound.
— ZEN SAYING

Of God and wind I have not seen, yet I am touched by both.
— JAMES RANDALL MILLER

1

"LOOK AT YOUR SAILS, Jon David! They're flapping like a flag in the wind. In nautical terms, you're 'in irons,' which means if you keep doing this, we'll just sit here all day looking like idiots. Remember, it's futile to sail straight into the wind. Your sails need to divert wind to move the boat."

"Okay, Chance, what the hell should I do?" the novice sailor asked.

"Find a point on the horizon and zig-zag the boat back and forth toward it," his father-in-law replied. "It's called tacking."

"It still doesn't seem possible that a boat will move forward when you're heading into the wind."

"Let me throw a little physics at you. Moving into the wind requires the boat's sail and keel to work together in harmony. The sail is an airfoil, like the wing of an airplane. Wind takes longer to travel over one side of the sail than the other, and this creates a pressure difference called 'lift.' It pushes the sail perpendicular to the wind direction. The keel provides resistance to this sideways movement, and the combined forces of the keel and sail create forward motion. So, with your sails flapping, there's no pressure difference and no lift. Got it?"

"I do. Being 'in irons' means it's time to have a soda."

Chance rolled his eyes. "Yeah, I suppose you're right. We might as well eat, too. Try not to sink us while I get the cooler."

"Aye, aye, Cap'n, sir."

Jon David leaned back and let the sunshine bathe his face. The gentle Chesapeake Bay waves lapping against the boat added to the peace of the moment. He sighed, knowing this feeling was fleeting. There was news to share that Chance wouldn't take well.

"Here, grab the Cokes before I drop them."

Jon David plucked the ice-cold bottles from Chance's hand.

"I have a powerful thirst, so crack one open for me," said Chance.

"It'll be my pleasure. What's on the spit for lunch?"

"Well, Mr. Landlubber, thinking you might be retching over the side all day, I packed nothing but blandness. Are you ready to eat your weight in saltine crackers?"

"Ugh. Actually, I'm craving a greasy pizza right now. And thanks for your lack of faith in my seaworthiness."

Chance chuckled. "I'm giving you a hard time. I made some killer sardine sandwiches. It's the perfect meal for sailing." He tossed one to his son-in-law.

Jon David removed the sandwich from the plastic bag, took a large bite, and swallowed it with a swig of Coke. "Excellent grub, Cap'n Ahab."

The older man smirked. He gulped down the rest of his drink. "I'm enjoying our time together."

"Me, too. And, with all the progress I'm making today, it'll only take sixty more years of your schooling for me to become a decent sailor."

Chance laughed. "You're doing okay. Riley is the one who impresses me. At the age of three, my grandson is a natural-born sailor. He'd blow a gasket if he knew we were sailing today without him."

"He loves being with you."

"Yeah. I never thought I'd be much of a grandfather, but that little guy worked his way into my heart."

Jon David sighed. Those words made the news he was about to share even worse.

Chance fetched a couple more Cokes from the cooler. He passed one to Jon David and then went to work on his sandwich.

"Mmmm, man, that's tasty. Hey, there's a reason for having you alone with me today. I wanted to tell you straight up how proud I am of you. It's amazing how you made it through medical school with a wife and two children. Also, I want you to know that I couldn't have a better son-in-law. Sara loves having you as her husband and being a mom. Thanks for making my only child a happy woman."

Jon David smiled humbly. "I appreciate you saying that. I feel the same about you. You're a hell of a father-in-law. I can't thank you enough for being an active part of my kids' lives. You've practically been their surrogate father while I was going through school. I'll never forget what you've done."

"Hey, they're my grandchildren. I'd walk through fire for them. So, Dr. Luke, now that you've graduated, do you have any ideas on where you'll do your residency?"

Jon David stopped eating. He swallowed hard and took a while to reply.

Chance noted his mood change. "Did I say something wrong?"

"No, no. I, uh, I have some news to share with you that you won't like. Do you remember when I first asked you for Sara's hand and said, among other things, that I wanted to become a doctor for disadvantaged children? You said you wouldn't have your daughter traipsing all over the world, living in squalid conditions."

"Yeah. Is that what you plan to do now?"

"No, I can't do it with a family."

"Jon David, we both have a habit of speaking directly. Some would say it's a flaw, but we are who we are. Don't dance around what you have to say. Tell me straight up."

"I will, but let me dance just a little."

Chance nodded. Jon David fidgeted a few moments and then looked Chance in the eye.

"You know I've been touched by something holy, right?"

Chance nodded again.

"I've been praying a lot lately. You know that Spirit has called me to work with disadvantaged children. I can't abandon that calling, no matter how much I love being here with you and my parents."

"Damn. You're moving, aren't you? Damn."

Jon David nodded. He took a long swig of his drink before continuing. "There's a three-year pediatric residency program in Seattle run by the University of Washington. It's called the Alaska Track, and in each of the three years I'm there, I'll spend eight months of the year in Seattle and four in Alaska. The time in Alaska will focus on serving the Alaska Native population. After my residency, there's a good chance the Alaska Native Medical Center in Anchorage could hire me. If that happens, we could live in a nice, relatively big city, and I could do what Spirit is calling me to do."

Chance's eyes welled up. "I assume Sara has agreed to this?"

"Yes, sir. She knows the enormity of this decision and how hard it will be on all of us. On the plus side, she loves Seattle, and Anchorage is a wonderful place to raise children."

"When will you leave?"

"In about six weeks. I can't even begin to tell you how much we'll all miss you and Maggie."

"I have to ask. Is there any way I could talk you into finding a residency program on the East Coast? It'll break Maggie's heart to lose her grandkids. It will break my heart, too," Chance said in nearly a whisper.

"Sara and I prayed long and hard over this decision. Just know you'll always be welcome to visit us."

"Damn."

Jon David sighed. "Residency will be the most trying time of my entire training. Eighty-hour work weeks will be the norm, and I'll see many extremely ill children. It'll be as rigorous as West Point but with suffering kids thrown in. And my residency won't be easy for Sara and the kids as well."

"Then why don't you stay here? Maggie and I will help out with your family, and you know we'll gladly do it."

"I know you would, but staying here won't get me to Alaska, which is where I need to be. Chance, I'm being called to do this, and it's a powerful calling. I can't ignore it. Sara knows what I'm talking about. Spirit once spoke to her, guiding her to be with me. She understands more than most how compelling God's callings can be. I hope you can fathom what I'm trying to say."

Chance nodded and sighed. "You know, it's not just about me missing Sara and the grandkids. It's about me missing you, too."

"The feeling is mutual. We've come a long way since you pointed that pistol at me and told me to leave your daughter alone."

"That we have. I still smile at how you looked down the barrel of that pistol and didn't flinch. You were fearless, my boy."

Jon David laughed. "I was crazy in love. I still am. If some arrogant, young buck ever acted like me and demanded Kelly's hand, I'd do the same as you."

Chance laughed. "What fathers won't do for their little girls." He finished his drink. "I can't tell you how many times I dragged Maggie all over the world during my Army career. So I have no right to argue with you about your decision. How do you plan on telling Maggie the news?"

"Sara's doing it today. She wanted some alone time with her to explain why we have to go."

"Man, there'll be some heaviness at my house tonight, I guarantee you that. Have you told the kids yet?"

"No, sir. We'll tell them when we pick them up at my parents' home. I still need to break the news to my mom and dad. Damn, I never thought change could hurt so badly."

"I know. It'll take a long time for me to get over this. Maggie, too. Come on, let's head in before it gets dark. I'll show you a technique called reaching, where you maneuver the mainsheet and jib sheet at right angles so the wind can fill the sails. She'll zip across the water after we do that."

"Sounds like a plan. Thanks for not keelhauling me after hearing my news."

Chance looked at him with a wicked grin. "Not so fast there, matey. There's a plank on board that I'm thinking about using."

2

CLANG, CLANG, CLANG …

"What happened!"

"Nothing, Rachel. I just dropped a pan."

She came into the kitchen. "Colt, look at Jekyll. That awful noise didn't affect him. He's still snoring away."

Colt looked at his dog and sighed. "His hearing is gone, and he had another bad day today. Rachel, I think the end is near."

She sighed. "With his appetite now gone, I'm sorry to say that I agree with you. He's in pain now, and we need to consider ending his suffering. It's time to let the kids know that Jekyll won't be with us much longer."

"I know. Let's talk to them after dinner."

At the dinner table, they took each other's hands, and Colt said grace. "Dear God, we thank you for this food, and we thank you for each other."

"Amen," said his family.

Danny lit up. "I love spaghetti! It's my favorite."

"I know, son. That's why I made it tonight."

"Thanks, Dad."

"I have some good news," said Rachel. "Grandpa and Nana are coming here for Christmas. They want to see the Rose Parade with us."

"Can we take them to Disneyland, Momma?" asked Christa.

"We sure can, and maybe Six Flags, too. We can try out the new roller coaster ride."

"Cool!" said Danny. "I'll bet Christa will puke."

"No, I won't. You will!"

"Hey, kids, your mom and I have something important to talk to you about after dinner."

"Is it about our hike this weekend?"

"No, son. Let's just eat, and we'll talk about it later."

"Momma, I told everyone at school today that you work on the Mars Rover. They want to know if you found any aliens."

"Tell them no aliens, Danny, but we've found lots of interesting soil."

"How can soil be interesting?"

"Well, Martian soils will help tell us how the planet formed. Plus, we're looking to see if there's any water in the soil. We'll need water if we ever send people to the planet."

"Why not take water with you?"

"Because water is heavy, and our rockets couldn't carry all we would need. The only practical way to sustain life is to use the water that's already there."

"Jekyll wouldn't like Mars. With no McDonald's there, he couldn't have fries." Danny smirked.

Tears welled up in Colt's eyes.

After dinner, Rachel took the lead. "Danny and Christa, let's go to the family room. It's time for our talk."

Colt came in with Jekyll in his arms. He sat and sighed. "Jekyll is very ill, and he's getting worse. Your mom and I talked to the vet, and he said there's nothing else we can do for him."

"Will he go to heaven, Daddy?"

"I'm sure he will, Christa. I'll bet he'll love meeting my mom and dad, who are already there. They'll care for him and love him as much as we do."

"I don't want Jekyll to die, Daddy."

"None of us do, Danny. But he stopped eating two days ago. It's his way of saying it's time for him to go."

In tears, Danny leaned into his mother. Christa followed his lead and did the same.

Rachel kissed them. "Let's take a few minutes to tell Jekyll how special he is and how we'll miss him. Let's tell him it's okay to go to heaven."

They all got up and gently patted their beloved dog. He didn't respond to their touch. "You can go to heaven if you want, Jekyll, but I'll miss you," Danny whispered to him.

Colt gently kissed Jekyll's head. "I'm going to take him to our bedroom and be with him for a while. He can sleep with you tonight, Danny, just like he always does."

Colt crawled under the sheets and brought Jekyll close. "I know you can't hear me, boy, but I'm going to talk anyway. I love you more than words could ever say. You've taught me so much, and all that I have is because of you." He gently stroked his friend's fur as he spoke. "My life won't be the same without you. I won't ever forget you."

Jekyll opened his clouded eyes. He feebly licked Colt's cheek, saying goodbye to his old friend. His breathing soon slowed and then stopped. Colt held him against his chest and wept.

3

One month later …

"I'M WORRIED ABOUT HIM, Momma," Rachel said into the phone. "He hasn't been able to shake off the grief of losing Jekyll. I often find him sitting dejectedly on the patio when I come home from work. Some nights, I hear him sobbing. And it's not just Colt. We all have chronic sadness. It's like a dark cloud is over us, and it won't go away. We need you and Dad to brighten our spirits. I hope you two will talk to Colt and help him out of the darkness."

"Of course we will. Rachel, it sounds like all of you could use family therapy to get past this. Why haven't you gone to see someone?"

"I suggested it, but Colt wants nothing to do with counseling."

"Just love him, Rachel. Jekyll meant the world to him, and he'll need time to make his peace with the loss. Your dad and I are grieving, too. Will you put Colt on the phone so I can say hello?"

"Sure. Hold on a second while I find him. Thanks, Mom."

She found Colt pruning a tree in the backyard and handed him the phone. "It's Mom."

"Hello, Annie. How are you and Pat doing?"

"We're fine, Colt. We're worried about you."

He glossed over her comment. "I look forward to seeing you two at Christmas. I plan on scoping out some sites for us to see the Rose Parade."

"Colt, Pat and I know how much you're hurting. We have you in our prayers."

"Thanks." He hesitated before continuing. "It . . . it's a powerful, unrelenting hurt. I miss him so much."

Annie sighed. "Colt, you can't afford the indulgence of extended grieving. It's dragging you and your family down. You're doing Jekyll a disservice, too. He wouldn't want you to grieve for so long."

"You're right."

"You know what might help? Writing a book about your life and how Jekyll changed it. Something like that would be the highest honor you could give Jekyll."

"Interesting idea. I'll give it some thought."

"Do it, Colt. Tell the world about your beloved friend."

"I should go. Do you want to talk to Rachel some more?"

"No, we finished our conversation before she handed you the phone."

"Thanks, Annie. Say hello to Pat for me."

"I will. Goodbye."

That night, Rachel stirred from her sleep. She opened her eyes to see her husband typing away. The glow of the laptop screen highlighted the concentration on his face. "What are you doing, Colt?"

"Writing."

"What are you writing about?"

"Jekyll and me—back before we met you."

"That sounds like a great idea."

"It wasn't my idea. Your mom suggested it."

Rachel smiled. "Thanks, Mom," she whispered.

Colt typed through the night.

4

"MY GOD, HOW DO you endure this traffic? Everyone driving seems to be in touch with their inner maniac."

Colt laughed. "Pat, once you leave downtown LA, it's not as bad."

"I've lived in Anchorage too long. I think I'd have a nervous breakdown if I lived here."

"You get used to it, Dad," said Rachel. "Pasadena's not nearly as crazy as LA."

Her father remained unconvinced and shifted to another subject. "So, Rachel, are you going to give your mom and me a tour of the Jet Propulsion Laboratory?"

"Yep. We can do that tomorrow morning. Plus, Colt has volunteered to watch the kids so I can take you to the observatory on Mount Wilson. It's given us some incredible pictures of Mars."

"We're looking forward to it, Dr. Mercer," he said with a smile.

"Rachel," said Annie, "your dad loves to brag to his buddies about his daughter being an astrophysicist at JPL. Be prepared for him to take lots of pictures of you at your job."

"I'm not the only one who has something to show you two. Colt's been typing away like a madman—his Jekyll novel is almost finished."

"Congratulations, Colt!" said Annie. "Have you come up with a title yet?"

"I have. Do you remember how Jekyll had that peculiar penchant for howling whenever we crossed a bridge on the Harley and how I joined him, and we'd howl in unison over bridges? That's the inspiration for the book's title. How does *Howling Across Bridges* sound to you?"

"I love it," laughed Pat. "When I was traveling across Texas with him on the Trike, it scared the hell out of me when he first did it. But then you said to howl with him the next time it happened. I did, and it was hilarious. I loved howling across bridges with him."

"I loved it, too," said Rachel. "Howling at the top of your lungs is curiously uplifting."

"Pat, I'd like you and Annie to critique the draft. Writing a novel is much more challenging than writing a children's book, so your feedback will be important to me."

"I'd love to read it," said Annie. "I'm sure it'll trigger some wonderful memories of when we first met you and Jekyll."

"I look forward to reading it as well," said Pat. "I still can't believe you're a bestselling children's author."

"I know. I'm blessed to make a living from writing. Our kids are clamoring for me to write some new stories with them in it."

"Speaking of them," said Rachel, "they're so looking forward to seeing you when we get home. Our neighbors are watching them so we could have you two to ourselves for a little while."

"I can't wait to see Danny and Christa," Pat replied. "Since we're alone right now, Colt, do you mind if I ask how things are going in terms of Jekyll?"

"I'm doing better now, sir, and so is the family. Writing about Jek has deflected some of my grief. I smile when I remember his antics, but I've cried, too."

"At dinner each night, Colt shares some of the things he's writing about," said Rachel. "It's been therapeutic for all of us."

A few days before Christmas, the family went on a four-mile hike to nearby Eaton Canyon. No one seemed to mind the creek crossings and boulder-hopping required to get to a stunning forty-foot waterfall. Danny and Christa tossed rocks in the water while Rachel and Annie unpacked the picnic basket. It was a little chilly, but nothing they couldn't handle. Pat motioned for Colt to come to him by the waterfall.

"I never thought there'd be an oasis like this after driving through LA."

"Pat, California is loaded with beautiful places. You just have to know where to find them."

"You don't mind living in a big city?"

"Well, truthfully, I miss Alaska a lot, but JPL is a world-class scientific organization, and Rachel loves working there. So, I'll do what it takes to make her happy. I do wish the kids could experience Alaska's wilderness, but I make sure they learn to appreciate nature right here in California. They love being outdoors."

"You're welcome to visit us anytime. As a writer, you can work anywhere. Why don't you and the kids come for an extended stay this summer? I don't think Rachel would mind."

"Thanks for the offer. It's tempting."

"Hey, tell me the truth. Are you getting past your grief over Jekyll?"

"I am. I still have some tough moments, though."

"Will you ever get another dog? That might help."

"No. I mean, how could any dog top Jekyll von Bickerstaff? I'd hate to be the pet following in his footsteps."

"Give some thought to the dog being for your children, not you. They need something to love on after Jekyll."

"I'll give it some thought."

"Great. Hey, my stomach's growling. Let's eat."

As Christmas morning dawned at the Mercer's home, the quiet of the night ended.

"Mommy, let's open our gifts!"

"Yeah, just like Christa says! Come on, Dad!"

Rachel opened her sleepy eyes. "Hey, kids. Merry Christmas. We're going to have breakfast before opening gifts, so you need to be patient."

"Why don't you two wake up Grandpa and Nana," said Colt. "I'm sure they'll want to get an early start on the day with you."

They charged out of the room and pounced on their sleeping grandparents. "You're so bad, siccing them on my poor parents," Rachel said, shaking her head.

"I know, but it gives me time to say Merry Christmas to you. I love you."

She kissed her husband. "I love you, too. We're blessed to have each other."

"Hey, can you cover for me so I can run to the Durans and get my gift for the kids?"

"What kind of gift needs to be kept at our neighbor's home?"

"It's a surprise for you, too. I'll slip out through the garage after I get dressed."

"Okay. I'll delay things by taking a shower, but knowing my mom, she'll have breakfast on the table in no time."

"I'll be back in ten minutes."

A while later, Colt banged on the front door with his foot while holding a cardboard box adorned with a big, red bow. Danny opened the door.

"Help me in, son. I have a special Christmas gift for you and Christa." Colt put the box in the middle of the living room floor. "Hey, everyone, let's open this gift before breakfast. Danny and Christa, please do the honors."

Inside, they found a puppy wagging his tail. "Yip, yip!"

"It's a dog!" yelled Danny. He reached in and scooped up the puppy. "Look, Mom, he's tiny!"

His sister put out her hands. "Let me hold him, too!"

"He's a terrier mix. I found him at the animal shelter. They said he'll weigh about fifteen pounds when fully grown. He'll never win a beauty contest, but that's how I prefer my dogs."

"He's perfect," said Rachel.

"What should we name him, Dad?" asked Danny.

"How about Harley von Bickerstaff?"

Pat laughed. "It's perfect. The von Bickerstaff line of fine mongrels now continues." They all agreed it was a worthy name.

5

JON DAVID SLUMPED ONTO the couch. He massaged his temples and then wearily gazed at his wife. "I'm spread way too thin. How can I learn anything when I'm flying at Mach 2 with my hair on fire?"

"It's part of the residency experience. They're teaching you to make decisions quickly because someday, someone's life might depend on it. As an ER doc, I know indecisiveness can kill."

"I feel I'm not getting the doctor-patient relationship that I want. It's as if I'm on an assembly line. I guess I was hoping for something more. Before residency, I had no clue what terminally ill children go through. Seeing them suffering and fading away breaks my heart. I wish I could spend more time with them and their families."

"Jon David, children magnify the hurt when you see them ill because it's a primal thing to want to protect the young. But there's a fine line when it comes to compassion. If you get too involved with your patients or their families, you'll intrude on a counselor's duties. A good bedside manner is important, but your main duty is to be their doctor. If you get more satisfaction from interacting with people, you should consider psychiatry."

"No, I like what I'm doing with kids. But, in my opinion, the whole residency program needs a major revamping."

"On the bright side, you're in the homestretch. In six months, it'll be over, and when you're practicing, you can do things more as you want. A year from now, I'll bet you'll look back and see how good this program is. So, tough it out and have faith."

He sighed. "I suppose you're right. Thanks for your support. I couldn't do this without you."

"You're welcome," she said with a smile. She helped him remove his prosthetic leg. "Uh, oh. You're getting some hot spots." She rubbed his leg and looked at him with concern. "You should consider using a wheelchair at work. It would be much easier on your leg."

Jon David shook his head. "Patients and their parents expect a doctor who appears to be invincible. Seeing me in a wheelchair or even using crutches wouldn't go over well."

"You could leave it outside the room and walk in. That would save a lot of walking."

"Yeah, but for now, I'll try using more talc to help with the chafing."

"Okay, but I'm keeping an eye on your leg. If it gets worse, you'll use a wheelchair."

He nodded, too tired to argue.

6

One year later …

SPRING IN ALASKA USHERS in a phenomenon known as "breakup." It's the time of year when the subzero cold finally wanes, allowing the snow that's accumulated for months to melt. Puddles of muddy water take over yards and fill abundant, newly formed street potholes, creating perfect splashing opportunities for kids equipped with "breakup boots." It's impossible to keep a car clean during this time of year, and carwashes do a brisk business.

Jon David smiled as he exited the Alaska Native Medical Center, located in midtown Anchorage. Not even breakup could suppress his happy mood. He just completed his first month as the medical center's newest pediatrician, and this accomplishment called for a celebration. Taking the family for dinner and a movie at the Bear Tooth Theatrepub seemed a worthy reward. Already, he was making a difference in people's lives. Helping Alaska's native children agreed with him, and the appreciation of their parents touched him. He glanced back at the ultramodern facility, which served thousands of Alaska Natives and American Indian people. He felt honored to be part of the medical team.

As he drove home, he thought about how proud he was of Sara for landing a part-time ER position at Providence Alaska Medical Center. While they were in Seattle, the urge to heal people awoke in her, and she completed the training required to practice again.

He pulled into the Spell's driveway, which was in the part of the town known as Hillside. They'd been staying with Jamie and Penny every summer during his residency and would continue living there until they found their own house. Sara greeted him with a kiss at the door. "Did you have a good day?"

"I did. My first month has gone well. Would you be up for dinner and a movie at the Bear Tooth? We could invite Jamie and Penny."

"You must be reading my mind. If we hurry, we can have dinner and then catch the latest Ice Age movie at six o'clock."

"Great! It's hard to imagine that we're going to see a movie. These forty-hour workweeks sure beat my previous eighty-hour marathons. I almost feel like I'm on vacation."

At the Bear Tooth, Jon David smiled at Jamie and Penny. "Okay, you two, dinner and the movie are on us."

"Well, thank you, son. This is a nice break from the daily routine."

After the waiter took their order, Jon David put Kelly on his lap and kissed her cheek. She snuggled in. "Jamie, this is a good time to say thanks for all you and Penny have done to help me through residency and for letting us stay with you until we can afford a house. Now that I'm employed, we're going to increase the rent we pay you each month."

"JD, my boy, you may not be blood kin, but you've been part of our family for years. Penny and I were lonely in our big, empty home. We love having you guys with us. As far as we're concerned, you can stay for as long as you like."

"Jamie's right," Penny added. "We've bonded to Riley and Kelly." She reached for Kelly, who eagerly went from Jon David to her.

Sara smiled. "We feel the same about you. Speaking of that, I'll be starting a part-time job at the Providence ER in a couple of weeks. I'll have odd hours at first, filling in for other doctors. I was wondering if you'd consider watching the kids while I'm at work."

"Of course," said Penny. "But I'll need car seats so I can take them to run errands or maybe go to McDonald's for a treat."

"Sure, that's no problem. Would three thousand a month be acceptable for rent and watching the kids?"

Jamie choked on his soda. "Sara," he rasped, "it would be a huge income boost for us. It's more than okay."

Penny patted her husband on the back to clear the soda that went down the wrong pipe. "We could use it to update our house and fix the cabin."

"Grandpa, could you take me to my soccer practices this summer?"

"I'd love to, Riley. It sounds like fun."

After the movie, they headed home as the sun set over the Alaska Range. With the change of season, they were gaining five minutes of daylight each day, on the way to twenty hours of sunshine in the summer. It was good to see more sunshine after a mere six hours of daylight in December. The kids were tired and didn't complain about going to bed.

In their bedroom, Sara looked at her husband. "Hey, is everything okay? You've seemed distracted since dinner."

"Nothing's wrong. I just need to check on something. Do you mind if I go up and talk to Jamie for a while?"

"No, not at all. Would you ask Penny to come down so we can chat about how she wants to fix up the place?"

"Sure."

He sighed as he headed upstairs. After Penny went to be with Sara, Jon David sat with Jamie.

"So, my boy, what's up?"

"How long have you had that tremor, Jamie?"

"What tremor?"

"The one in your right hand. I saw it while you were eating. How long have you had it?"

"I don't know what you're talking about. Here, see for yourself. There's no tremor." He held out his hand. It looked steady.

"So, you're indirectly saying that it comes and goes. How often does it happen during the day?"

"Jon David, once more, I have no idea what you're talking about. I think you're taking your doctoring a little too far." He sounded defensive, which was quite unlike him.

"Should I ask Penny to come up so I can ask her?"

Jamie's jaw tightened. He didn't respond.

Jon David stood. "I'll be back in a few seconds with Penny."

"Wait. Sit back down. I'll tell you what's going on."

Jon David sat and looked Jamie in the eye. "I'm listening."

Jamie sighed. "I don't want to lose my pilot's license. If they find anything wrong, I could get grounded. You know how much I love going to the cabin. If they revoke my license, I'll never see the cabin again."

"Living matters more than seeing the cabin. How long have you had the tremor?"

Jamie sighed again. "The tremors come and go. They started a few months ago. At the cabin last month, my whole body began shaking uncontrollably, and, odd as it sounds, I swore I smelled fresh-cut alfalfa like when I was a kid on our farm. After a few minutes, it went away. I'm also having some difficulty seeing with my right eye, and my right leg and arm sometimes feel weak. It all comes and goes. There's something else." He paused and looked scared. "I tried to sign a birthday card for Penny last week, but I couldn't hold a pen in my hand. So I ordered flowers for her instead. What do you think it is? Am I just getting old?"

"No, it's not about aging. You probably had a seizure at the cabin. A seizure is like an electrical short circuit in your brain. From what you described, it's occurring in the part of your brain that involves movement. That would also explain the weakness in your leg. Damn, Jamie, what if you'd been flying at three thousand feet and had that seizure? What else? Do you have any other symptoms?"

He grimaced and nodded. "Yeah, I've been having a lot of headaches. They're worse in the morning and then go away as the day progresses. A few mornings, it's been so bad that I vomited. Getting up too quickly can cause me to have one. What's wrong with me, Jon David?"

"Without testing, it's hard to say for sure. It could be a hundred different things, many of which are treatable. We won't know until you get a full neurological workup."

"And what does that entail?"

"I'm a kid doc. Sara knows a whole lot more than I do regarding this. Let me get the ladies so we can all discuss it."

"Before they come up, don't sugarcoat it, son. Is it bad?"

"Jamie, this needs immediate attention. As I said, it could be something easy. But, from what you've described, these are symptoms you can't ignore."

Jon David found Penny and Sara laughing about something when he walked in. "Jamie and I need to speak with both of you upstairs." He turned around and left without waiting for a response. From the tone of his voice, Sara knew something was wrong. She took Penny's hand and followed her husband. In the dining room, Jamie gave them a sad smile.

"What's wrong?" Sara asked.

Jon David motioned for her and Penny to sit.

"While we were eating tonight, I noticed a slight tremor in Jamie's right hand. I just talked to him about it, and he said it comes and goes. But there's more. From what he described, he likely had a seizure when he was last at the cabin. Plus, he's been having episodic vision problems in his right eye. These symptoms are troubling, and I told him he needs a neurological workup as soon as possible."

Penny touched her husband's hand. "At night, I've noticed him shaking in bed. I thought he was dreaming, or maybe he was just cold. The shaking never lasts long. Jon David, did Jamie tell you about his bad morning headaches and vomiting?"

Jon David nodded.

"I agree about getting an exam," said Sara. "Jamie, you need a full workup. Give me a second; I want to take your blood pressure right now." She ran downstairs and brought back a portable monitoring device and a flashlight. "Okay, let's see what we have." She pushed a button on the machine. "It's 140 over 80. A little high, but not bad. Now, I'm going to shine this flashlight at your pupils, and after that, I'll see how well your eyes track the light." She performed the exam. "Jamie, your right pupil's contraction is a bit off. Are you having any problems with bright lights?"

"Yeah, I've been sensitive to them and the sun lately."

"You should be seen as soon as possible. The VA can do the basic stuff, but we need to find a top-notch neurologist. Jon David and I can ask around."

"Is this bad, Sara?" asked Penny. "Please tell us."

"Penny, Jamie's symptoms are troubling."

Jon David put his hand on hers. "Penny, I told Jamie the same thing."

"What kind of tests will they need to do, Sara?"

"Well, Jamie, if it were me, I'd do a thorough neurological exam, including a CT scan and a complete blood workup."

A tear ran down Penny's cheek. Jamie gently wiped it away. "Sweetheart, I survived Vietnam, so I can survive this, too. Let's not sit around fretting all weekend. I'll get the tests, and then we'll go from there." He stood. "I suggest we call it a day." His request wasn't open for debate.

Jon David stood and hugged him. "You know we'll all be here for you."

"I know, son, and I'm grateful." Sara hugged Jamie as well.

Downstairs, in bed, Sara kissed Jon David. "I can't believe you noticed his hand tremor. I'm with him all the time and never saw a thing."

"Well, residency teaches you to be hyper-alert, and I'm still in that mode."

"Are you thinking what I'm thinking?" she asked with a sigh.

"Unfortunately, yes. All the signs point to a tumor, probably on the left side of the brain."

"I agree. Dear God, let's hope the tests prove us wrong."

7

"ARE YOU SURE YOU won't mind Colt and the kids staying with you and Dad for the summer?"

"Rachel, this is like a thousand Christmas gifts rolled into one. Pat will be doing cartwheels in the street when I tell him. What about Colt—when will you give him the news?"

"He'll be back from his book signing tour next week. I think I'll wait and tell him in person."

"Knowing how much he loves Alaska, he'll flip at the news. Are you sure you'll be okay being away from them for so long?"

"It'll be tough, but this sabbatical will keep me super busy, and hopefully, that'll take my mind off missing them. I still can't believe they invited me to spend the summer there."

"Tell me more about it."

"Well, the new Atacama Large Millimeter Array is amazing. We'll be able to see some of the most distant galaxies in the universe. Not only that, but we can better look for protoplanets and even see how new stars are forming. For an astrophysicist, it doesn't get any better than this."

"Where is it located again?"

"In Chile. A place called San Pedro de Atacama. At 16,400 feet, we'll need to breathe supplemental oxygen to work there. The Atacama Desert is the driest place in the world, which means a cloudless environment that's free from light-distorting moisture. The only place better for an observatory is in space."

"We loved the tour you gave us of the Mount Wilson observatory. Is this one bigger?"

"It's much bigger. And, unlike Mount Wilson, ALMA will look at the skies in the millimeter and sub-millimeter wavelengths, which are longer than optical light. This will allow us to view inside gas clouds and study star formations—we'll even be able to see distant light that's been shifted toward the red end of the light spectrum."

"Rachel, you are way over my head with what you're saying. I'm so proud of you and what you've accomplished."

"Thanks, Mom. I couldn't do all this without Colt. I know he prefers living in Alaska, but he agreed to move here so I could work at JPL. And he does more with the kids than I could ever do. He never complains about anything. I think spending the summer in Alaska will be the perfect gift for him."

"You really love him, don't you?"

"I do. Our marriage seems to get better with each passing year."

"After all he's been through as a soldier, it warms my heart to see how happy he is now. You're a good wife to him, Rachel. Switching subjects, I'm glad his new novel is selling well. He has the perfect job as far as I'm concerned. As an author, you can live anywhere, and with people buying your books, you can make money even while you sleep."

"Yep, I agree. Colt loves the time it gives him to be with the kids. Hey, do you think he could coach Danny in soccer up there?"

"I don't know. Let me check around, and I'll get back to you."

The following week, Rachel picked up her husband at LAX. On the way home, after he told her about his book tour, she casually mentioned her sabbatical and her parents inviting him and the kids to spend the summer with them. After the initial shock of her announcement subsided, his reaction was utter joy.

8

THE NEUROLOGIST LOOKED GRIM as he motioned for everyone to take a seat in his office. "Thank you for coming today, doctors," he said to Jon David and Sara. He opened a folder, turned his attention to Jamie and Penny, and got down to business.

"I have the results here, and, unfortunately, the news isn't good. Mr. Spell, the biopsy revealed you have what's known as malignant glioma, and the CT and MRI scans show that it has spread from your left parietal lobe and created satellite tumors elsewhere in your brain. It's like an octopus with tentacles going everywhere. There are two types of gliomas: anaplastic astrocytoma and glioblastoma multiforme. You have the latter, which is far more aggressive. The main difference between the two kinds of gliomas is how long you will live. Studies have shown that glioblastoma multiforme does not respond well to surgery. In your case, with it weaving through your brain and forming ancillary tumors, it would be impossible to remove."

The news brought Penny to tears, but Jamie sat stoically.

"How long do I have, Doc?"

"My guess is a few months, at best. We might be able to prolong your life a little longer with radiation and chemotherapy that hopefully will shrink the tumor. There's also an oral drug called temozolomide that sometimes makes the tumor receptive to radiation therapy. Some experimental drugs are available, but they only extend life by a few weeks and have unpleasant side effects."

Jamie nodded. He took Penny's hand. "It sounds like the best course of action is 'no action.' The last thing I want is to be irradiated and chemo'd to death, with little hope of it being effective. So, if I do nothing, how long can my current quality of life continue?"

"Jamie, you can't just give up," Jon David interrupted. "Let's at least give radiation a go. If we can shrink the tumor, you'll likely live longer."

"I appreciate what you're saying, son, but let the man answer my question."

"Mr. Spell, quality of life is governed by the rate of tumor growth. Your tumor is growing and spreading rapidly. It's already affecting your speech and body movements. In the days ahead, you could experience memory, vision, auditory, cognitive, and more gestural disturbances, along with personality and behavioral changes. Plus, your headaches and seizures may become more severe due to increased intracranial pressure. As I said, I believe you have a few months to live, but your quality of life will soon decline."

The doctor closed the medical folder and glanced at Jon David before returning his attention to Jamie. "Mr. Spell, choosing 'no action' doesn't mean your medical care will end. We can try to control future seizures with medication, and corticosteroids will help with your headaches for a while. But, as your disease progresses, you'll need hospice care. They provide many services such as pain control, home and inpatient care, emotional and spiritual support, as well as support for your family and other loved ones."

Jamie sighed. "Thanks for your assessment and recommendations. I appreciate your candor. What do you think caused it?"

"We don't know. There are no known risk factors for this type of tumor. It seems to target people between the ages of fifty and seventy."

"Should I expect a lot of pain in the days ahead?"

"Every person is different. Just know that if your pain becomes severe, we have medications to keep it under control."

"Thanks for your time. You've addressed all my questions. These two fine young doctors live with me, so I'll be in good hands."

The physician stood and shook Jamie's hand. He gave Penny, Sara, and Jon David a nod and excused himself.

Outside, Penny latched onto her husband and wept. He showed no emotion as he hugged her. Jon David and Sara embraced them.

"Okay, okay, that's enough sadness," said Jamie after a few moments. "I have one order for all of you to heed. I don't want to discuss my situation for one week, and Penny, do not call our children. I need time to digest everything and decide what I want to do."

A week after the doctor visit, Jamie waited for the kids to go to sleep and then called the family together. He looked upbeat as they took seats around him at the dining room table.

"C'mon, you all, cheer up. I have good news to share." Jamie's remark perked them up. He touched Penny's hand. "I had a dream last night that lifted the heaviness I've felt all week. I want to tell you about it." He took a sip of hot tea. "The spirit people came to me in the dream. They said God is calling me to begin my next journey, and it will be just as glorious as my time here on Earth. They wouldn't say what the new journey would be, but my time to leave is near. They said I shouldn't be afraid during my remaining days here. Penny, I asked if you could come, but they say you have more work to do here. They promised we'll be together again, and we'll be just as happy as we've been here. They said not to have radiation and chemotherapy, and that's good enough for me. I woke this morning feeling completely at peace. My hope is you all will accept what I'm saying and will help make my last days as pleasant as possible. I don't want your sadness."

Jon David cried as he listened to his friend. "Jamie, if that's what you want, I'll support your decision."

"I will, too," said Sara. "We'll make sure you're comfortable."

"No," said Penny, shaking her head. "No."

Jamie wiped his tears away. "God is calling me home, and we need to accept it. We need to have faith. Sweetheart, would you mind if I go out on the deck with Jon David? I have something to discuss with him." She nodded.

Outside, he motioned for Jon David to take a seat on an Adirondack chair and moved the other one around to face him. "I have something I'd like you to do for me. It's big, so I expect you'll need to talk first to Sara before giving me a reply."

"Just tell me what you want, and I'll do it."

"Thanks," Jamie said with a sad smile. "Jon David, I want you to buy our home and have Penny live with you. I'll get the home appraised and inspected. From there, we'll come up with a fair price. Penny can use the proceeds to live comfortably for the rest of her days. She could live on her own here in Anchorage in a smaller home or condo, or she could move to the Lower 48 to be with one of our kids. But I know she'd thrive being with you and your family. Talk to Sara and let me know if you can commit to it."

Jon David stood. "Wait here. I'll be back in five minutes." Inside the house, he looked at Sara. "Will you please join me downstairs? I have something I need to ask you."

In their bedroom, Jon David told her of Jamie's desire and got an immediate yes. He dashed upstairs and told Jamie. Tears poured down Jamie's cheeks, knowing that Penny would be okay after he passed.

Over the next several weeks, the Spell children came and went. It was a time of love in the home, with many memories exchanged and a father saying goodbye to those he held dear.

9

COLT HERDED THE KIDS into the airplane. "We're in seats 17 A, B, and C. See if you can find them, Danny." His son, who was carrying Harley in a pet carrier, walked down the aisle.

"They're here, Dad."

"Great. You two get in and buckle up. I'm so excited about seeing Grandpa and Nana. Man, are we going to have fun this summer!"

"When can we climb a mountain, Dad?"

"This week, if the weather cooperates. Oh! Grandpa says the reds should soon be in the Russian River. Catching a salmon will be a blast for you two."

Shortly after the airplane was in the air, the kids fell asleep. Taking the red-eye flight proved to be a smart choice. Colt took Harley out of the pet carrier and put him on his lap. Soon, the pup fell asleep, too.

Annie met them at the airport. She looked at Colt and smiled. "You look tired. After you all unpack, I'll take the kids for a bike ride so you can rest."

"Thanks, Annie. I could use a nap, although Harley will probably keep me occupied."

"He's doubled in size since we last saw him."

"Yeah, he has. Be sure to put your shoes up because he's fond of them. I hope his teething phase will end soon."

"Is Harley working out all right? I mean, are you bonding with him?"

"I like Harley, and the kids adore him, but Harley's not equal to his predecessor. Jekyll was a once-in-a-lifetime dog."

"I hear you. You know, I'm so glad you're here. Pat can't wait to see you again. He's taking next week off to be with you guys, and he'll take another week off toward the end of your stay. He wants us to go to the Alaska State Fair."

"That sounds fun. I love Alaska in the summer."

Annie turned her attention to Danny. "Hey, after dinner, Grandpa wants to climb Flattop with you and your dad."

"Cool! Where's Flattop?"

"Look over there. See the mountain with the big flat top? That's Flattop. It's 3500 feet high. Oh, Colt, I almost forgot. I signed Danny up for soccer starting next week, and the local soccer club would be delighted to have you coach his team."

"Perfect. Danny, what do you think?"

"Thanks, Nana. I brought my soccer shoes."

"Great! Colt, you might want to call the soccer club president today. I'll give you his number when we get home. Oh. Scotty says that he and Maggie expect you over for dinner this week. He can't wait to see you. By the way, the kids love him at school. He's the most popular School Resource Officer we've ever had. As a counselor, I tell the rowdy students that I'll send them to see Officer Morey if they don't straighten up. They get real cooperative fast. I feel safer knowing he's on the job."

"I'm so glad he found a rewarding job after retiring from the Army. I'll call him. Thanks for doing the legwork on soccer. Danny and I appreciate your efforts."

"It's no problem. Christa and I will watch him play. Danny, you can show Grandpa your soccer moves in our backyard today."

"Does Grandpa play soccer?"

"No, he prefers American football and roots for the Seahawks."

"I like the Chargers."

"Don't tell him that, or he'll try to convert you to being a Seahawks fan."

After their bike ride with Nana, Colt played with the kids outside to give Annie time to prepare dinner. Soon, Pat arrived home.

"Hello, everyone! Welcome to Alaska again."

"Grandpa! Grandpa!" The kids latched onto him.

"Let me see how much you've both grown. Wow!" He hugged Colt. "It's good to see you again, son."

"Same here. I hope you can tolerate us for the summer."

He laughed. "We have a lot of catching up to do."

"I'm looking forward to it."

"Hey, congrats on your novel. Rachel said it's selling well."

"It is. I'm indebted to Annie for coming up with the idea."

"I love how you wrote the story."

"Thanks. It felt good to write about how I came to meet you two. We've come a long way since those days."

"We sure have," said Pat. "Now, you're a great dad. I couldn't ask for more than that. How's the new pup working out?"

"I call him Harley von Nightmare. Look at him. His engine is always red-lined. He never stops. Actually, he's a hoot to watch."

"It'll get better after his puppy phase."

"Well, remember you wanted me to get another dog. I'll remind you of that when Harley chews on one of your favorite shoes."

"I consider myself forewarned. I'll pick up all my valuables. Is he housebroken yet?"

"Most of the time. He does have his moments."

"Argh. Well, let's hope for the best."

"Dinnertime!" Annie yelled from the kitchen.

"You know how much I've been looking forward to her cooking, right?"

Pat laughed. "Yeah, I do. She plans on making a double batch of cannelloni on Friday."

Annie greeted the hungry crew as they came in. "Okay, everyone, wash your hands and then take a seat. Colt, I made you a meatloaf with mashed potatoes."

He hugged her. "That's a 'welcome home' meal if ever there was one."

She kissed his cheek. "It's good to have you here."

An hour after the delightful dinner, Pat, Colt, and Danny headed out to climb Flattop. Even though it was now late to go on a hike by "Lower 48" standards, in the Land of the Midnight Sun, they'd return home with the sun still shining.

After a twenty-minute drive, Pat parked at the Glen Alps trailhead. "Okay, let's get our gear," he said. They got out and geared up. "Look, Danny, there's Flattop. We'll first head to Blueberry Knoll and then catch the Flattop trail. It'll take us to the top."

Danny adjusted his ball cap and ran to the trailhead. "C'mon, you guys!"

Pat took a deep breath and looked at Colt. "Ever since Annie said you were coming, I've spent my lunches on the treadmill at the base fitness center. Let's hope all my huffing and puffing has helped."

"Hey, you and Danny will probably be dragging me up the hill. My days of being in decent shape are in the past."

"I'll try not to humble you."

Colt smiled and followed his son. An hour later, they were standing on top of the mountain.

"Give me a high-five, grandson. You did good. So did your father, although he looks a little winded."

"I see how your treadmill time has paid off," said Colt. He turned his attention to Danny. "Look, son, that tall peak on the horizon is Mount McKinley, the tallest mountain on the continent at 20,320 feet. Alaskans call it Denali. Over there is Mount Redoubt, and to the right is Mount Spurr. Both are active volcanoes. I was here when Spurr last erupted. We got a dusting of ash from it in Anchorage. To the north is the Talkeetna Range. That's where your grandpa married your mom and me. Right across the valley is Wolverine Peak, which we can climb if you want, and to the south are the Kenai Mountains. Over here is Anchorage, and Grandpa's house is right there, to the south of the airport. Can you see Nana waving to us?"

Danny laughed. "No. Everyone looks like ants down there."

Pat patted Danny on his back. "We're kings of the world up here."

10

WHILE SITTING IN HIS wheelchair on the back deck, Jamie enjoyed the early morning sun. Sara came out with a blanket. "If you don't put this on, Penny says you'll have to deal with her."

He smiled and nodded for her to put the blanket on him. "It is a little chilly out here. Care to join me for a while?" He slurred the words, and she struggled to understand what he was saying.

"I'd love to. How's your pain?"

"So, so. I have a headache."

"I can get you an ibuprofen tablet if you want."

"No, I'm fine. Look, Sara. Look at the mountains. The mountains. The wonder of it all. Can you see the wonder of it all?"

"I do. It's beautiful. Jamie, I'm sure Penny told you this, but we closed on the house yesterday. She and I are going to a financial counselor this week to discuss ways for her to conservatively invest your home's equity money. Jon David and I will ensure that no one takes advantage of her."

He smiled as best he could. "Thank you, Sara. What are your plans for today?"

"Well, I signed Riley up for soccer, so I'll be with him this afternoon. They play on Tuesdays and Thursdays. Kelly will stay here with Penny if you don't mind."

"No, I don't mind. Kelly brightens my day. Sara, I have something to say."

"What's on your mind, Jamie?"

"I'm fading. I can almost feel the tumor growing in me. It's hard to form words now, as you can tell, and my memory is going fast. It won't be long now. I might need to go to extended care soon."

"Let's take it one day at a time."

He took her hand and gazed at her in tears. "My-my-my kids c-call me on the phone, and I can't remember their n-n-names. I can't remember what they look like."

"It's okay, Jamie. They know this is part of the process you're going through. Don't worry. Just know they love you."

He nodded and tried to smile. The right side of his lips no longer moved. "Go on and get ready for your day. I'll stay out here for a while longer." Sara gave him another hug and went back inside.

Penny was in the kitchen. She looked at Sara. "He's losing control of his bladder. Did he tell you?"

"No, but he told me he's fading. He mentioned going to extended care at Providence."

"I don't want him to be in a sterile room by himself, possibly dying alone."

"We could rent a hospital bed and put it in the living room. That way, he can be with us until the end."

"It sounds perfect."

"I'll check on it after soccer today."

"Thank you. How much longer do you think Jamie has?"

"He's down to weeks now, if that. It's time to speak any remaining words you may want to say to him."

"We've already said our words to each other. We've been saying them for over forty years."

"I hope Jon David and I feel the same after that many years. You and Jamie inspire us."

"You will. I see the love between you two." They hugged each other.

"If you ever need to talk, I'm here."

"Thanks, Sara. I thank God every day for you and your family being part of our lives."

"We'll be here for you and Jamie. That's something you can count on."

11

"OKAY EVERYONE, FORM a line here. My name is Coach Mercer. How many of you have played soccer before?" All but one of the six-year-olds raised their hands. "Good. I plan on challenging all of you to play better, but in a way that'll be fun. Today, we'll go over basic moves like dribbling, ball control, and passing and receiving. Next Thursday, we'll work on our shooting skills and one-on-one soccer moves. Okay, let's get to it."

Colt ran the kids through a series of drills, making sure they stayed engaged and focused. They looked like they were having fun. He blew his whistle. "All right, everyone, huddle around me." They did as he asked. "For the next fifteen minutes, we'll do something called 'Around the World.' It's a dribbling exercise that'll start at that corner of the field. We'll set up a square with the traffic cones in each corner and name each cone after an Alaska animal. You there, what's your name?"

"Riley Luke, Coach."

"All right, give me the name of an Alaska animal."

"A bear."

"Good. Give me three more animals."

"An otter!" another kid yelled.

"A moose!"

"A caribou!"

"Okay, we have our names. That cone is Bear, that one is Otter, that one is Moose, and the last one is Caribou. I'll call out one of their names, and you'll then dribble the ball to that location. I'll mix it up, so you need to pay attention to what I'll call next. Got it?"

"Yes, Coach!" they yelled in unison.

"Good. Is everyone ready?"

"Ready!"

"Caribou!" They took off toward that cone, dribbling the ball like madmen. "Otter!" Off they went again. After fifteen minutes, they were panting. "Good job, everyone. I'll see you on Thursday, and we'll do some other cool things. Our first game is next Tuesday, so work on what we did here today if you can. Okay, practice is over. I'll see you in a couple of days."

Danny and Riley stayed on the field and kicked the ball back and forth. The rest of the kids headed to their parents.

A woman approached Colt, smiling. "Hello, Coach Mercer. I'm Sara Luke, Riley's mom. The kids looked like they had fun today."

He shook her hand. "Pleased to meet you, Ms. Luke. You're welcome to call me Colt. Danny's my son. He's over there with Riley. They seem to have hit it off."

"Please call me Sara. Yes, it's nice to see Riley making new friends. We recently moved here from Seattle, so he's feeling lonely."

"That can be tough, but young kids usually adapt well to change. I'm sure he'll meet a lot of new kids when school starts again."

"I'm sure he will, too, but so far, he has no close friends. How about Danny?"

"Well, we're not from here either. We live in California. My wife is on a sabbatical, and her parents live here in Anchorage. My kids and I are spending the summer with them."

"That sounds like fun. Does your wife often go on sabbaticals?"

"No, this is her first. She's an astrophysicist and got invited to a fancy new observatory in Chile. We've been apart just a few days, but it already seems like years."

"I'll bet she's thrilled to go to Chile. You don't get invites like that every day."

"She is. For her, it's a once-in-a-lifetime opportunity."

"Are you a teacher? Is that how you get the summer off?"

"No, I'm an author. Children's books, mostly, but I just completed my first novel."

"That sounds like an interesting line of work. I read children's books every night to my kids. I have a daughter who's five. She won't go to bed unless I read to her. Riley's getting a little old for children's books, but he still joins us each night. Give me the name of one of your books. Maybe I've read it."

"Well, my first book is called *Jekyll von Bickerstaff.* It's a book about a dog."

"Oh my God, we have that book! That and *Finley von Bickerstaff* and *Seymour C. Sparrow,* too. We love those books."

"Thanks. That's good to hear. My new book, *Howling Across Bridges,* is for adults. It's a story about Jekyll and me traveling across North America on a motorcycle. I called it my 'Grand Adventure.' It was released a few months ago and is in most bookstores."

"I'll look for it. Wow, it's an honor to meet you."

"Thanks, Sara. It's nice to meet you, too."

"You'll have to pardon me for saying this, but when I saw you on the field today barking orders, I thought you could've been in the military or perhaps be a physical education teacher. Being an author never occurred to me."

"You're very perceptive. I was an Army Ranger, but that seems so long ago."

"My husband was a Ranger, too. He was medically retired after losing his leg in Iraq. His name is Jon David."

"I did two tours in Iraq and one in Afghanistan. A lot of my friends never made it back. Is your husband able to work?"

"Yes. He and I are doctors. After he got out, he went to medical school and became a pediatrician. He works with Native kids at the Alaska Native Medical Center."

"What type of doctoring do you do?"

"I'm a trauma surgeon. I just started a part-time job at Providence. I used to be in the Air Force Reserve and accompanied critically wounded soldiers and airmen to Ramstein on C-17 medivacs."

"So, you, too, have seen the aftereffects of war."

She nodded. "It was hard. I've taken the last few years off to recharge and be a mom. This ER job is my first foray back into the field."

"I hope it works out for you."

Danny and Riley came running over. "Dad, I mean, Coach, can Riley come over sometime?"

"Sure, if it's okay with his mom."

"That would be fine. Where do you live?"

"We're over by Campbell Lake. A place called Resolution Pointe."

"I've never heard of it. We live on Hillside, off Abbott Road."

"That's a nice part of town. I'll bet you get good views of the Alaska Range."

"We do. The sunsets are glorious."

"Well, maybe the kids can get together next week. After her sabbatical, my wife, Rachel, is flying up. We'd love to have your family over for dinner."

"That's a great idea. It's been a pleasure meeting you, Colt. I'll look for your new book."

"Thanks. Please tell your husband *'Rangers lead the way'* for me. He'll know what it means."

"I will."

He turned to Danny. "We need to head over to the Moreys for dinner. Riley, I'll see you and your mom here in two days."

"Well, actually, I'm working on Thursday," said Sara, "so Riley will be coming with Tommy's mom."

"Sounds good. It was a pleasure meeting you, Sara. Take care."

"Bye, Riley," said Danny.

"See you this Thursday," he replied.

Colt and Danny pulled into the Morey's driveway shortly after three. Scotty came running out and bear-hugged his friend. "Man, I've missed you. Welcome back to Alaska."

"Thanks, Scott. It's good to be home."

"How you can live in that rat race down there escapes me. What's it like to breathe fresh, clean air again?"

"I love it here; you know that. But Rachel's work is down there. Happy wife, happy life is my motto."

"Yeah, I hear you. She sure scored with that Chile gig. Plus, she won't have to see your mug for a whole summer."

"Yeah, she's liking life. Say hello to Danny."

Scotty hugged him. "Hi, Danny. It's great to see you again. You've grown a good six inches since I last saw you. Did your dad ever tell you about our Army days together? I've known him since he was seventeen."

"Hi, Uncle Scotty. My dad says he always outran you in Ranger School and that I shouldn't make you mad because you eat kids for lunch. I know he was kidding about you eating kids. Did you know that we climbed Flattop the other day?"

Scotty grabbed Danny and pretended to bite his head. "Hey, your dad was right about me eating kids. They taste better with mustard." Danny giggled at his antics. "I'll bet you enjoyed the hike."

"I did. We got to see Mount McKinley, I mean, Denali."

Scotty laughed. "Yep, we call it Denali up here. If anyone calls it McKinley, we'll know they're not from Alaska. Come on in, you two. Maggie's getting the food ready for the barbeque."

Colt had a great time catching up with his old friends. Scotty suggested they go on a two-day hike in the Chugach Mountains over the weekend. Colt and Danny eagerly said yes.

After dinner and talking, they didn't return to the Brennans' home until well after eight. It was a good day, the type of day Colt had hoped the summer would bring. Tomorrow, he planned to go with the kids and Annie on a drive along Turnagain Arm to see Portage Glacier.

12

SARA AND RILEY WERE in a good mood after soccer practice. She was glad her son made a new friend.

"Riley, let's stop at the bookstore to see if they have Coach Mercer's new book. After that, we need to check into renting a hospital bed for Grandpa Jamie. Then, let's go to McDonald's for an ice cream cone."

"Okay. Mom, can I have Danny over to play?"

"Honey, Grandpa Jamie is extremely ill. It won't be long before he goes to heaven. We need to make sure he's comfortable, so we can't have company for a while."

"I can't understand what he's saying anymore. He just mumbles."

"I know. It doesn't matter if you understand him or not. What he needs is your love. Just being with him comforts him a lot."

"When will he die, Mom?" Riley asked with tears in his eyes.

"Soon, Riley. Probably within the month. Hey, let's not dwell on that now." He nodded. She turned on the radio, hoping a little rock and roll would lighten the mood.

At the bookstore, she asked an employee if they had Colt's new book and was delighted to hear that they did. On the way to the register, she decided to tell Colt about what was happening at their home and ask if Riley could go over to his place and play with Danny. Her son needed a best friend more than ever.

At home, Sara told Penny she had found a place that rents hospital beds. Jon David arrived home from work shortly afterward. "Riley and I had a great day today," she said. "He had a blast at soccer. I didn't realize how down he's been about Jamie, and all that running around did him good. He made a new friend. His name is Danny, and his father is the team's coach. They're here for the summer while his wife is on a sabbatical to Chile. He said to tell you 'Rangers lead the way.' I haven't the slightest idea what that means. Oh! He's a children's author now, and he just wrote a novel. I bought it today at the bookstore."

"*Rangers lead the way* is a greeting Rangers say to each other. He sounds like an interesting guy. I'd like to meet him someday. Regarding Riley, we need to talk to him more about dealing with Jamie's illness."

"We do, but not tonight. He's feeling so good right now. Jon David, Penny told me that Jamie's losing control of his bladder. She doesn't want him to go to a nursing home. She wants him to die here if it's possible."

"That's fine with me. It's time for us to call Hospice of Anchorage. After he passes, I think our family and Penny will need their bereavement support."

Sara hugged him. "I know how hard this is on you, but we'll get through it. Let's talk about hospice with Penny after the kids are asleep. I'm so glad that Andrea's coming this weekend. Seeing his daughter will delight Jamie. I'm sure Penny is looking forward to seeing her, too. Let's go up and say hello to him. Keep your spirits up around him, okay? He doesn't need to see us moping around."

"Yeah, okay. It's hard not to look at him and cry."

"I know. I feel the same way." She kissed her husband, and they headed upstairs.

"Do you want to join us for dinner, Jamie?"

"No, Jon David, I don't feel like eating, but after dinner, would you sit with me on the deck?" He struggled to get the words out.

"Sure, I'd love to."

Jon David ate quickly and pushed Jamie in his wheelchair to the deck. After putting a blanket on his friend, he pulled up a chair and placed it facing Jamie.

"I'll miss seeing this view every day."

Jon David leaned over and squeezed his hand. "I love you. Not having you in my life will create a huge void within me."

"And just what m-makes you think I will no longer be in your life when I'm gone, young m-m-man?"

Jon David smiled meekly.

"When I was a soldier in Vietnam, I met a Buddhist monk. He said to me, 'Knock on the sky and listen to the sound.' I spent years trying to figure out the meaning of those w-w-words. After what happened to me at the cabin, I finally knew what he meant. I have something to tell you, and you need to hear." With much effort, he touched Jon David's hand. "I slur my words, so I will speak slowly." Jon David nodded. "You are my son. I expect you to talk to me after I'm gone. If you need help, I will be there for you. Knock on the sky and listen to the sound. It will be me. Do you understand what I'm saying to you? Knock on the sky and listen."

"I do. Thank you, Jamie."

"I want you to tell my kids the same thing."

"I will."

"Jon D-David, I want to be cremated and have my ashes scattered at the cabin. Will you do that for me?"

"Yes."

"I have one more request. Ice cream. Will you bring me some ice cream?"

"Yes, sir. We can all have ice cream on the deck if you want." Jamie nodded and gave him the best smile he could muster. The conversation left him exhausted.

That night, Sara started reading Colt's book. She didn't put it down until four in the morning. Jon David got up a short while later. Before heading upstairs, he kissed his wife goodbye. She stirred and opened her eyes. "Have a good day at work, my love."

"Thanks. You sure were up late."

"I know. I love Colt's new book. You've got to read it."

"Unless it's a textbook, I'm not much of a reader. But, if you like it that much, I'll try to get to it. I've got to go. Love you."

"I love you, too. Call me during your lunch hour, and I'll tell you how things are going around here." He nodded and left.

13

THURSDAY ARRIVED, AND THE kids were back on the practice field running around. Annie and Christa were there to see them play. Colt eyed his players carefully as they moved through the drills. He blew his whistle and gathered them up. "Okay, guys, today is the day for me to assign positions. First off, does anyone want to be the goalkeeper? It's an important position."

"I do, Coach. I played goalie last year."

"Okay, that's cool. Tommy is now our goalkeeper. Danny and Riley, you'll be forwards, our primary scorers. Jake and Rashad, you're our midfielders. Your job is to play the middle third of the field as our 'stoppers.' You'll try to get the ball to Danny and Riley so they can score a goal. Max and Zeke, you're our fullbacks. You'll work with Tommy to stop our opponents from scoring. Even though all of you will be defenders, the fullbacks and goalie are the big dogs when it comes to defending our net. Assume your positions, everyone, and let's give it a go."

They spent the rest of the day learning their assignments on the team. Colt was happy with what he was seeing. He looked at his watch and blew the whistle. "Gather up, everyone. Be sure to drink some water to rehydrate. Our first game is next Tuesday, and I can't wait to test our skills against another team. Keep practicing at home, and I'll see you next week."

Many of the team's parents came to Colt wanting to talk, including Annie, with Christa in tow. "Danny looked good out there today," she said. "I'm impressed that you have them playing together as a team already."

"Yeah, they're doing well. Hey, do you mind keeping an eye on Danny so I can talk to the other parents? He's over there with his teammates. They're trying to score goals."

"Sure."

Colt smiled and turned his attention to the waiting parents. Some acted like next week's game was akin to the World Cup. He patiently answered their questions. At the other end of the field, Danny and his two friends galloped toward the goal. Danny kicked the ball, and it soared over the net and rolled into the street. Not missing a beat, he chased after it.

In the street, a lady driving an SUV spotted a blur of motion to her right. Before she could jam on the breaks, there was a sickening thud. Something sailed through the air and landed on the pavement in front of her. She screeched to a halt, jumped out of her SUV, and screamed in horror at the sight of an unconscious boy.

Annie heard the woman's screams and scanned the field for Danny. "Oh God, no!" She raced into the street and spotted Danny lying motionless, his head covered in blood. "Colt!" she screamed with a bloodcurdling cry.

Colt sprinted to her and gasped when he saw his son. "Danny! Someone call 911! Call 911!" Many already had their phones out. "Oh my God! Oh my God!" He kneeled next to Danny and tried to feel for a pulse, but his hands shook too much.

One of the parents raced in and felt Danny's neck. "He has a weak pulse. Don't move him. Does anyone have a blanket?"

"Is he breathing?" Colt gasped. "We have to make sure his airway is open."

The man felt Danny's chest. "He is, but it's sporadic. DID ANYONE CALL FOR AN AMBULANCE!"

Several people shouted, "Yes!"

"We have to stop the bleeding," said Colt. He ripped off his T-shirt and put it on Danny's head. There were pieces of skull bone sticking out of his head. Colt nearly vomited. "Dear God, please don't let him die!"

Annie gave Christa to another parent. She touched her grandson, sobbing. "Oh Danny, oh Danny ..."

Colt glared at her. "You said you'd watch him!"

She gasped at the anger in his voice. "It happened so fast—" The enormity of what occurred hit her with full force. "I'm so sorry." Another parent stepped in and led her back to the playing field, offering comfort along the way.

An ambulance arrived within minutes, and two paramedics raced to Danny. The dented SUV grill conveyed what had happened. They quickly assessed the injured boy. "His breathing is labored. We need to intubate." They worked to stabilize and immobilize Danny to prevent further injury to his spine. "Sir, are you the parent?" one of them asked Colt as he worked.

"Yes."

"We're taking him to Providence ER; you can come with us."

The paramedics rushed Danny into the Providence emergency room. "His blood pressure is all over the place," one of them said to the trauma physician. "The last reading was 80 over 40."

"Thanks for getting him here so quickly." She looked at the unconscious child and flinched. He was wearing a soccer uniform— the same colors as her son's team. She lifted the head bandage and saw pieces of bones protruding from the child's scalp. Then, she removed the bandage covering his face and gasped. It was Danny Mercer. "Oh my God, I know this boy. He's on my son's soccer team. Get the resident neurologist down here now. Tell him it's a diffuse axonal brain injury. You—get me a priority for a CT scan. Let's cut off his clothes and check for other traumas."

Sara Luke fought the urge to cry while waiting for her staff to cut Danny's uniform away. The left side of his chest was deeply bruised and lacerated. She spotted lumps in his ribcage, a dead giveaway for broken ribs. "We need to be careful that one of his ribs doesn't puncture his lung. Let's get his vitals nailed down. I need rectal temp, blood pressure, heart rate and pulse, respiratory rate, and oxygen saturation." She opened Danny's eyelids. His pupils were non-responsive. "Danny, can you hear me? Open your eyes if you can hear me." Nothing. She moved down to his feet and checked for any motor response to stimulation. Again, nothing.

The neurologist raced in. Sara looked at him. "Car accident. Severe skull fracture. Comatose. Both pupils are dilated and unreactive to light. His Glasgow Coma Scale score is six. BP is holding steady at 90 over 60. Pulse is weak. The CT scan will tell if bone frags penetrated the brain. He has multiple co-existing injuries and chest trauma with rib fractures. Too soon to tell on cervical injuries."

He shook his head. "Light a fire under the CT staff—we need the scan done ASAP!"

A nurse got off the phone. "They're ready for doing the CT."

Three hours later, Sara wearily walked out of the ER. "Hello, Colt. Do you remember me? I'm the trauma physician here."

He nodded. "Is he going to be okay?"

"It's not good. Danny suffered a traumatic brain injury and is in a deep coma. His brain is swelling, which is called cerebral edema. If this intracranial pressure continues, we'll have to perform a decompressive craniectomy—it's a procedure where we remove part of the skull to allow the brain to expand.

"His EEG shows activity, which means he isn't brain dead. Since being here, he's had three seizures, and we're giving him medicine for that. He has a fractured skull, but none of the bone fragments penetrated his brain."

Sara sighed. "Unfortunately, there's more. "Danny has three fractured ribs. The trauma that fractured his ribs caused a pulmonary contusion, or bruise, to his left lung. This damaged the lung's capillaries, causing blood and other fluids to accumulate in the lung tissue. It's now interfering with his breathing. Infection is a possibility with this type of injury. Also, trauma to his spine and neck is a possibility. We all need to pray for Danny. The next few days are critical."

"I'm his grandfather. Should we call his mother to come? Is it that dire?"

Sara looked at him and nodded.

"Can I see him now?" asked Colt.

"Let me check. If something happens while you're with Danny, I want your word that you'll stay out of the way."

"You have it."

"Give me a few minutes to make it happen."

She returned a short time later. "A nurse will soon take you to see Danny." She reached into her pocket, pulled out a scrap of paper, and wrote something down. She handed it to him. "My shift is over, and our hospital policy requires me to leave when being off duty. If you have any questions, call me at home at this number." She hugged him and left.

In her car, Sara looked upward. "Thank you, God, that it wasn't Riley." She broke down.

Scotty and Maggie arrived at the hospital and found Colt and Pat in the ER waiting room. "Colt, I'm so sorry. Maggie and I will watch Christa at a moment's notice. Call us anytime."

Maggie then hugged him. "Anything you need, you call us."

"Thanks, you two. Pat, please call Rachel and tell her to come."

"Sure. God help our little boy."

A nurse came out and motioned for Colt to follow her to the ER room. After he left, Pat turned to Maggie and Scotty. "He's going to need you two in the days ahead. We all will need you."

"I'm glad you called us. You can count on us, sir."

"Let me call Annie and fill her in," said Pat. "If she wants to come here, will you care for Christa and their little dog, too?"

"Of course we will," said Scott. "We'll go for a walk and return in ten minutes to see what you two decide. Colt's part of our family, too, Pat. Anything you need, we'll do it. It's that easy."

"Thanks, Scotty. I'll call Annie now and get back with you."

"See you in a few." He and Maggie left to give him time to make the call. When they returned, Pat had a plan. "Annie wants to come so we can make the call to Rachel together. She'll have a bag packed for Christa when you come. You remember how to get to our house, right?"

"Yes, sir, we do."

"Pat, don't worry about Christa. She and the dog can stay with us the whole summer if necessary."

"Thank you, Maggie. Please pray for Danny."

"We will," said Scotty. "Sir, will Annie be okay driving here? If not, I'll drive her over."

"You driving her here is a good idea."

"No problem. I'll drop off Maggie and Christa at my house and then come back here with Annie."

"Thanks, Scotty."

An hour later, Scotty brought a distraught Annie to where Pat was sitting. She ran to her husband and hugged him.

Scotty looked at Pat. "Any change, sir?"

"No. Nothing to report."

"I'll leave you guys alone so you can make the call to your daughter. Do you need anything else?"

"No. I'll call you in the morning with a progress report or sooner if anything happens. Thanks for all you're doing."

He nodded and left.

Annie took a seat and stared at the wall.

Pat sighed. "Are you ready to call Rachel?"

"It's my fault. Colt asked me to watch Danny. All this is my fault. He told me so, and he's right."

"Who told you so?"

"Colt. When he was holding Danny, he looked at me and said it. He's right. It's my fault."

"Look at me, Annie." He waited for her eyes to meet his. "There's no way you could've prevented what happened. A cop came by earlier and said many parents saw the whole thing. Danny darted onto the street to get the ball. You couldn't stop that split-second act—no one could. The police aren't citing the driver of the car. It was an accident."

"It's not that simple. Colt asked me to watch him."

"Damn it, Annie, shit happens. Pardon my language, but it's the truth. There's no time for you to wallow in self-pity. Danny's fighting for his life, and our family needs your strength, not your whimpering. Whatever Colt said to you was said in the heat of the moment. It was his anguish talking, not him."

She wiped her eyes and nodded. "You're right. Let's make the call."

14

SARA DROVE HOME AFTER collecting herself. No one was there when she walked in. She knew something was wrong. A note pinned on their bedroom door confirmed it: *Jamie's having multiple seizures. We're at the VA hospital. JD*

"Oh God, not now, not now." She turned around and, with Danny's blood still on her scrubs, got back in her car. Tears rolled down her cheeks as she drove. Twenty minutes later, she found her family. They were quietly sitting around Jamie in the hospital room. Penny was holding his hand, talking to him in hushed tones.

Jon David stood and greeted her. He moved close to her ear and whispered. "It's not good. After the last seizure, he lost consciousness. His breathing is labored, and with his DNR directive, they aren't going to do anything if he crashes. I've called their children and told them he probably won't make it through the night. Do you want the kids to witness his passing?"

"No!" She said the word loud enough for all to hear. She gathered herself and leaned toward her husband's ear. "I'm sorry for the outburst. I've had a dreadful day. Danny Mercer, Riley's soccer friend, was hit by a car, and he has massive brain trauma. He also may not last the night."

"Oh my God! Riley said he got hurt, but he didn't know how badly."

"This is all too much. I'm close to losing it right now. I kept picturing Riley being the one injured when I was working on Danny."

Jon David nodded and turned his attention to his family. "Kids, after your mom says goodbye to Grandpa Jamie, she's going to take you home. Grandma Penny and I will stay here with him."

Sara squeezed his hand and mouthed a silent "thank you." She looked at Penny. "I've been dreading this day."

Penny nodded. "It's time for you to say goodbye to Jamie."

Sara tenderly put Jamie's hand in hers. She squeezed it as she whispered something into his ear and kissed his forehead. "God bless you, dear sweet Jamie," she said aloud. She turned around and faced her children. "Kids, say goodbye to Grandpa. We need to go home."

While they said their goodbyes, Sara hugged her husband again. "I'll be better in the morning."

"We'll get through this. Go home and try to rest." He kissed her and hugged the kids goodbye.

The night passed slowly. Penny and Jon David took turns speaking to Jamie. He was unresponsive, but it didn't matter to them. At four that morning, his soul left his body. There was no rally where he awoke and spoke his last words. He just faded away.

The attending physician entered the room, alerted by Jamie's life support monitor. He turned off the monitor and noted the time of death.

Jon David kissed his friend's forehead and said a final goodbye.

Penny put a hand on her husband's chest. She looked at the doctor. "May I have a few minutes alone with him?"

"Of course, Mrs. Spell," said the physician. "Take your time."

Jon David hugged her and left the room. He thanked the doctor for his condolences. Alone in the hallway, the enormity of what had occurred hit him. The man who saved his life was gone. He sank to the floor and wept.

15

THE MORNING BROUGHT NO joy in the ICU room. Colt sat at Danny's bedside, holding his hand, mentally saying every prayer he had ever learned. A doctor came in. "Mr. Mercer, we'll be doing a follow-up CT scan later this morning to see if the diuretics and a drug called mannitol are working to reduce Danny's intracranial pressure. His vital signs are stable, which is good. We'll keep him on mechanical ventilation due to the pulmonary contusion."

"If the CT shows no more swelling, does that mean he'll be okay?"

The doctor shook his head. "Mr. Mercer, traumatic brain injury, or TBI, is a severe condition. We use something called the Glasgow Coma Scale to classify TBI severity. It grades a person's level of consciousness on a scale of three to fifteen. Anything below eight is considered severe. Your son's rating was six. He won't get over this in a day or two. Many people with severe TBI don't die right away but rather days to weeks following the event. Even with hospitalization, forty percent of TBI victims will worsen. Just imagine how delicate a brain is. It can't handle sudden acceleration/deceleration within the skull or have its blood vessels being stretched, compressed, or traumatized. Little can be done to reverse the damage caused by trauma. If he survives the next few days, we'll move him from ICU to the neurosurgical ward. It's likely that Danny will never regain consciousness. You need to prepare yourself for that. For now, all we can do is wait and see."

Colt felt nauseous.

An hour passed, and a nurse came in. "Sir, we have to work on Danny's wounds, and then he'll be off for a CT scan. His grandparents are out in the waiting area. After the scan, one of them can take your place. This is going to be a long, hard battle, Mr. Mercer, so you need to take care of yourself."

He looked at her and sighed. "Okay."

She led him to the waiting room. Katie, his sister-in-law, had flown up from Oregon. She was there with Pat and Annie. They jumped to their feet when they saw him.

"He's still alive," Colt said wearily. "The doctor said he might never regain consciousness."

"I'm so sorry, Colt," said Katie. "We're all here for you; you know that."

He hugged her. "Thanks for coming. Rachel will need you."

"I'll be here for the next week."

He nodded and turned his attention to Pat. "Sir, they said you can stay with Danny so I can get some sleep. Where's Christa?"

"She's with the Moreys. They're taking good care of her and Harley," said Annie. "Rachel is on her way. It could take two days."

"Colt," said Pat, "the police were here. They said eyewitnesses told them that the driver of the car had no chance to stop. She wasn't speeding or driving recklessly; it was an accident, pure and simple."

He nodded. "Annie, please forgive me. My anger had to lash out at something, and you were there. I know there was nothing you could've done."

She kissed his cheek. "I understand why you reacted that way. From now on, our focus needs to be on Danny's recovery. Looking backward and playing the 'what if' game serves no purpose. All that matters now is doing whatever it takes to get him well."

"You're right."

"Colt," said Katie, "let me drive you home. Dad and Momma will stay here."

Too tired to say anything, he nodded.

16

JON DAVID AND PENNY returned home at six in the morning and went to their respective bedrooms to rest after their long night. He undressed and snuggled in with his wife. She awoke and looked at him, wanting news. "He passed away at four o'clock." There was nothing else for him to say.

"God rest his soul. Is Penny okay?"

"She's exhausted and wants to get some sleep."

"You need to rest, too."

"I know. I'm beyond tired."

"I'll wait on telling the kids. We should tell them as a family."

He didn't reply. He was already asleep.

She eased out of bed, went upstairs, and called Providence for an update on Danny. The news wasn't good, but at least he was alive. She looked in on the kids, and both were sleeping peacefully.

At ten-thirty, they came upstairs, hungry for breakfast. Sara whispered for them to be quiet so they wouldn't disturb their father and Penny. She put some instant waffles in the toaster and cut up bananas and strawberries.

Riley sat on a barstool and looked at his mom as she sliced the fruit. "How's Grandpa Jamie? Is he okay?"

"We'll talk about that later when Dad and Penny are awake. After we eat, let's go swimming. It'll be fun, and then we can go to the Lucky Wishbone for lunch."

"Okay," said Riley. "Mom, what about Danny? Is he okay?"

She sighed. "He's in the hospital now and will be there for a while to heal. We need to keep him in our prayers and ask God to help him recover."

After they ate and got dressed, Sara left a note on the fridge telling Jon David where they'd be.

A while later, Jon David stirred from his sleep. Thoughts of how Jamie delighted in sitting on the deck during his last days crowded his thinking. He felt compelled to write these thoughts down before they escaped him. He got out a pen and paper and started writing.

The fabric of his existence worn thin by the motion of days, blurred memories of the seasons; youth distant now, distant, lost when he knows not. Frailty coats his tired body, and reflection seems more key than action. Time, once a friend, now a silent, stalking foe. The pull of the earth appears more pronounced in the twilight of his being—perhaps the heavens too are pulling, and the earth refuses to release. Still, he finds himself looking more at the stars than the flowers, and a feeling of anticipation settles in; a yearning deep within stirs. Each moment he measures, savoring its pleasures and rewards; he sighs when remembering how often he forgot the present in favor of the past or future. But not now. One last look at the clouds—puffy, dancing, dreaming in the sky; squirrels hustling about, another season to prepare for; mother bird feeding her young. He stares for hours, the present triggering golden moments of the past. The feeling is utter contentment. He watches knowingly as the sun slips under the horizon, going, going, gone.

He read what he wrote and was satisfied that he captured the words in his thoughts. Then, he turned the paper over and wrote one more sentence:

In the end, he peacefully released his delicate grip of earth and floated effortlessly into the heavens.

He put the paper on his nightstand and looked up. "Goodbye, Jamie. I love you."

He shaved and showered. As he headed upstairs, Sara and the kids returned. He greeted them with hugs. Sara whispered in his ear. "I said we'd talk about Jamie after you and Penny were up. Is she awake yet?"

"Good idea. No, she's still asleep."

She leaned in. "I want to be with her. Will you watch the kids?"

"Sure." He turned to them. "Hey, you two, let's go downstairs and watch a movie so your mom can be with Penny for a little while."

Sara tiptoed into Penny's room and found her sleeping on her side. She crawled under the covers, snuggled next to her, and kissed her cheek. Penny took her hand and squeezed it. Neither said a word.

Although the kids knew it was coming, the news of their beloved grandfather's passing had them in tears. Grandma Penny assured them that Grandpa Jamie would now be happy in heaven.

17

TWO DAYS AFTER GETTING the phone call from her parents, Rachel's airplane touched down at the Anchorage airport in driving rain. She'd been awake the whole time, praying and aching to be with her son. She sprinted down the long concourse and spotted her parents. The grief in her erupted. "Momma! Momma!" Her spine-chilling screams shocked those nearby. Annie hugged her daughter with all her might.

Pat was shocked at the haggard condition of his daughter. "Danny's still alive, Rachel. We'll go straight to the hospital."

Annie took her hand and guided her toward the exit. "Colt's been with him constantly. Katie flew up, and she's at the hospital, too. Christa's with the Moreys. They're taking good care of her."

For the rest of the way, they tried to prepare her for what she'd be seeing.

In the ICU room, Rachel gasped at the sight of her son. The ventilator, electronic monitors, and tubes confirmed the worst was indeed true. She dashed to her little boy. "Danny, it's Momma! I'm here now." She kissed his cheek and put her hand on his chest. "Momma's here."

Colt touched her. "I'm so sorry, Rachel. I'm so sorry."

She hugged him. "It's my fault. It was my selfishness that caused this. If I hadn't left, none of this would've happened."

"Don't say that, sweetheart. It's no one's fault."

"Colt's right," said Annie. "None of this is anyone's fault. An accident can happen anywhere. Colt, what's the latest news on his condition?"

Katie answered her question. "The doctors were here just a few minutes ago. There's no change. Danny's still extremely critical. There's nothing we can do but wait."

"Rachel, how long has it been since you've slept?"

"That's not important, Dad. I want to speak to Danny's doctors."

"There'll be plenty of time for that tomorrow. Both you and Colt are exhausted and need to sleep. Stay with Danny for the rest of the evening, and then Annie and Katie will take you both home. I'll stay with him. It's not open for debate from either of you." His voice was firm. He was taking charge of his family. They didn't argue. "Colt, one more thing. Please give me the ER doc's phone number. Remember, she gave it to you when she met with us. I'm going to ask her to meet with you and Rachel tomorrow to discuss Danny's condition and what we can do for him. I don't know why, but I trust her." Colt reached into his pocket and handed him the paper.

Later that night, Pat called the doctor.

"Hello." It was a man who answered.

"Um, hello. My name is Pat Brennan, and I'm the grandfather of a patient Dr. Luke saw the other day. May I speak to her?"

"Sir, it's not a good time to talk to my wife. My father just passed away."

"I'm so sorry to hear that. Thanks for your time. No, wait. I really need to speak to her. She gave us this number and said we could call at any time. Sir, Dr. Luke knows my grandson. He's your son's soccer teammate."

"Oh my God, you're talking about Danny. We've been praying for him. Hang on a moment, and I'll get her."

"Hello, Mr. Brennan. This is Sara Luke. What can I do for you?"

"I'm sorry to hear of your loss, Dr. Luke, but I have an enormous favor to ask you."

"Go on."

"Danny's mother just arrived from Chile. I was wondering if you'd come by the ICU tomorrow and meet them so you could explain Danny's condition in detail. You're the mom of a little boy the same age as Danny. I know your words would mean a lot to them."

"Mr. Brennan, I'm no longer your grandson's caregiver, and I cannot interfere in any way. I also couldn't give them any advice due to medical insurance restrictions. I recommend talking to his current doctors. They're specialists and are up to date on his condition."

"Dr. Luke, I'm asking you to come as a mother to help console another mother. I understand you won't be coming in any official capacity. I'll tell them that."

She hesitated before replying. "Mr. Brennan, since I know Danny and his father, I'll come as a family friend. Will one o'clock tomorrow work?"

"Yes, that time is fine. Thank you, Dr. Luke."

The next morning, Annie had breakfast ready when Colt and Rachel awoke. She told them Pat had called and said Danny's status was unchanged. On the way to the hospital, they stopped at the Moreys to see Christa. She was surprised to see her mom.

"You both look better than yesterday," said a weary Pat as they entered the ICU. "I called Dr. Luke, and she's coming to meet with you at one o'clock. She's here strictly as a family friend and can offer no advice. It's all about medical insurance crap. One more thing: her father-in-law just passed away, so her family is going through a tough time."

"When did she become a family friend?" asked Rachel.

"Her son is on my soccer team," said Colt. "His name is Riley. She's the ER doc who first saw Danny. Thanks for asking her to see us, Pat."

"You're welcome. I hope she can help make sense of all this."

Annie touched her grandson's chest and kissed his cheek. "It's me, Nana. I love you, little man."

She took Pat's hand and looked at Colt and Rachel. "I'm going to run Pat home, and then Katie and I will spend the rest of the day with Christa. Call me if anything changes." She hugged them goodbye. Pat was too tired to say anything more. He absently followed his wife out of the room.

Sara arrived at the hospital early and met with Danny's neurologist for an update. She told him about seeing the Mercers strictly as a friend, which was okay with him. She then walked to the ICU and found Colt and Rachel sitting on each side of Danny. She looked at Rachel. "Hello. You must be Mrs. Mercer. I'm Dr. Sara Luke. I wish we could be meeting under better circumstances."

Rachel stood and shook Sara's hand. "I'm pleased to meet you."

"Hello, Dr. Luke," said Colt. "Thanks for coming. Please accept our condolences for your loss."

"Thank you. Jamie was a special man to my family and me. I hope Mr. Brennan told you I'm here in an unofficial capacity."

"He did. As far as anyone's concerned, you're just a friend," said Rachel.

"Good. In that case, please call me Sara."

"You're welcome to call me Rachel."

"Okay. Rachel, I'm not sure if you know, but my son Riley is on the same soccer team as Danny. They became fast friends. I was the one who first cared for Danny in the ER here. You're supposed to be unemotional as an ER doc, but my heart ached when I saw Danny. It could've been my son."

Rachel hugged her. "Thanks for caring for our son, Sara, and thanks for coming here today."

"You're welcome. All right, I'll put on my unofficial doctor hat. I'll begin by saying I've been a board-certified trauma surgeon for several years. A trauma surgeon specializes in resuscitating and stabilizing people who've been in a serious accident. I worked at Harborview Medical Center in Seattle, which is the only Level I adult and pediatric trauma center in the Northwest, including Alaska. I was also in the Air Force Reserve and headed a medical team that accompanied critically wounded soldiers and airmen from Iraq and Afghanistan to Germany. I tell you this, so you'll know that I'm qualified to address the issues with your son."

They nodded. "Okay. I'll first discuss what these tubes and monitors are for, so they won't intimidate you." She took her time explaining them. Following this, she spoke in detail about Danny's physical injuries.

"Sara," said Rachel, "please talk to us about him being in a coma. Will he regain consciousness?"

"That's a good question. Let's start with the basics. In medicine, a coma means 'deep sleep.' It's a deep state of unconsciousness. The degree of unresponsiveness usually correlates to how well the brain is functioning. Two players in the brain work in concert with each other to produce consciousness. One is in the brainstem, and it's called the reticular activating system. The other is in the cerebral cortex, which covers the cerebrum. In Danny's case, we can't tell which of these neurological components is malfunctioning. It could be both."

"Is he going to die, Sara? That's all we need to know."

"I don't know, Colt. No one can tell. Some patients seem to get well, and then they crash. Children seem especially vulnerable to condition swings. How the brain works is still a great mystery to medical science."

"Should we take him to Seattle? Do they have better medical care there?"

"Rachel, right now, I don't think he'd survive the flight. It could do more harm than good. The neurosurgeon here is quite skilled. I'd trust having my son in his care."

"Can you give us a time estimate for him being out of the woods?"

"No, Colt, I can't. You need to accept the possibility that he'll either succumb or be in a permanent vegetative state." Her words brought tears to them. Sara sighed. "I so wish I had better news to give you."

18

SARA DROVE HOME IN tears. A block away from her house, she parked her car on the street, turned off the engine, and reached for her phone.

"Hello, Dad. I need to talk to you and Mom."

After talking to her parents, Sara drove home. Upstairs, she found the family feasting on pizza and laughing. Jon David stood and kissed her. "We were talking about Jamie falling into the river when he tried to land Andrea's first fish." He leaned in and lowered his voice. "How did it go?"

"As good as can be expected," she whispered back.

"Do you want to join us for pizza? I ordered your favorite."

"Sure, but afterward, I need to talk to you." He nodded, knowing that something wasn't right.

Sara sat and did her best to converse and eat. Penny saw her struggling and took the lead. "Hey, kids, let's play Monopoly so your mom and dad can catch up on things. Andrea always won when she was a kid, so let's see if she's still as good as she used to be."

"I'm even better than I was as a kid," her daughter responded with a devilish smile. "Do you still keep the games in the hall closet?"

"We do."

Sara mouthed a "thank you" to Penny. Downstairs, she closed the door and looked at her husband. "I, I just can't do it anymore."

"Do what, Sara?"

"Be a trauma surgeon. When Danny came into the ER, I could barely function. I need to ask for your concurrence to quit at Providence. I can't do it anymore. I was fooling myself into thinking I could. I'll figure out some other way to earn money."

"I'll support whatever you want to do."

"Thanks. I talked to my dad and mom on the way home. I have a huge favor to ask of you. I want to fly home with the kids and spend a month there. Between Jamie and Danny, there's been too much pain here. I need a break from it. The kids do, too."

"That's fine with me. Are we doing okay?"

She hugged him. "We're more than okay. I love you so much. I'll call you every day."

"I'd love to head east too, but I have no leave built up. Let's get online now and book a flight. After that, we'll tell Penny and the kids."

"Thank you," she said with palpable relief in her voice. "Oh. I forgot to mention that I saw what you wrote about Jamie. It's beautiful. Would you mind sharing it with Penny and Andrea? I know they'd cherish it."

"Sure. I don't know why, but the words just came to me."

Two days later, while Jon David was at work, Penny drove Sara and the kids to the airport. The day before, Sara gave her notice to Providence. They were sympathetic regarding her decision. The burnout rate for ER docs is substantial, so they were used to seeing physicians come and go. While at Providence, she saw Danny and told his parents about her month-long trip back east. She promised to see them after she returned. Danny was still unconscious, and with each passing day, the odds of him remaining in a permanent vegetative state increased.

19

One month later ...

JON DAVID AND PENNY greeted Sara and the kids at the airport. They looked tanned and happy. "Guess what, Dad? Grandpa says I'm now a better sailor than you!" said Riley. "We had a blast out on the ocean."

"I'll bet you're a great sailor. Your grandpa's a terrific teacher."

"I learned how to ride a bike, Daddy. Momma taught me."

"Wow, Kelly. I envy all of you. All I did here was work. And Grandma Penny has kept me busy in the yard."

At home, Jon David helped Sara unpack. She pulled a book from her bag and handed it to him. "You've got to read this."

He looked at the title. *"Howling Across Bridges.* Isn't this the book you wanted me to read a while ago?"

"Yes. Danny's father wrote it. Trust me; you'll love it."

"I'll put it on my 'to-do' list. By the way, a couple of weeks ago, I called to see how Danny was doing. He's off the ventilator but is still comatose. Given the length of time since the accident, my guess is he'll remain in a permanent vegetative state. He's now at the Providence Transitional Care Center."

"Thanks for checking on him. Sadly, I agree with you. Maybe tomorrow I'll go see him and his parents." She kissed him. "I've missed you so much. You won't be getting much sleep tonight."

He smiled. "I hoped you'd say that."

The following morning, Jon David stepped out of the shower to see his wife greeting him with a smile. She had Colt's book in her hand. "After you get dressed, go out on the deck and start reading. I'll call you when brunch is ready."

"What about the kids?"

"Penny took them to see a movie."

"God bless that woman. You really want me to read this, don't you?"

"I do."

"Well, after all you did last night to show how you missed me, how can I refuse?" he said with a sly smile.

"That's the spirit."

When Sara poked her head out of the sliding glass door to announce that brunch was ready, Jon David reluctantly closed the book.

"I just finished chapter four, where Scotty told him about his friend Manny getting killed in Afghanistan."

"After we eat, you're welcome to keep reading. I've got a lot of things to do around here."

"Thanks, but I plan on spending every minute I can with you before Penny and the kids return."

She took a sip of coffee and smiled. "That sounds a lot better than doing chores."

The next day, Sara drove to the transitional care center. She found Colt and Rachel sitting in the room with Danny. They looked even more haggard since she last saw them. "Hello, you two. How are you doing?"

They were surprised to see her.

"Hello, Sara," said Colt. "As for how we're doing ..." He pointed to his motionless son and shrugged his shoulders. He looked so tired.

"We have some big decisions to make," said Rachel. "I've been on an extended absence from work, and the medical bills are piling up, as you can imagine. We'll probably head back to California and find a place for Danny there. Sara, I talk to him all the time, but it does no good." She started crying.

"I'm so sorry."

"Do you think he'll live much longer?"

"I don't know, Colt. I'd have to talk to his caregivers to answer you."

"Don't bother," he said with bitterness in his voice. "All they say is every patient is different."

"Unfortunately, what they're saying is true. I just came here to say that I'm thinking about all of you."

"Would you consider being his doctor? We trust you."

"Thanks for your confidence in me, Colt. But, before I left to see my parents, I turned in my notice at Providence. After years of seeing shattered bodies, I can't deal with it anymore. My husband is a pediatrician. I can ask him to give an informal assessment of Danny."

"Thanks. Rachel and I would appreciate it," said Colt.

"We would," said Rachel. "I wish I'd met you under different circumstances. I think we would've become friends."

"I do, too, Rachel. We can still be friends. I'd love to have lunch or maybe go on a walk. I'll give you my number, and you can call me anytime, just to talk if you want." She touched Rachel's hand to emphasize the point.

"Thanks. That sounds good."

Sara hugged her. "I'll say goodbye for now. God bless you all."

On the way to her car, she looked at her watch. There was still time to catch Jon David on his lunch hour. She headed there.

Jon David was eating a sandwich when she walked into his office. He stood and kissed her. "Well, this is a surprise. What brings you here?"

"I just came from seeing Danny and his parents. There's no change in his condition. They're considering moving him to a facility in California. Like you said the other day, his coma is probably permanent."

Jon David shook his head and sighed. "That's too bad. I can't even begin to imagine how I'd cope if it had been Riley."

"I know. I think about the same thing all the time. Jon David, will you examine Danny? Maybe there's something that's been overlooked. You're quite good at spotting subtle things, like Jamie's tremor." She teared up. "His parents are hanging on by a thread.

They have major decisions to make about what to do with Danny. I know they'd appreciate you talking to them, even if it's just to say there's little hope."

"I just finished Colt's book. What a tough life he's had. His parents were killed by a drunk driver when he was just seventeen years old, then being an Army Ranger and sniper. Three tours in Iraq and Afghanistan, losing so many of his friends to combat, and then meeting that stray dog and traveling across North America with him on a Harley to try to get his life back in order. And then, he becomes a bestselling children's book author. His story is inspiring, and I feel I know him as if we've been friends for years. Man, his dog Jekyll was something. Heck, look at me—I'm tearing up. So, yeah, I'll see his son. I doubt I can do much good, but I'll give it a go."

"That's all I ask. Thank you. I feel so attracted to Colt and Rachel. Under different circumstances, they could've been our best friends. Can you see Danny soon, maybe in the next couple of days?"

"Sara, it's more than just doing a physical exam. I'd first need to go through his medical records before assessing him, and for that, I'd need his parent's permission. Plus, Danny's primary caregiver would have to give me the okay to do it. That's not going to happen fast."

"I have both their numbers right here. I'll call the parents if you call Danny's physician," Sara said with an eager smile.

He chuckled and looked at his watch. "I have an appointment in a half-hour, so we need to hurry."

While talking to Danny's physician, in the background, Jon David overheard someone yelling, "Dr. Luke has my permission to see my son's records!" Obviously, Sara was successful in her quest to contact Colt. The doctor agreed to Jon David coming by later in the day to review Danny's charts. Sara beamed when he relayed the news and kissed him goodbye.

Jon David arrived at the transitional care center at two o'clock and poured through Danny's medical records. He grimaced after closing the folder. Nothing was lacking in the care Danny had received. He and Sara were right—the outcome was bleak. Armed with the medical facts, he walked into Danny's room at four-thirty. Only Colt was there with Danny.

"Hello, Colt. My name is Dr. Jon David Luke. Rangers lead the way."

Colt rocketed up from his chair and hugged him. "Thank you for coming, Dr. Luke."

"Please call me Jon David. I finished reading your book today. It touched my heart."

"Thanks. That part of my life seems so long ago now."

Jon David hiked up his pant leg, showing his prosthetic leg. "Part of me didn't leave Iraq. You're right; it does seem like long ago. Do you mind if I examine Danny?"

"Please do."

Jon David pulled a stethoscope from his coat pocket and listened to Danny's heart and then his lungs for any signs of pneumonia. He asked Colt to help turn him on his side and checked for decubitus ulcers, or bedsores. He then did an impromptu neurologic examination.

Afterward, he turned his attention to Colt. "I need to review Danny's records further, and then I'll get back with you."

"That's it? That's all you have to say to me?"

"For now, yes."

Colt's jaw tightened. "You know, you're just like all the other clowns around here. They drop by and do the same cursory exam you just did, and it all comes to nothing. You guys are quite adept at running up the bills to support your lavish lifestyles. Just for once, I'd like to see some action instead of the same disingenuous 'let's wait and see' crap."

Jon David gave him an icy stare. "Do you think I'm a magician who can snap my damn fingers and have your son suddenly wake? This little boy had major trauma to the most delicate organ in his body. As for my 'lavish' lifestyle, you seem to forget that I'm not charging you a damn thing for my time. So shut the hell up and let me do my work."

His blunt response startled Colt. His lips quivered. "Sir, please forgive my outburst. I … I'm struggling right now."

Jon David eased his stance and nodded in empathy. "I know you are, Colt. Just know this: You have a new friend in me, and Rangers never leave another Ranger behind. And that includes their children."

Colt smiled meekly. "Thank you." A tear rolled down his cheek.

Jon David hugged his new friend. "Give me your number so I can call you."

Colt wrote it down. "When do you think I'll hear back from you?" he said as he handed the paper over.

"I don't know. Soon, I hope. I promise nothing regarding Danny's recovery, is that clear?"

"It is."

"Good. I'll say goodbye for now."

After leaving the facility, Jon David drove to Kincaid Park, which bordered Cook Inlet. He took a trail that led to the inlet and climbed to the top of a glacier-deposited boulder offering grand views of the Alaska Range. After making sure he was alone, Jon David looked upward.

"Hello, Jamie, it's me. I'll bet you never thought I'd be talking to you so soon. Dear friend, I need your help. There's a boy named Danny who's been in an accident. He's the same age as Riley, and he's in a vegetative state from brain trauma. I fear his condition is permanent.

"I'd like to bring Danny to the cabin and have the spirit people heal him. I'm asking you to persuade them to do it. They told me we all have a part to play in the divine plan, and I know I should accept this, but I have such trouble accepting it for children. Please talk to them, Jamie. Give me a sign if they'll help, and I'll do my best to get Danny to the cabin." He sighed. "I miss you so much."

On the way home, as Jon David drove up Abbott Road, he noticed rain-laden clouds hugging the tops of the nearby Chugach Mountains. Just before turning onto the street leading to his house, a spectacular double rainbow appeared in the valley between the

Flattop and O'Malley peaks. "YES!" he shouted at the top of his lungs. He banged the steering wheel in total delight. "YES!"

At home, Jon David threw open the front door and rushed in. "Sara! Penny!" The whole family ran up from downstairs, wondering what was going on. "Sara and Penny, I need to see you right now. Kids, can you give us some time to talk?"

"We just started a movie so they can keep watching it," said Sara. "Kids, do you mind?"

"Is everything all right, Dad?" asked Riley.

"Yes. I figured out a way to help Danny!"

Riley's eyes went wide. "I'll watch Kelly so you can talk."

Jon David charged upstairs. "What did you find?" Sara asked as she ran after him.

"I have something important to share with both of you."

After they took a seat, Jon David began. "I spent the afternoon reviewing Danny's records, and then I gave him a cursory examination. In my professional opinion, he's hopeless. He'll be comatose until he dies."

"Well, why did you call us up here acting so excited?"

"Sara, hear me out, but first, let me digress a little. Shortly before he died, Jamie said he expected me to talk to him after he was gone. He said he'd 'search the heavens' and find the spirit people if I ever needed help. After looking at Danny and knowing with all my heart that it would take a miracle to heal him, that's when it hit me—take him to the cabin. I told Colt I needed to review Danny's medical records further and then I'd get back to him. He expected to hear a lot more from me, but that's how we left it.

"After leaving the facility, I went to Kincaid Park and talked to Jamie. I told him I wanted to bring Danny to the cabin so the spirit people could heal him. I asked him to give me a sign if they would help. Well, on the way home, just before I turned onto our street, a magnificent double rainbow appeared over the Chugach. The sign from Jamie couldn't have been clearer."

"Oh my God!" said Penny. "We have to take Danny to the cabin."

Sara wasn't as enthusiastic. "Jon David, I believe you, but if we say, *Let's take your comatose boy out of the hospital and bring him to a remote cabin to be healed,*' his parents will think we're crazy."

"I've thought about that and have an answer. It will take all of us to convince Colt and Rachel to do this. Penny, you can give them the cabin's history, Jamie's healing there, and how you came for me in DC. I can tell them my story, and Sara, you can speak of how Spirit told you to find me."

"Do you realize how long it would take to do all that?" asked Sara.

"It would take a long time. We'd need to bring them to our house where we can talk uninterrupted."

"What about our kids? Who will watch them?"

"I don't have everything worked out, Sara. There are lots of details to nail down."

"You can't just pull Danny out of the transitional care center. He has a feeding tube and needs round-the-clock monitoring."

"Sara, I reviewed his records closely. His condition is relatively stable. As parents, Colt and Rachel have the right to withdraw Danny from the facility and care for him at their home with an in-home nurse. That's the easy part. The hard part is we both know he could crash at any time, and we have no advanced equipment to deal with a medical emergency. Even the altitude changes to and from the cabin could trigger something bad. But that's a risk we'll have to take."

"How will you get him there?" asked Penny. "None of us are pilots, and we don't have an airplane."

"We'd have to charter a plane or helicopter."

"My God, Jon David, the logistics are staggering, and you're right—just getting him there is risky. More importantly, you can't guarantee he'll be healed."

"I know, but I have faith."

"I do, too," said Penny.

Sara remained unconvinced. "I'm sorry, but if it were Riley and a couple of strangers proposed flying my critically ill son to a cabin in the middle of nowhere to be healed by a bunch of spirit people, I'd think they were whackos trying to dupe me. We barely know his parents. What we're suggesting they do will sound absurd to them."

Penny put her hand on Sara's and looked her in the eye. "Sara, with that rainbow, my Jamie told Jon David what to do. On faith, we flew to Washington, DC, to rescue your husband, even though we didn't know who he was or where he was. Faith said we would find him, and we did. Spirit told you to fly up here to meet Jon David, and you did. They deserve to hear our stories, and then they can decide what to do. I know you want to get that little boy to the cabin as much as we do."

"You're right."

"Then, it's settled," said Jon David. "In my opinion, we should talk to them here at our house. As for all the decisions that need to be made, the only one requiring immediate attention is who will watch our children. Maybe the Brennans could. From Colt's book, they seem like fine people."

Sara tried to put the pieces together. "Should we invite them in person or call and ask them to spend a day here?"

"Inviting them in person is a must," Jon David replied. "It's important for them to see our sincerity. I'll call Colt now and ask to meet him and his wife in Danny's room at six-thirty tomorrow."

Sara nodded an okay.

He dialed Colt's number and put it on speaker.

"Hello?"

"Hello, Colt, this is Jon David. Sara and I would like to meet with you and your wife tomorrow at 0630 in Danny's room. Will that work for you?"

"Can you come now? We're both here. We really need to talk to you and Sara."

Jon David looked at his watch. It was nearly seven. "Hold on a minute." He looked at Sara and Penny. They both nodded yes. "Sara and I will be there in fifteen minutes."

"Thank you," said Colt. "I'll meet you and Sara at the reception desk."

When they arrived, Colt led them to Danny's room.

"Jon David, this is my wife, Rachel, and here are Pat and Annie Brennan, my parents-in-law."

Jon David was surprised to see his parents-in-law there but didn't miss a beat. "Hello, Rachel." He turned to Pat and Annie. "Pleased to meet you two as well. This is my wife, Sara."

"Hello," said Sara warmly as she extended her hand to Annie. She then shook Pat's hand and hugged Rachel.

"I brought in a couple more chairs so we can all sit," said Colt.

Jon David took the lead. He looked at Pat. "Sir, I read Colt's book and felt an immediate kinship to him and with you and Annie. I was also a Ranger like Colt before getting wounded and being medically retired. I was a lieutenant, a West Point graduate.

"After the Army, I went to med school and am now a practicing pediatrician. My father was an Army colonel. Sara is a board-certified trauma surgeon and was also a captain in the Air Force Reserve, heading critical care teams that accompanied wounded soldiers from war zones to military hospitals in Germany for further care. Her father is also a retired Army colonel.

"I've told you this so you'll know that we're both highly qualified professionals. After examining your grandson, I have a plan that could heal him. Sara agrees with my proposed action."

"Oh my God!" Rachel wailed. "They said today he'd be in a permanent vegetative state."

"What's the plan?" Colt excitedly asked.

"It's something non-conventional. Nothing can ever be guaranteed, but Sara and I are optimistic that it will work."

Sara put her hand on Jon David's. "I agree with my husband's plan completely."

"What is it, and why do you believe it'll work, Jon David?"

"Because, Colt, what we propose doing for Danny also healed me."

"What worked on you? What are you suggesting?"

Jon David looked at all of them before replying. "What Sara and I propose will take your undivided attention for an entire day. We want you to come to our home so we can talk without interruption. Mr. and Mrs. Brennan, we have two children, ages four and six.

Would you consider watching them while we speak to Colt and Rachel? If what Colt said is true about you two in his book, we'll rest easy with them being in your care."

Annie spoke. "Dr. Luke, if this involves making a life decision regarding our grandson, Pat and I want to be there, too.'

Jon David looked at Sara. She nodded. "Okay, that's fine. But you'll have to give us time to find daycare for our children."

"I know who can watch your kids," said Colt. "My friends Scott and Maggie Morey. He's a retired Ranger, and I've known him since I was seventeen. They have three girls and have been watching our daughter Christa since Danny's accident."

"I read about Scotty in your book. Sara, is it okay with you?"

"It is."

"Good. Oh. One more thing. I expect you all to have a good night's sleep before coming to our home. I need you to be lucid and thinking clearly. Colt and Rachel, a good night's sleep means going to your parents' home and sleeping in a bed. Am I clear, Sergeant Mercer?"

"Yes, sir."

"Now, we need to come up with a day. Will Saturday work?"

"Why so long?"

"I'm a doctor, Colt. I have patients scheduled to see me." Jon David saw the desperation in Rachel's eyes and relented. "Okay, I'll call the hospital and see if someone can cover for me."

"Will you call us back tonight and let us know?" Rachel asked. "Jon David, I'm begging for you to meet with us as soon as possible."

"I will, Rachel. We have a son, Riley, who's the same age as Danny. That's why we're here."

"Jon David and I love your family," said Sara. "I don't know if it was because of Colt's book or seeing what extraordinary parents you are, but you've touched our hearts, and we're here to help you."

"My wife is right. We feel a strong kinship to you."

"You're the only ones who've thrown us a lifeline. I can't thank you enough," said Colt.

Rachel said nothing more. Hugging Sara did all her communicating.

Sara drove home, allowing Jon David to call the hospital. He got the next day off. The Mercers were elated at the news. They gave him directions to the Moreys and said they'd meet him there at ten. After that, they'd form a caravan and drive to the Lukes' home.

Jon David, Sara, and Penny stayed up late, going over what they'd say the next day. A young boy's life was their incentive to get it right.

20

THE LUKES ARRIVED AT the Moreys' home a few minutes early. They wanted to check them out and ensure their children would be safe in their care. Earlier, they explained to Riley and Kelly how important it was to talk to the Mercers about Danny getting better. Riley understood and was ready to do anything for his friend. Kelly wasn't such an easy sell. She protested the whole way and clung to her mom as they got out of the car.

The Moreys and their children were playing Frisbee in the front yard. He and Maggie walked over to greet them. "Hello, Dr. Luke. My name is Scott Morey. *Rangers lead the way.* My friends call me Scotty." He shook Jon David's hand with authority. "This is my wife, Maggie, and the cutie she's holding is Christa, the Mercer's daughter."

"Hello, Scotty and Maggie. Please call me Jon David. This is my wife, Sara, and this is Riley and Kelly."

Scotty looked at them and smiled. "Hello to you all, and welcome. Here are our children, Julianna, Sophie, and Amy. The odd-looking dog Julianna is trying to control is named Harley von Bickerstaff."

Jon David and Sara said hello to them. The oldest girl looked to be in her early teens, and the youngest, maybe eight. The family seemed eager to see them. Scotty was right about the dog looking odd, but he appeared to be friendly. Jon David flashed on the image of Colt's dog, Jekyll, and smiled.

"I'm so pleased to meet you, Sara," said Maggie. "Thank you for trying to help Danny get better. His parents have suffered so much from this ordeal."

"We'll do our best with Danny. Maggie, Jon David and I read Colt's book and feel we already know you and Scotty. That's why we're confident you'll take good care of our children."

"Sara, I promise your children will be safe with us. We have the day planned for them. We're going to have a barbeque, and there's a playground right down the street. Plus, we have tons of computer games and movies to keep them entertained. Christa, do you want to show Kelly your new LEGOS?" The little girl nodded. "Okay, let's go inside and first show the Lukes our home."

Sara and Jon David were pleased with what they saw. Their house was spacious and showed pride of ownership. Maggie brought Sara, Christa, and Kelly into Christa's room, which used to be their office. On the floor was a huge LEGO set. Kelly and Christa dug into the brightly colored pieces and, seconds later, were oblivious to anything else. Maggie motioned for Sara to leave the room and let them play.

There was a knock at the front door. Colt and Rachel walked in, looking refreshed. He hugged Scotty and thanked him for watching the Luke children, and then he hugged Jon David.

"You both look like you got a good night's sleep," said Jon David.

"We did and are eager to go to your place. Pat and Annie are out in the car."

"Okay. Give us a second to say goodbye to the kids." Colt nodded, hugged Maggie, and went outside with Rachel.

Jon David and Sara waved to the Brennans as they walked to their car. It took fifteen minutes to reach their hillside home. Penny came out to greet them, and Jon David introduced her.

"Please come inside, and we'll get started," he said. Sara led them upstairs to the living room, where they moved the furniture to form a circle.

Colt and Rachel looked around to see a house that appeared bright and cozy but perhaps not as lavish as one would expect for well-paid doctors.

Jon David "assigned" them seats with the Brennans and Mercers on one side, and he, Sara, and Penny sat on the other. Colt appeared surprised by Penny joining them since Jon David made no mention of her being there before.

"Okay, let's begin," said Jon David. "What to do with Danny will be the most important decision you'll ever have to make. I told you we believe we know how to heal Danny and that it will be unconventional. We ask that you listen to us with an open mind and heart." His voice was clear and firm. "Sara, Penny, and I have stories to share with you, and we swear they're true. But before we do that, let's talk about Danny's condition. I reviewed his medical records to see if they missed anything that could make a difference in his healing. There wasn't. I then examined him and agreed with Sara regarding his long-term prognosis. Colt and Rachel, it's a near certainty he'll be in a vegetative state until the day he dies."

Rachel gasped at his words. "Then, why are we here?"

Sara passed her a tissue. "You're here because my husband and I feel there's another way to help Danny. Please listen to us, Rachel. What we have to share is something incredible."

"Hold on a minute," said Pat. "I'm getting the feeling you're about to suggest something that has nothing to do with medicine. Are you two involved in some kind of faith-based healing scheme?"

Jon David verbally pounced on him. "Mr. Brennan, we're not snake-oil hucksters trying to make a buck at your expense if that's what you're implying. We are two highly qualified doctors who have a son we love as much as you all love Danny. That's why we asked to see you today. To answer your question, yes, what we're about to propose is based on faith. I have been touched by something holy, and it saved my life. If you can't handle that, please leave and let us speak to Danny's parents. If you stay, I won't tolerate any cynical interruptions. After hearing us, all of you can decide on the merits of what we've said. Am I clear?"

Pat started to get up to leave. Annie grabbed his arm. "Pat, we'll hear what they have to say, and you *will* honor Dr. Luke's request to stay quiet."

Startled by Annie's uncharacteristic demand, he reluctantly yielded to her dictate.

"I'm at my wit's end," said Colt dejectedly. "Without Danny, I don't want to continue living. Lately, I can't keep my thoughts from drifting that way. Jon David, please look me in the eye and tell me you're not messing with me or my family. If you are, just know that any more letdowns could do me in."

"Colt! My God, don't leave Christa and me!" Rachel gasped in panic.

Jon David motioned for Colt to stand. He went to him and stood face-to-face. "I'm looking you straight in the eye. What we have to say is the rock-solid truth, as God is my witness."

Colt stared into his eyes for several moments, looking for any hint of deception.

"I believe you."

"Good. It'll be okay. Have faith, my friend. We'll get through this. Sit back down and hear what we have to say."

Sara, in tears, leaned on her husband when he sat next to her. He kissed her cheek and then looked at his guests. "Okay, here goes. Our story begins during the Vietnam war at a place called Khe Sanh. Jamie Spell was a young Marine stationed there. Penny, please show them a picture of Jamie."

She held up a picture of him for all to see. "This is my husband, Jamie. He died just a few weeks ago."

"I'm so sorry, Mrs. Spell," said Annie.

"Thank you, Mrs. Brennan. Please, everyone, call me Penny."

"You're all welcome to call me Annie."

Jon David resumed the story. "There wasn't much to do at Jamie's isolated post, so they spent a lot of time playing poker. One of his friends ran out of money and offered land in exchange for playing chips. His family homesteaded a hundred and sixty acres in Alaska in the late 1940s and willed the land to their only son when they passed.

"After some haggling, the poker players decided an acre in godforsaken Alaska was worth ten bucks. Jamie won the pot and thirty acres. His friend dutifully drafted a deed for the land in Jamie's name and sent it to the state. Three days after the official deed arrived, his buddy died when a Viet Cong mortar shell hit his foxhole. A week later, another round landed near Jamie and took his leg.

"After being discharged from the Marines and getting equipped with a fake leg, Jamie visited his property in Alaska. He was stunned at how beautiful the land was and decided to make Anchorage his home to be close to his acreage. He found work teaching high school math and a year later met the love of his life, a third-grade teacher named Penny. They married and had three children. Sara and I have never witnessed a more powerful love than the two of them shared." He looked at his watch. "Let's have a quick lunch, and then Penny will share her story with you."

Sara stood and pointed to the kitchen. "Please come this way, everyone. Help yourself to the food and drinks. The bathroom is down the hall."

Jon David excused himself and went downstairs. He returned, wearing short pants that exposed his prosthetic leg. As Pat came out of the kitchen with a sandwich and drink, he couldn't help but gawk at the fake leg. Jon David noticed. "I'm glad they were able to save my knee. It makes a lot of difference with mobility."

"Sorry for staring. I promise I'll hear what you have to say with an open mind."

Jon David nodded. "You know, I've always had trouble with colonels, and now I seem to be surrounded by them in my family. Sometimes, though, you guys can appear to be human."

Pat laughed. "We're allowed to be humans again after retirement. Please call me Pat."

"Thank you, sir. Please call me Jon David."

Colt and Rachel ate quickly. Breaking for lunch seemed so unnecessary, given the matters at hand.

After everyone finished, Jon David invited them back to the living room. "Okay, I'll turn the floor over to Penny."

Penny's infectious smile made them feel at ease. "I'm so glad you came here today. This is the home where Jamie and I have lived since the late seventies. Jon David and Sara recently purchased it from us, and they invited me to stay with them. Before I begin my story, I want you to know how much I've come to love them and their children. When Jon David was single, Jamie and I 'adopted' him, and we consider him to be our son. Mr. Brennan, I know you're skeptical, but I want you to know that these two are wonderful, honest people. I love them dearly." Sara smiled and mouthed "thank you" to her.

"My story centers on the cabin we built on the land Jamie won. We scrimped and saved until we had enough money for materials. We spent three summers constructing the cabin. It's hard to believe all the years that have passed since then. There were no roads, and our makeshift airstrip was too short for a heavy-lift airplane, so we had to haul the building materials to the site in the dead of winter by snow machine.

"Construction of our cabin was a family affair involving our two boys and daughter. Building a cabin is a wonderful way for a family to bond. We all have an affinity for the little place we call 'the cabin.' I wanted to name it something grand, but no eloquent name ever stuck."

She took a sip of tea and continued. "I wish I could tell you my relationship with Jamie was good back then, but in truth, the demons of war haunted him. Drinking was his way of subduing them, and this caused him to be isolated from the kids and me. He began spending more time at the cabin alone, drinking.

"One night, something happened there. He flew home and described to me what had occurred, but I was very skeptical. I thought he must've fantasized the whole thing during a booze binge. But I changed my mind in the following days and months. His demons never haunted him again, and alcohol was no longer part of his life. He went on to be the best husband and father a woman could ever hope to have." She pointed to his picture. "I've treasured every day with him since that event. Jamie was an exceptional man and partner.

"Let me tell you how he changed. After his experience, there was a dramatic shift in how he approached life and living. It's hard to describe, but he began listening to his intuition, or what he called his 'inner knower.' Others refer to it as the Higher Self, divine essence, or indwelling Holy Spirit. Things that once bothered him became trivial. He was so much at peace inside that it radiated from him. Just being near him would brighten your day. His intuition never let him down. I learned to trust him and listen to the still, small voice in me as well. Our home was filled with love. The years passed, and they were wonderful."

She paused for a moment to wipe away her tears.

"Now, I'll tell you how we came to meet Jon David. For many months, Jamie kept having a vague dream about someone needing to be rescued. Then, one evening, when we watched a national news story about wounded soldiers at the Walter Reed National Military Medical Center, he intuitively knew he was supposed to go there. I learned to trust and rely on his intuition, so we flew to DC without hesitation.

"In DC, Jamie went to Walter Reed and started walking the halls. When he saw Jon David sitting in a waiting area looking forlorn and dispirited, he knew he was the one God wanted him to help. He *knew* it."

She looked at the guests. "Jon David will now continue the story."

21

"DOES ANYONE WANT a break before I begin?" asked Jon David.

Annie raised her hand. "May I use the bathroom?"

"Sure. While you're doing that, the rest of us can get some fresh air out on the deck."

Pat walked to the edge of the deck and gazed at the horizon. "You have a nice view of the Alaska Range," he said to Jon David. "We're down by the inlet near Campbell Lake, so we have nothing like this."

"It is nice. Coming out here after work helps relax me."

Colt stood at the far corner of the deck, looking anxious. Jon David walked over to him. "Patience, grasshopper."

"It's hard to be patient when you have a comatose child."

"You're right. Forgive me. Let's get started again." Colt nodded and hurried back inside.

After they took their seats, Jon David began speaking.

"I'll begin with my Army days since they are critical to my story. I was a cocky lieutenant, full of piss and vinegar, so arrogant that any colonel would've loved using me for target practice. I went by the Hollywood name 'Cool Hand Luke.' In an Iraqi city called Taji, I led a fifteen-man squad equipped with four Humvees armed with machine guns. I always began patrols with my rules and expectations. Rule one was to stay together; rule two was to be vigilant at all times; and rule three—the most important rule—was don't die. After rule three, I'd say a simple prayer: *'Sweet Jesus, please bless us with your divine protection.'*

"Forgive my language, but Taji was a hellhole, a dangerous place with foul-smelling open sewer trenches and dirt roads. Bags of rotting trash were everywhere, and lots of dead animals added to the insufferable stench. We had to be hyper-vigilant—the garbage, dead animals, and fresh digging in the street were perfect places for hiding improvised explosives.

"I always liked kids, and a bunch of them followed me during my patrols. I got to know a lot of their names. I still remember some of them—Haady, Badar, Na'eem, Pir, Ja'far, and Aban, to name a few.

"One day, as part of my patrol activities, I went into a pottery shop and looked around. The owner, a potter, did exquisite work. I complimented him on his wares and told him he was a master at his craft, which delighted him. We then headed toward the center of town with me on point. That's when I saw a flurry of activity ahead. Several insurgents piled out of parked vans and began attacking us with AK-47 automatic rifles and RPGs—sorry—rocket-propelled grenades. An RPG hit one of the Humvees, instantly killing the crew. I shot and killed of the several insurgents, so the remaining ones focused on me.

"One pointed his RPG at me and fired. The grenade passed inches away from my left side and exploded when it hit a two-story stone-walled building behind me. The entire wall came crashing down, killing most of the children and slamming me to the ground.

"Momentarily stunned, I willed my eyes to resume seeing. An Iraqi boy, Haady, lay beside me, mouth open, his lifeless eyes staring directly at me. That image of him is seared forever in my memory. Dust and smoke filled the air, mixed with the strong stench of cordite. Blood oozed from my ears from burst eardrums. Stone and grenade shrapnel peppered my body. My sergeant ran to help me. An AK-47 round caught him in the neck, dropping him dead in his tracks."

Jon David reached for a tissue, wiped his eyes, and continued.

"Rangers leave no one behind, so I hoisted him to my shoulder and began running back to my men. A bullet slammed into my left arm, spinning me around, causing me to fall hard again. I felt something snap in my jaw when my face hit the ground. I was fifteen meters from the nearest squad members, which wasn't good. When I looked back toward my attackers, they were closing in on me. I shot the pack's leader with my pistol and then the one behind him. The others ducked behind cars for cover.

"I picked up my sergeant again. An insurgent rolled a hand grenade down the sidewalk toward me. It exploded and sent me cartwheeling through the air. I landed hard on my left shoulder and screamed in pain from the blazing hot metal chunks perforating my body. When I looked down, I was horrified to see shiny white bones protruding from my left leg. My uniform was scorched and smoking. Pulsing jets of blood shot into the air from my leg. I tried to reach down to stop the blood flow, but my left arm wouldn't work. A tsunami of panic rolled through me. I screamed, 'Oh Jesus! Oh Jesus!' —I knew I had to get back to my men who were pinned down by a barrage of gunfire.

"The insurgent who threw the grenade came at me. I fired my Beretta multiple times and dropped him. Then, as my vision blurred from a lack of blood, I crawled to a shop doorway with all my remaining strength. The insurgents focused on getting me. 'Don't shoot him!' one of them screamed in Arabic. I knew what they wanted—a live American soldier to behead in front of an internet audience. I heard them racing toward me. My sight was gone now, and I knew I didn't have enough bullets to kill all of them, so I decided to shoot myself rather than be captured and decapitated. I labored to get my pistol to my head.

"Just then, an AK-47 blast rang out from the doorway behind me. I heard the insurgents drop. Someone touched me. *Not worry, Lieutenant, I take care you! I take care you!*' It was the potter I met earlier. He grabbed me by the collar and pulled me into his shop. He then tied an extension cord around my left leg as a makeshift tourniquet. That was the last thing I remembered of my time in Iraq. I learned later that the potter threw me in his car parked behind his shop and drove like a maniac to Camp Taji, the American post just outside of town. The Americans manning the gate mistook him for being a suicide bomber racing toward them. They shot and killed him."

"Oh my God!" gasped Annie, shocked.

Jon David sighed. "I'm sorry, but I need a break. Please give me a few minutes alone." He went outside and paced back and forth on the deck. Through the windows, his guests could see the anguish on his face.

"Sara, I'm sorry we're putting you all through this," said Rachel.

Sara kept her eyes on Jon David while replying. "He never told me some of the things he's speaking about." She wiped tears from her eyes.

Jon David returned and took a seat. The others followed his cue looking eager for him to resume his story.

"I awoke in unimaginable pain. A chaplain came by and told me I was in Germany. He said they had to amputate my leg, and I lost four of my men. Three others were wounded, one severely. He pointed to a Purple Heart pinned to my pillow and said our country was indebted to me. I wanted to scream, but my jaws were wired shut.

"My wounds were extensive. In addition to my amputated leg and the jaw fracture, I had perforated eardrums, a severe concussion, dislocated left shoulder, broken collarbone, nasty arm lacerations, a bullet wound in my left bicep, and a fractured wrist. Oh. I also had a gunshot wound in my upper right leg, lots of embedded shrapnel in both legs, and burns from the grenade. Damn, just saying it hurts."

In tears, Rachel leaned on Colt for emotional support. He looked at Jon David. "My combat wound seems trivial compared to yours. I only got a bullet in the arm."

Jon David nodded. "After returning to the States, I started having dreams about that awful day. Wicked dreams. The word 'nightmare' isn't adequate to describe them. I'd wake up gasping for air. The recurring image of Haady looking me in the eye shook me right down to my soul. My severe wounds never really healed. Some of the shrapnel embedded in my legs would periodically work their way up to the surface, creating abscesses that required surgery to remove. These flare-ups brought back the memories of the searing hot, razor-edged shards of metal tearing into my body. This touched off more nightmares. The flashbacks were hideous and frequent. I'd wake up drained and in a bed of sweat-soaked sheets. When I went to a store, I scanned everyone for weapons. Going outside meant having to eye the street for IEDs and looking for potential snipers.

"The pain from my wounds was constant and unrelenting. At first, two shots of vodka at night would dull the pain and my bad dreams. Then I needed three shots and then four. Eventually, drinking a fifth in the evening became the norm. My doctors warned that alcohol was incompatible with my medications, but I no longer cared. The once cocky, arrogant warrior was reduced to a pain-riddled, nightmare-plagued mess.

"Between the pain, consuming countless pills, nightmares, and booze, my life descended ever deeper into a dark hole. One night as I sat in my apartment, I put a pistol to my head. I started to squeeze the trigger, but then I thought of my parents. Dying is one thing, but suicide would've broken their hearts. That's the only reason I didn't shoot myself that night.

"The next morning, while lying in bed, an idea flashed in my head. All I had to do was find a way to end my life and make it appear like an accident. My parents could handle an accident better than suicide. I went to Walter Reed to get my pain prescriptions renewed. While waiting to see a doctor, a man came in and sat next to me. Much to my dismay, he wouldn't stop talking. But, after a while, I found myself beginning to like him. He'd also lost a leg in war. Out of the blue, he invites me to visit him in Alaska. Yes, it was Jamie. He and Penny were in DC on vacation. Well, that's what he told me then. Anyway, he gave me his phone number. I'd been stationed at Fort Richardson on my first tour of duty, and it hit me that Alaska would be the perfect place to stage an accident.

"I called Jamie the next day and accepted his invitation. I then went to Virginia to see my parents and kid brother and told them I was going to see some friends in Alaska. I just needed time to myself—an adventure, I called it. Little did they know I was seeing them to say my last goodbyes.

"I came to Alaska in December. After staying a few days with Jamie and Penny in this house, he flew me to their cabin. I asked to spend Christmas alone there to have time to think.

"Jamie showed me how to use the cabin's cast iron stove. At thirty below, it sure becomes your friend. While using the stove, the perfect way to end my sorry life came to me. I remembered my Army training about never having charcoal grills inside your field tent because it would cause dangerous levels of carbon monoxide to build up. From that came an epiphany—use the stove to fill the cabin with carbon monoxide. This would be simple—close the damper on the chimney and open the stove's fire door. Stay outside and let the gas rise to lethal levels. Go back in, open the damper, and close the firebox door to make everything look normal. Then, head upstairs and go to sleep, never to wake again.

"My 'check out' time was going to be the night before Christmas. Later, when Jamie came to pick me up, I'd be a frozen corpse in the loft bed. An autopsy would reveal carbon monoxide poisoning, which is common in Alaska during the winter.

"On Christmas eve, I put my plan into action and went upstairs to let the gas do its job. I removed my pants and prosthetic leg and crawled into bed. I remember what I thought before I fell asleep: There was nothing more to say, to think about, to cry for, and to hope for. I failed my men, those little Iraqi boys, and ultimately, I failed at the game of life. I was ready for the peace that would come shortly—sweet, dream-free, pain-free, worry-free peace. I closed my eyes on the last night of my life."

Jon David shut his eyes and took a few deep breaths before looking at his guests again.

"Forgive me. I needed a few moments to collect myself."

"Take your time, Jon David," sat Pat. "What you went through—it's heartbreaking."

22

JON DAVID TOOK a sip of water and stared at the ice floating in the glass. The others waited for him to summon his words. He set the glass down and looked at them. "This is the meaty part of the story—the part that changed my life.

"Around two a.m., I awoke with a start. Something was wrong. I wasn't dead—and I heard voices downstairs! A peculiar soft-colored light emanated from down there as well, bright enough for me to see without a flashlight. I put on my prosthetic leg, grabbed my pistol, and climbed down the stairs. When I got to the bottom, my gun was up, and I was ready to shoot. My mouth dropped open in shock at what I saw."

"What was it?" Rachel asked, wide-eyed.

"There were five human-like figures, and each of them glowed in different colors from head to toe with auras as bright as neon lights. They sat in chairs moved from the dining table to the cabin's center. The chairs formed a semicircle, with an empty chair being placed on the opposite side, facing them.

"The one on the left, a middle-aged man, shimmered in a purple color with flashes of sky blue. To his left sat an ancient-looking man with a stunning silver-colored aura. Around the edges of his aura, gold hues danced. At the center of the semicircle was a younger man ablaze in a bright gold-colored luminescence. Next to him was an older woman, angelically aglow in white with flits of green and orange. The one on the right radiated a soft yellow. I couldn't tell if the yellow one was male or female.

"The gold one motioned for me to sit in the empty chair. Pissed by the interruption of my suicide, I demanded to know who they were and what they wanted. The gold one said they were friends. I asked if they were aliens and, if they were, they should find another person who gave a damn. I pointed to my amputated leg and told them they might want to beam up an undamaged human.

"The white-glowing lady laughed and said they weren't aliens; they just wanted to talk to me. I said I had nothing to say and told them to get the hell out of the cabin. I glanced at the stove. The gold one caught me looking at it and spoke. I remember his exact words: *'One who doesn't enter by the door, but climbs up some other way is a thief and a robber.'* I nearly fainted after hearing that. They knew what I was doing.

"The purple one then spoke, saying that for many, a longing for death comes when they hear Spirit calling them home. He said in my case, all I had was a desire to escape and nothing more. I angrily told him what I did with my life was my own business.

"That fired up the yellow one, who said, 'What is rule number three?' My mouth dropped open. How did they know my Army pep talk rules? My mind raced back to my patrol ritual. Rule one: Stay together. Rule two: Vigilance. Then rule three: Don't die.

"I was speechless. The yellow figure spoke again. 'What comes after rule three?'

"My overloaded brain struggled—after rule three, what? The answer came to me: *'Sweet Jesus, please bless us with your divine protection.'*

"I asked if they were there to help me. The gold man nodded. I sarcastically asked where the hell were they when I lost my four men and the children following me that day in Iraq. The purple one replied with a Bible verse: *'For everything there is a season, and a time for every purpose under heaven.'*

"I asked what they wanted from me. The silver one said it was time to fulfill the purpose of my existence—my divine contract.

"I told them I no longer believed in God after what I've seen and been through. I asked what their names were, and they said it didn't matter; their words were all that mattered. I decided to name them by the color of light each was emitting. I looked at them, one by one, and issued a demand: 'Prove to me there is a God.'

"The ensuing conversation lasted for hours. We'd be here all night if I covered everything they said, so I'll pare it down to a few essential points.

"Yellow told me this story: *There is an old parable that goes like this: Once upon a time, there was a far-away land that was ruled by a vicious tyrant. His iron-handed rule reached into every nook and cranny of his subjects' lives— every corner, that is, except one. Try as he might, the tyrant could not destroy their belief in God. But, oh, how he wanted to. In his frustration, he finally summoned his sages and asked where he could hide God so the people would end up forgetting about him. One suggested hiding God on the dark side of the moon. This idea was debated but was voted down because the sages feared that scientists would one day discover a way to travel into space, and God would be discovered again. Another suggested burying God in the deepest part of the ocean. But there was the same problem with this idea, so it too was voted down. One idea after another was suggested and debated and rejected. Finally, the oldest and wisest sage had a flash of insight—Why not hide God where no one will ever even think to look? And where would that be? They asked. The old sage smiled and replied, if we hide God inside the people, they will never find him! And so it was done. They say that even today, people in that land are still looking for God.'*

"That's what Penny was trying to tell you regarding what Jamie learned at the cabin. The 'spirit people,' as we call them, told both him and me to go inside ourselves, for God is there. When I asked what my divine purpose was, they said I should listen to the still, small voice within me.

"I have one other thing to share with you. Purple said it to me: *Jon David, if I could move beyond the negatives of your situation, I would ask not why it is happening, but rather, what the circumstance is possibly providing—perhaps a chance to address and explore the stories of your old scars, bestowing the grace of forgiveness if merited. Or maybe the chance to discover the true essence of living which may have been neglected in the dash of the years; the chance to touch the tenderness of each moment that life presents; the chance to cry unrelenting tears to see what is washed away and what becomes uncovered; the chance to discover in the rawness of your pain any message it is telling you; the chance to embrace and heal your faltering body with gentleness and compassion; the chance to meet, in quiet stillness, the source of your being, perhaps for the first time on terms not dictated by you.'*

"After we said our goodbyes, they departed through the cabin's front door. Curious to see where they were going, I grabbed my parka, opened the door, and stood on the deck. To my amazement, they simply vanished. There were no tracks in the freshly fallen snow.

"I stood outside for a long time, eyeing the winter panorama. The only sound breaking the stillness was the noise of my teeth, chattering in the subzero cold. Overhead, a brilliant aurora lit up the night. In a flash of insight, I realized where my friends had gone. They were dancing across the heavens."

Jon David coughed to clear his throat. "Excuse me; I need another glass of water." He went to the kitchen, giving his guests a few moments to ponder his story.

23

JON DAVID RETURNED TO his guests, who eagerly waited for him to continue his story. He got right to it.

"I slept soundly that night for the first time in years, the kind of sleep that comes from being free of dragons and full of angels. I awoke feeling refreshed and in no pain. I can't even begin to explain what it's like to be in ceaseless pain and then how it feels when it stops. Imagine a colossal, deafening noise suddenly being turned off. Without looking, I reached for the bottles of pain pills on the nightstand. I wanted to swallow several to prolong the pain-free sensation. The bottles weren't there. I panicked—I couldn't live without my pills.

"I always started my mornings by massaging my leg to get it ready for the prosthetic and to check for any shrapnel working its way out on both legs. Even my panic attack couldn't stop this routine. As I rubbed my stump, it didn't protest with the usual sharp, stabbing pain. I shifted to the right leg, and my fingertips felt none of the shrapnel bumps under my skin. I threw the blanket off and stared wide-eyed at my legs. The bumps were gone, and there was only smooth, scar-free skin on both legs. I was dumbfounded. Then, I realized what had happened. I closed my eyes, bowed my head, and said a humble 'thank you.'

"Since that morning, I've never taken a pain pill or had a drink. I put on shorts so you can see that my legs are scar-free and how there are no longer any bumps from embedded shrapnel. Sara is going to talk more about this in a moment.

"I have another thing to say before Sara speaks. Penny told you that Jamie, too, had been haunted by the horrors of war and, like me, had fallen into a deep, dark abyss. He almost drank himself to oblivion. At his lowest point, the spirit people visited him at the cabin. So, he knew that once he got me to Alaska, he had to get me to the cabin. I hope you can see why Jamie and I shared an unbreakable bond. He saved my life. Can you imagine—he and Penny flew to DC from Alaska only on a notion that someone needed to be saved? My love for him and Penny is boundless." Tears flowed down his cheeks. The others were crying, too.

Jon David gently touched his wife's hand. "Sara will now tell you her story."

Sara stood. "Now I need some fresh air. Let's take a quick break."

After the break, Sara looked relaxed and calm. With a smile, she began speaking.

"My story also begins in Iraq, at Joint Base Balad. I was an Air Force trauma physician aboard a C-17, leading a critical care team. We operated the aircraft's portable intensive care unit during the flight from Iraq to Ramstein Air Force Base in Germany. That day, all our efforts would focus on just one person, a critically injured lieutenant. They carried him into the aircraft on a stretcher, and we strapped him in. He was heavily sedated and in dire condition. Red-stained bandages covered his body, and there was a void under the blanket where a leg should've been. After hooking him up to monitors, I remember whispering into his ear, 'rest well because I'll be taking good care of you.'

"Two hours into the flight, alarms started beeping. We removed his blanket and saw fresh blood oozing from his stump. I had to do emergency surgery, which is hard when flying in an aircraft. I found and repaired a bleeding artery and re-sutured the stump.

"Three hours later, we landed in Germany. The lieutenant, along with the other non-critically wounded soldiers, were transported by ambulance to the Army hospital in Landstuhl. The lieutenant was unconscious the entire time, so we never spoke to each other. My job regarding him was officially over.

"I caught a military hop back to Seattle, where I lived with my then-husband. I took a taxi home, and when I walked in, I found him in our bed with another woman. That was the end of my marriage. I swore off men and focused on my job. When I wasn't working as a civilian trauma surgeon at Harborview in Seattle, I was flying across the globe as an Air Force doc. After three years, I was burned out. I began therapy and was told I had 'compassion fatigue.'

"Another reason for therapy was to address a recurring dream I was having about the grievously wounded lieutenant I cared for on that flight from Iraq to Germany.

"The dream began invading my days. *'That young lieutenant, so injured. How is he doing now? Did he recover from his wounds?'* my inner voice kept asking. Finally, I could take it no longer. I decided to find him. Maybe seeing and talking to him would end the 'lieutenant obsession' in me. Through my mission notes and an Air Force friend stationed in Germany, I tracked him down. His name was Jon David Luke.

"In his medical record was the contact information for his next of kin. I dialed the number, and his mother answered. She said he had just left for Alaska to spend the summer with the Spells, and she gave me their phone number. I called, and Jamie answered. He said Jon David was at their cabin, and there was no phone reception there. I told him about my dream and why I needed to find him. He suggested flying up to meet him. Before I could say no, he got Penny on the line. The two of them were just so friendly. They convinced me to get on a plane that evening. I was ready to do anything to end my obsession, so off I went.

"Jamie flew me to the cabin the following day to meet Jon David. An hour later, Jamie left, saying he had some errands to run and would be back to pick me up in a little while. The crafty old guy told Jon David, just before taking off, that he'd return the next day. When Jon David conveyed that to me, I thought, oh, this isn't good.

"Jon David asked if I liked salmon. I nodded, and he said, good, let's catch one for lunch. I said, before we go, I need to tell you something. We sat on the deck, and I told him about my dream, which was why I sought him out, and that I was glad he had recovered and was doing so well. He told me he'd been praying to meet his perfect partner, and God answered his prayer by planting the dream in me.

"Needless to say, I was incredulous and basically told him that he was nuts. He said something extraordinary had happened to him at the cabin a couple of years before and asked if he could share the story with me. When I said yes, he smiled and touched my cheek. When he touched me, it was like my whole world shook. We went to the river, and I caught a salmon. I was so excited that I kissed him without thinking about it. That was the exact moment I fell in love with Jon David Luke.

"After lunch, we went on a hike. I was shocked to learn he was in med school at Georgetown. I thought he was simply a former gun-toting soldier. He told me of his desire to spend the rest of his life helping disadvantaged children. He was so sure of what he wanted to do with his life.

"That night, he shared his story. He showed me his legs, and I was shocked—there were no scars. As a surgeon who operated on him, I can assure you his legs were riddled with shrapnel-induced lacerations and gunshot wounds.

"That night, he fixed a bed for me downstairs, and he slept up in the loft. While trying to sleep, a voice boomed in my head. *'Go upstairs and be with the man you love!'* I tried to resist, but the voice just kept getting louder. I went to him, and we made love. It was the most beautiful thing I'd ever experienced. I asked Jon David to marry me right then and there. Imagine, just hours before, we were strangers. Jon David Luke is the love of my life."

"Wow," said Pat. "What an amazing story."

Jon David nodded. "I have just one more thing to say, and this is specifically about Danny. Before he died, Jamie said he expected me to talk to him after he was gone. He said he'd 'search the heavens' and find the spirit people if I ever needed help. After examining Danny and knowing there was so little hope for his recovery, I asked Jamie to give me a sign if the spirit people would heal Danny."

"Did he give you a sign?" Colt asked.

"Yes. After talking to him, I drove home. It was raining along the face of the mountains. Just before I turned onto our street, a spectacular double rainbow formed in the valley. So, did Jamie give me a sign? Yes, he did."

"I think he did, too," said Colt.

"Well, that's our story," said Jon David. "The decision regarding how to proceed is yours to make."

No one spoke for a while.

"Thank you for what each of you shared," said Annie. "They're amazing stories."

"I agree," said Pat. "I've never met someone who's been touched by something holy."

"We can say goodbye, and you all can discuss what you want to do by yourselves," said Jon David.

"No, there's nothing to think about. I want to do it," said Colt.

"I'm sorry, but as touching as your stories are, why didn't Jamie return to the cabin for another healing?" asked Rachel.

"I can answer that," said Penny. "Jon David discovered Jamie's illness when he noticed a slight tremor in his hand. We had it checked out and found he had an aggressive and inoperable tumor in his brain. Shortly after getting the devastating news, Jamie called a family meeting. He looked so upbeat. He said he had a dream the night before, and it lifted the heaviness that had dogged him all week. He said the spirit people came to him in the dream. They said God was calling him to begin his next journey, and it would be just as glorious as his time here on Earth. He said they wouldn't say what the new journey would be, but his time to leave was near.

"They told him not to be afraid during his remaining time here. He asked if I could come with him, but they said I had more work to do here. They promised we'd be together again, and we'd be just as happy as we've been here. He said after having this dream, he woke feeling completely at peace."

Penny locked her eyes on Rachel. "I now know what part of the work I have left to do here is. It's to help get Danny healed. Spirit blessed my husband. Spirit blessed Jon David. I'm asking you to give Spirit a chance to bless and heal your son."

Rachel nodded. "Why can't the spirit people cure Danny in his hospital room?"

"Rachel," said Jon David, "I don't know why they require us to come to the cabin to be healed. That's where faith comes in. Also, when I asked why bad things happen to people, they replied, *'All human beings are of equal importance in God's eyes and have a purpose.'* That's what Jamie was trying to tell us when he said it was time for him to go. Sometimes, a person's time to go is early in life. This could be part of Danny's divine contract with God."

"I don't accept that."

"Colt, as a father, I wouldn't accept it either," said Jon David, "But we can't see the grand picture."

"So, if you feel everything happens as part of a divine contract, why did you invite us here?"

"We invited you here today to share our stories of divine intervention being possible. Can I guarantee a miracle will happen with Danny? Of course not. But Jamie, Sara, and I have been touched by something holy, and Jamie gave me a sign to bring Danny to the cabin."

Colt nodded. "I understand what you're saying."

"I ask each of you to find a quiet spot, close your eyes, and listen to the still, small voice within you. That is how your decision should be made. I suggest we leave it at that." Jon David stood. "When you've decided what to do, let us know. God bless all of you. God bless Danny Mercer."

24

ON THE WAY HOME, Pat spotted a fast food restaurant. He ordered four burgers with drinks at the drive-through without asking anyone what everyone wanted. After getting his order, he drove around the building, parked, and handed out the food.

"I'm not hungry, Dad."

"I'm not either," said Colt.

Annie didn't say a thing. She put the sandwich on the dash.

"I will not start the car's engine until you all eat something. No discussion. We can't make a good decision without having some energy in our bodies. Eat. That's an order, and I'm not kidding."

Colt frowned but then opened the wrapper and absently began eating. Rachel followed his cue, chewing while staring into space. Annie knew her husband was right and retrieved her sandwich.

After everyone ate, Pat started the engine and headed home. "Since I'm barking orders, I have one more. Your mom and I will watch Danny tonight. You two will stay at our house. You need time to think and, like Jon David said, search your souls for an answer." Neither responded, which he took as their concurrence.

After dropping Colt and Rachel off, Annie fell asleep on the way to the care center. Pat glanced at her. "Dear God," he whispered, "please speak to me and my family."

Rachel was sound asleep when Colt came to bed after showering. In bed, he stared at the ceiling, trying to quiet his mind. "Please, God, tell me what to do. Tell me what to do …"

After tossing and turning, Colt drifted off to sleep. He dreamed he was floating like a balloon over the Alaska wilderness. As he came to a grassy knoll, he spotted Danny standing with his deceased parents, who were now alive. The three of them were playing and laughing. Colt's dad spotted him and waved—he then pointed to a cabin near a river. Danny gave him a 'thumbs up,' and his mom blew him a kiss. Danny looked so happy.

Colt awoke with a start. Rachel was staring at him. Neither said a word for a few moments. She broke the silence. "I had a dream. I dreamed Danny was with your parents."

Colt gasped and put his hand over her mouth to stop her from speaking. The gesture startled her. "They were standing on a knoll in the wilderness. Dad saw me floating overhead like a balloon and pointed to a cabin near a river."

Rachel recoiled in shock. "Oh my God! Colt! Oh my God!"

"Thank you, God, for speaking to us," he said as he looked upward. "Thank you."

He excitedly embraced and kissed his wife. The kissing quickly turned passionate. They made love for the first time since Rachel left for Chile.

Pat sat next to Danny and stroked his sandy blond hair. He wondered what he would've looked like when he became a man. Probably quite handsome and smart, like his parents. He sighed. Annie stirred, came over, and hugged him. She massaged his shoulder muscles. "Oh, that feels good," Pat said wearily. "Did you wake with any revelations?"

"No. How about you?"

"Nothing for me either. Annie, I can't say what we should do. Jon David had a remarkable story, and I'll admit something holy touched him, but expecting a miracle for Danny—I'm sorry, that's a notion too hard for me to embrace. I'm sure a spiritual person would call this a character flaw, but the dictates for actions in my life were always logic-driven. Taking Danny to a cabin in the middle of nowhere and hoping some supernatural force will touch him negates every rational circuit in my brain."

She sighed and continued massaging his shoulders. "I've already decided to support Colt and Rachel's decision without prejudice."

"Annie, forgive me, but that's a fancy way of saying you're copping out."

"I just hope they won't ask what we think."

"How could they not on a decision this big?"

"Then we'll tell them we don't know." She looked at her watch. "It's past eight, so let's go home."

Both were too tired to speak as they drove home. Just before turning left on Minnesota Drive, a flatbed truck pulled out of Spenard Builders Supply loaded with a small, prefabricated cabin. It blocked both lanes of the intersection, trying to make a turn. Pat turned to Annie. "Oh my God! Annie, look at that cabin! God is giving us a sign."

"I know! I know!" She hugged her husband and looked to the heavens. "Thank you, my dear God."

When traffic cleared, Pat drove home like a madman. They raced into the house, finding Colt and Rachel eating breakfast. "We have to take Danny to the cabin! We saw a sign."

"God spoke to us, too, Dad," said Rachel. "We called the Lukes and told them of a dream we both had about Danny and Colt's parents telling us to go to the cabin. Jon David and Sara are coming here tonight at six."

25

COLT AND RACHEL SPENT the day with Danny. Eager to meet with the Lukes that evening, he paced the floor all day as if it could make time pass faster. He understood Jon David had to work, but damn, the healing of his child should trump everything else. At four-thirty, they hurried home.

After dinner, Colt looked at Pat. "I just can't work out the logistics. I mean, how will we fly him there? What medical supplies do we take? How will we get him out of the facility? What if something happens to Danny? How can we get help—"

Pat motioned for him to stop. "Normally, I'd be on the same bandwagon as you, worrying about the details. But you know what, I say screw it. Now is the time to have faith. Colt, we'll find a way to make it work."

The Lukes arrived, and Rachel welcomed them in. "We're so glad you're here," she said. "Getting through the day has been hard for us."

Colt shook Jon David's hand. "Thanks for coming. I know you must be tired after working all day."

"Actually, I feel invigorated, like an athlete getting ready for a big game." He turned his attention to Pat and gave him a wry smile. "Good evening, sir. So, were you the voice of reason, trying to dissuade the others from doing this irrational endeavor?"

Pat hugged Jon David. "Thank you both for coming. On the way home from being with Danny, a flatbed truck carrying a small cabin blocked the road. God gave us a sign. So, consider Annie and me to be all in."

"I'm glad to hear that. Sara's been busy today, and she's got the logistics nailed down. We're excited to share with you how we can make this work."

Pat looked at Colt and winked. His son-in-law nodded and smiled.

After sitting in the living room, Jon David looked at them. "Before Sara begins the mission details, I have something that you all must agree to, or the whole thing is off."

Rachel gasped. "Do you want money?"

Jon David looked at her, shocked. "No! I told you before we want nothing from you, Rachel. Nothing." He saw her lips quivering and softened his tone. "Forgive me. I keep forgetting you hardly know us. One day, I hope our deeds will prove our genuineness."

"I'm sorry for jumping to that conclusion."

"Rachel," said Sara, "we understand the pressure you've been under. Please let Jon David speak, and you'll realize why you all must agree to something."

She nodded meekly and leaned on her husband.

Jon David resumed. "There's a place called Lourdes in southwestern France near the Pyrenees Mountains. Apparently, the Virgin Mary appeared to a young girl named Bernadette on eighteen different occasions in the mid-1800s. Because of this, Lourdes has become a major Roman Catholic pilgrimage, where five million people come each year seeking miraculous healings. Can you imagine if word of Danny's healing at the cabin gets out? Our cabin would become a tourist attraction, which is the last thing Jamie would want. I told you before—the spirit people say we each have a divine contract, and usually, it's not up for alteration. Up to now, I was the only one that Spirit chose to bring to the cabin. Do you understand what I'm saying?"

"We do," said Pat. "We'll tell no one about the cabin and what happened there." The others nodded.

"Good. Sara, you're up."

"Okay, let's start first with our children. Would they be able to stay with the Moreys for the weekend?"

"I'm sure it won't be a problem," said Colt.

"Okay. Next is how to get everyone there. I assume you all want to go, correct?"

"Yes," said Annie.

"Penny wants to go, too, so we have a total of eight people. I called around and talked to several charter services. Trail Ridge Air has a DeHavilland Beaver that can hold six and a four-passenger Cessna 206. Both aircraft are available this Saturday and Sunday. It will be expensive. We're talking about two round trips."

"Annie and I will pay for it," said Pat.

"Good. Jon David can borrow a stretcher from his hospital that will fit in the DeHavilland. We can also bring basic first aid equipment, but I'm sorry, if Danny's condition deteriorates along the way, he'll most likely die. I know it's hard to hear, but we need to be realistic. Even the altitude changes from flying could adversely affect him."

"We'll take that risk, Sara," said Colt. "How do we get him out of the care center?"

"That's fairly easy. Danny is breathing on his own and only has a feeding tube in his stomach. He would be fine living at your home. So, tell them you're checking him out and taking him home, where you'll have an in-home nurse look after him. We'll rent an ambulance to bring him here to make it look official. We can then bring him to the airport in your SUV."

"You've worked hard on this. Thank you, Sara."

"You're welcome, Rachel. We'll have to book the planes soon. I asked for the Cessna to leave three hours before the DeHavilland to give us time to prep the cabin before Danny arrives."

"Let's book them now," said Colt. "We'll do the paperwork tomorrow to release Danny."

Sara held her hand up. "If there's no healing, Danny will have to come back here until you can re-admit him to the center. I have the number for an in-home nurse to care for him. You'll need to purchase liquid nourishment, diapers, etcetera. I've made a list of supplies you'll need and included the nurse's number." She handed it to Rachel.

"Sara's right to cover this," said Jon David. "As we all know, miracles are contrary to the established laws of nature."

The room went quiet. Jon David waited a while before ending the silence. "Okay, it's time for a reality check. If your heart is conflicted, then don't go. We can't have any negativity at the cabin. So, let's have a show of hands. If you believe a divine healing is possible, raise your hand."

They all raised their hands.

"Good. It's settled. First, let's call the Moreys and see if they'll watch the kids. Everything hinges on that."

Rachel went to the kitchen and made the call. She came back smiling. "They can. I told them it was for more extensive hospital tests and that you and Sara were part of the medical team. I said nothing about going to the cabin."

"Excellent. Pat, please book the aircraft," said Jon David. "Tell them it's for what Sara Luke tentatively scheduled."

"I'm on it." A couple of minutes later, he hung up and smiled. "It's done."

"Excellent." Jon David then turned his attention to Rachel and Colt. "Tomorrow, please do the release paperwork. After that, book the ambulance and get the supplies on Sara's list." Colt nodded. "Annie," he continued, "will you prepare the meals for us?"

"I'd be happy to."

"Thanks. Please keep it simple. We'll put the food in an Igloo and carry it in the Cessna."

"I understand."

"Lastly," said Jon David, "the cabin is a humble place, with only an outhouse and no running water, so keep that in mind. Bring a change of clothes and a raincoat. Does anyone have questions or comments?"

No one spoke.

"Okay then, please bow your heads, and let's pray. *Dear God, we're putting our faith in you. We ask that you heal Danny. In your name, we pray, amen.*"

"Amen," everyone replied.

26

ON SATURDAY MORNING, JON DAVID looked at the weather forecast and frowned. A front was moving in later in the day, with rain predicted by evening and continuing through the night. It wouldn't be the best weather for a miracle. He, Pat, and Penny formed the advance team that would leave early in the Cessna.

"Penny, are you ready to go?" he asked.

She came out with two backpacks. "Yes. My clothes are in this pack, and Jamie's urn is in the other."

Jon David nodded and took her packs. "Will you round up the kids while I say goodbye to Sara and load the car?"

"You bet."

Downstairs, he hugged Sara and sighed. "I hope this won't be a fruitless endeavor."

"Hey, remember what you said to everyone else—no naysayers."

"Yeah, you're right, but we both know this will devastate them if nothing happens. And Danny could die on the way." He paused and looked at her with a wry smile. I know what you're going to say— 'Have faith, Jon David.'"

"Kiss me, my dear husband, and hey, have faith." She smiled when she said it. "I'll see you shortly. Let's hope the cabin is in good shape."

On the road, Jon David appreciated Penny entertaining the kids as he drove. It gave him time to pray. At the Moreys, he hugged the kids goodbye. He was grateful that Kelly didn't put up a fuss. She seemed excited to spend the night with Christa.

106 | James Randall Miller

He and Penny drove to the Brennans. There, Annie had the Igloo packed and ready to go. They put it in the car and headed to the airport.

After the pilot gave them a safety brief, the Cessna took off and headed west, across Cook Inlet. Pat sat in the seat next to the pilot. Jon David and Penny sat in the back—they held hands the whole way, each silently praying for Danny's healing.

Following an uneventful landing and saying goodbye to the pilot, they walked to the cabin with gear in hand. Jon David sighed when the cabin came into view. Weeds had overrun the place. He wished he had a string trimmer but refocused his thoughts on tidying up the cabin's interior. He glanced at Penny, who also wasn't happy to see the weed invasion. She opened the door and went inside. It was stuffy and dusty, but getting the place ready for the others was why they came early.

Pat looked sad as he surveyed the cabin's interior. Jon David knew what he was thinking—this humble abode seemed unworthy for hosting a miracle. "Pat, just remember Jesus was born in a stable when there was no place at the inn." He responded with a simple nod.

Penny assumed command. "Okay, let's leave our gear on the deck until we clean up. Pat, please open all the windows, including those in the loft, to air out the place. Jon David, you know where the brooms and mops are, so please start sweeping. I'll do the dusting."

"Yes, ma'am," Jon David said with a smile. Pat repeated the words to her.

After two hours, the place looked sharp. Even the outhouse got some cleaning attention.

"Pat, will you help me with the kitchen table and chairs?" asked Jon David. "I want to move them to the middle of the room. We can put Danny on the table when he gets here."

"No problem."

They moved the furniture. Everything was now ready for Danny.

Pat sat on one of the chairs and admired the handiwork. "Did you make these chairs, Penny?"

"I did, from willows growing along the river."

"They're so comfortable."

"That they are," said Jon David. "Hey, let me give you a tour outside." They walked to the river, which was a hundred feet away. "This little slice of heaven is called the Talachulitna River, or 'Tal,' for short. It's teeming with fish throughout the year—kings, silvers, reds, pinks, and chum salmon, along with trout, grayling, and char. If you're a fisher, this is where to be. The Tal drains into the Skwentna, which is a shallow, braided stream, unsafe for many to traverse except for an occasional expert river captain in a jet-powered shallow-draft boat. So, few people get up here. If this were an ordinary trip here, I'd be fishing right now and loving life."

"I'd be right there with you. It's beautiful here. To think that Jamie won this land in a Vietnam poker game is amazing."

"Pat, Sara and I know if nothing happens, Colt and Rachel will be devastated. I pray to God they won't be let down."

"I agree. As you know, in the military, you're taught to act by reasoning and not heart-speak. Relying on faith is a poor way to run any operation."

"Sir, what you're saying was drilled into me at West Point, but even us old war dogs can learn new tricks. Of course, when it comes to colonels, it might be wildly optimistic to think that."

Pat laughed. "You really must've butted heads with the brass during your short career."

"The arrogance of my youth didn't mix well with seasoned commanders."

They heard an approaching airplane. Jon David turned in the direction of the sound and peered at the horizon. "It's them. Come on, let's get Penny and meet them."

After unloading the gear, the men carried Danny on the stretcher into the cabin and placed him on the table. Danny survived the trip and was doing fine, other than being unconscious. Rachel kissed his cheek. "We're here," she whispered in his ear.

"Welcome to our cabin," said Penny. "Please make yourselves at home."

"Hey, everyone," said Jon David. "I'll go over the basics. The food and drinks are over here, there are pillows and blankets up in the loft if you want more comfort, and the outhouse is on the left side of the cabin. This is bear country, so don't leave any food outside, and if you need to answer nature's call at night, I'll escort you since I have a pistol."

Sara saw Annie and Rachel squirming after her husband's remarks. "Hey, just so you know, I've never seen a bear here. When I first met Jon David here at the cabin, I think he told me about the bears so I'd cling to him all the time."

"Well," said Annie with a smile, "if you and Penny aren't worried, then we won't be worried, either."

Jon David looked at his watch. "Let's feed and hydrate Danny." Rachel hiked up Danny's shirt, revealing his G tube—a gastric feeding tube that led into his stomach. Jon David opened the cap attached to the tube, slipped in an extension tube, and connected a funnel at the other end. Rachel opened two cans of nutritional drink. She handed one to Jon David, who poured it into the funnel. He waited for gravity to drain it into Danny's stomach and then poured in the second can along with water to hydrate him. When the tube was empty, he removed it and closed the cap. They cleaned the tube and funnel with bottled water.

A rumble of thunder shook the cabin. Thunder is a rare event in Southcentral Alaska. The cool summers usually don't produce enough heat to generate lightning-producing convective clouds.

Jon David looked outside and saw the threatening clouds rolling in. "Hey, everyone, if you need to use the outdoor facility, now is the time."

Minutes later, a pouring rain began. The metal roof intensified the noise. Everyone sat on the willow chairs that surrounded Danny. Colt put his hand on Danny. Rachel did the same. Soon, they all touched Danny. No one said a thing; the rain did all the talking.

The afternoon gave way to evening. Jon David and Rachel fed Danny again, and Colt changed his diaper. After that, Penny helped Annie pass out dinner, which consisted of store-bought potato salad and an assortment of sandwiches. Bags of chips and bottled water completed the meal. As she promised, it was simple. Afterward, she passed around a big bag of M&Ms. There was no conversation during the meal. It was like they were in church. When a break in the deluge occurred, Pat joined Jon David and Colt out on the deck for some fresh air. Silence was observed there, too.

As the evening wore on, the rain lessened to a peaceful-sounding symphony. Penny lit large white candles toward midnight. She kissed Danny's forehead before taking her seat.

An hour passed. Then another. The quiet vigil continued around Danny. They seemed captivated by the rise and fall of his chest. His little-boy face conveyed the innocence of all God's children.

When three o'clock arrived, Colt cast a glance at Jon David. *'When will they be here?'* was his silent query. Jon David pretended not to notice by bowing his head and putting both of his hands on Danny. The peaceful rain ended.

Rachel greeted the fourth hour after midnight with tears. She broke the church-like silence. "Please, God, please. I'm begging you, please. Please, God. Please, God. Please, God. ..."

Annie put her arm around her and joined her simple prayer. "Please, God. Please, God. Please, God. ..."

At five, the first rays of the morning sun began shining through the windows at the apex of the cabin's front wall. A half-hour later, the sunshine bathed the room in radiant light. Rachel's tears spread to everyone.

As tears rolled down his cheeks, Jon David spoke. "I'm sorry. I'm so sorry," he said to no one in particular. Sara touched him in reply.

Pat lifted his hand from Danny. He stood and left the cabin, wiping his tears away as he went. A minute later, Annie followed him. Jon David looked at Penny and Sara and silently motioned for them to follow him outside. He wanted to give Colt and Rachel some private time with their son.

Outside, Pat and Annie were by the river, tearfully hugging each other. "Let's go be with them," Jon David dejectedly said to Penny and Sara.

Back in the cabin, an exhausted Rachel stood. "I'm going to the loft to lie down for a while." Colt didn't reply. He held Danny's hand and bowed his head. His tears dropped audibly onto the floor.

Minutes passed in silence. Colt wearily raised his head and gazed at his son. Danny appeared to be staring at him. He wiped the tears from his eyes and looked again. Danny *was* staring at him. "Can you hear me, Danny?" Colt whispered.

"Yes," Danny whispered back. "I thought you were sleeping and didn't want to wake you. Where are we, Dad?"

"We're in a holy place. A holy place." He started crying.

Danny put his hand on his father. "What's wrong, Dad?"

"Nothing. I'm just very happy."

Danny looked around. "Where are the colored people?"

"What are you talking about, son?"

"The colored people. They glowed in different colors. The green one is Grandpa Jamie. He's funny."

Colt hugged him, then stood and bellowed. "Ra-Rachel! Rachel!"

She flew down the stairs and found her husband holding their son with absolute joy on his face. "He's talking to me!"

"Hi, Mom. I'm hungry."

She brought her hands to her face in disbelief. "Oh God, oh God, thank you! Thank you!"

She pounced on Danny, showering him with hugs and kisses.

Colt bounded outside and screamed at the top of his lungs. "Come in! Come in!" He dashed back inside.

The others burst in. "He's talking to us!" Rachel shouted. "Danny's talking!" They rushed to him. Danny looked bewildered from all the commotion.

"Hi, Danny, it's Nana. Here's Grandpa."

"Hi, Nana. Why is everyone crying?"

"Because we're so happy to see you!"

Danny looked baffled as his family hugged and kissed him.

27

WITH THEIR COMBINED MEDICAL skills, Jon David and Sara examined Danny from head to toe. Reflexes, balancing, and a Glasgow Coma Scale assessment to check for his eye, verbal, and motor responses—all were normal. Sara motioned for the others, who were keeping a respectful distance away, to join them.

"He's perfect," said Jon David. "Sara, please lift his shirt." Colt and Rachel gasped. Danny's abdominal skin was perfectly smooth, with no sign that a C tube had been there. "That's not the end of it," said Jon David. "There are no head scars or signs of a skull fracture. It's like nothing ever happened. He's healed."

Penny lifted Jamie's urn toward the heavens. "Thank you, my dear man, thank you!"

Pat, with tears rolling down his cheeks, started clapping. He didn't say a thing. It was his way of letting out the pent-up tension that had accumulated since the day of the accident. Everyone joined him in clapping. They were a family again, a family that just had an enormous burden lifted from them. It was time to rejoice.

Jon David stepped away to let them renew their bonds with Danny. He suddenly felt weak. Sara saw him swaying on his feet and asked Penny to bring a chair out to the deck. She helped Jon David sit. Penny went back into the cabin with Sara, and they returned with food and water. "We all need to eat something," Sara said to her husband.

He ignored her and rocked back and forth with an absent look in his eyes. Sara kissed his cheek and looked into his eyes. "Jamie listened to you and brought the spirit people to grant our prayers. Now, it's time to take care of you. Please eat this."

He snapped out of his trance and looked at her. "You're right."

Colt came out from the cabin a while later, his face aglow with joy. Jon David stood, and Colt bear-hugged him with a rib-cracking intensity. He reciprocated the hug with equal enthusiasm. "Thank you, Jon David. Thank you so much."

"It's okay, Colt. It's okay. This was all due to Jamie. We have him to thank." Colt then hugged Sara and Penny. They, too, felt his unbridled joy.

Rachel poked her head out of the cabin's door. "Danny says he's hungry. Can he eat?"

"You bet he can," said Jon David. "Just tell him the Igloo is inedible."

Rachel smiled and returned to her son. A while later, she joined them on the deck. "He's eating like a hungry bear." She hugged Sara. "I love you so much." With tears of joy, she hugged Penny and then Jon David. "Thank you all for saving my son."

Jon David shook his head. "We didn't save Danny. God did."

"We'll be forever indebted to all of you," said Colt. "There's something I need to tell you all. When Danny first awoke, he looked at me and said, *'Where are the colored people?'* I asked what he was talking about. He said, *'The colored people. They glowed in different colors. The green one is Grandpa Jamie. He's funny.'*"

Penny's mouth dropped open. Tears of joy cascaded down her cheeks. "My husband is now one of the spirit people! It's the perfect thing for Jamie to be doing on his new journey." Colt's revelation brought the same astonishment and joy to Jon David and Sara.

"What does a green aura mean?" Colt asked.

"Green is the color of healing and renewal," said Penny. "It's the perfect color for Jamie. Before the planes arrive, I'd like to fulfill my husband's desire to have his ashes scattered here. I'd be honored to have you all witness his last wish."

Jon David hugged Penny. "He knew this would be the perfect way for us to say goodbye."

28

One week later …

"HELLO, JON DAVID, THIS is Colt. Um, do you have a minute?"

"Colt! It's good to hear from you. Sara and I are going nuts wondering how Danny's doing, but we've forced ourselves to give your family time to re-bond."

"Danny's fine. You're welcome to call anytime you want. I've spent the last few days resisting the urge to call you. We've already imposed so much on you." His hesitant voice conveyed distress.

Jon David motioned to his kids that he was going out on the deck. "Hey, I don't know you that well, but I can tell something's bothering you. What's up?"

There was a pause on the other end.

"Could I, uh, I mean, could we meet at a place where I can talk to you privately?"

Jon David sighed. Something *was* wrong. "No problem. We can spend the day together if you want. I've been anticipating your call."

"Thanks. There's a place up Arctic Valley Road near the Alpenglow ski area on Fort Richardson. I find peace and inspiration there. Would that work for you?"

"From my Army days on Fort Rich, I know the area well. If you drive, I'll bring sodas, sandwiches, and a couple of field chairs. Drop by anytime you want."

"That sounds good. I'll be there within the hour."

"Great. Hey, why not bring Danny? He can hang with Riley. Sara would love to see him. I'm sure she'll give him a quick once-over to see how he's doing."

"That'd be nice. If it's okay, I'm sure Rachel and Christa would love to come if it's okay with Sara."

"Sure. Sara will love to see them."

"Okay. We'll be there soon."

Colt didn't say much as he drove. Jon David decided to enjoy the scenery and let him be. When his friend was ready to talk, he would. Three-quarters up the mountain leading to Alpenglow, Colt pulled off the road. "This trail leads to a knoll that overlooks Ship Creek Valley. The views are amazing." He couldn't help looking at Jon David's artificial leg. "It's an easy trail."

Jon David laughed. "You know, you're as bad as my mother. I'll have you know I did the Polar Bear 5K run this year."

Colt raised an eyebrow. "I'm impressed."

As they headed up the trail, Jon David stopped for a few moments to admire the scenery. He adjusted a strap on his leg. "Most of the time, I do okay with my fake leg. In humid climates, though, I need to be careful where my skin comes in contact with the prosthesis. It can cause irritation, which can lead to sores, and the sores can get infected."

"I had a similar problem riding my Trike through the South. They call it monkey butt down there."

Jon David laughed. "I remember that from your book. You praised something called Anti-Monkey Butt powder, as I recall."

"Man, you really did read my book."

"I did. Your friend Jekyll was quite a dog."

"He was. He taught me how to be a human being."

"You're a gifted author, Colt."

"Thanks. I love writing. Who would've thought I'd be a writer one day?"

"No one would've pegged me as a future doctor when I was growing up."

They reached the top of the knoll and admired the view.

"This is one of my favorite places in Alaska," said Colt. "My dad was a fine amateur geologist, and he taught me how to get the lay of the land. I could teach Geology 101 from this very spot." He swept his arm across the valley that was surrounded by jagged mountains. "See how broad and U-shaped this valley is? It's the classic signature of a glacier-carved valley. In comparison, river-carved valleys are more V-shaped."

Colt reached down, picked up a rock, and studied it. "Check out the flattened grains in this rock," he said, pointing to some dark splotches in the gray stone. "This rock was first a sedimentary rock, probably laid down by a river, and over eons, it was buried to a depth of about 20,000 feet, where tons and tons of pressure and heat altered its minerals to form what you now see. Geologists call this a metamorphic rock because it 'morphed' from one type of rock to another. Then, after this happened, upheavals thrust these rocks back up to the surface and formed this mountain range. Imagine the forces that created a new rock and then thrust it up as high as 13,000 feet above sea level today. And then, the glaciers came, grinding and pulverizing the rock to create these valleys. I find it fascinating."

Jon David smiled. "Interesting. Hell, all I see is a spectacular, tree-filled valley that probably looks like it did ten thousand years ago. So, do you look at rocks a lot? If you do, maybe therapy could help."

Colt laughed. "Every rock has a story."

"Well, so far, no rock has ever told me its story. I don't understand cats either, so maybe I'm challenged in that way." He looked up the valley again. "Thanks for bringing me here. My emotional and mental batteries recharge when I'm out in nature."

Colt nodded and opened the folding chairs. "You want a soda?"

Jon David eased into one of the chairs. "Sure."

Colt handed his friend a Diet Coke and opened one for himself. Jon David raised his can. "Here's to us." He took a swig. "This hits the spot."

"So, are you a teetotaler in your old age?"

"I am. I guess the technical term for me is recovering alcoholic. I haven't had a drop since my healing at the cabin."

"Wow, that was years ago."

"Yep, and I don't miss drinking one bit. Alcohol is irrelevant to my happiness."

"Well, I still enjoy a good brew. The last time I got drunk was in the Army, so I'm not much of a drinker. You want a sandwich?"

"Nah, I'll wait a while." He took another swig of soda. "So, what's up?"

Colt frowned and ignored the question. He looked absently at another rock on the ground and touched it with the toe of his shoe. After several moments, he turned his gaze to Jon David.

"My life will never be the same."

"What do you mean?"

"My life will never be the same. Jon David, I witnessed a miracle. How can my life ever be the same?"

Jon David smiled. "I know. I felt that way after Spirit touched me."

"So, what did you do? I mean, how do you live when you know what we know? Please tell me what I should do."

Jon David leaned back in his chair and took his time to respond.

"I asked Jamie the same thing when he picked me up at the cabin the day after my healing happened. That's why I said I was anticipating you calling me. I figured you'd be asking me the same thing, too."

"So, what did he say?"

"He said, *'Do not look at me like I'm your guru because I'm not. I'm just like you, nothing more, nothing less. All the answers you seek lie within you.'* Colt, Jamie was right. So, to answer your question regarding what you should do, don't turn your power over to me or anyone else. There are a lot of people out there who'll be more than happy to give you 'guidance,' which is often self-serving. Listen to the still, small voice within you for the answers you're seeking."

Colt grimaced and shook his head. "If there's a 'still, small voice within me,' it must be pretty still and small because I've never heard it."

Jon David smiled. "On the contrary, my friend, you've heard it within you many times."

"How in the hell do you know what's happening inside my head? Excuse me, but you're sounding pretty damned arrogant right now."

Jon David laughed. "Hey, quit acting like I just pissed in your Cheerios. Calm down. I didn't say Spirit spoke to you. You did."

Colt looked puzzled. "Can you be any vaguer?"

"I read your book, remember? It's loaded with Spirit talking to you."

"I haven't the slightest idea what you're talking about."

"Well, then, I'll be happy to tell you. Remember when you and Jekyll were in the Yukon? You wrote Annie a letter—I'll paraphrase it. You said you had a dream where you rafted down the Colorado River again with your dad. As evening approached, the two of you built a fire at your camp on shore, and he told you the campfire tales you loved to hear as a child. Then he said that he and your mom were happy in heaven and that someday, you'd come to know the wonder of it all. You told him all that had happened to you since they died, but he said they already knew. You apologized for being a failure in life. He looked puzzled when you said that and took your hand while saying your mom and he would always love you.

"You told Annie how, in your dream, your mom suggested you go cross-country skiing, which enabled you to meet Jekyll. When the vet wanted to put Jekyll down, your dad told you to rescue him. Your mom said to turn left on the road after picnicking with Scotty's family because they wanted you to meet the Brennans.

"Your dad suggested you tour the land to rediscover your soul when Pat asked what you'd do if you bought his motorcycle. Your dad said he and your mom are the cool wind that caresses your cheek on a warm day, and they will never abandon you. He said they danced with joy when you opened your heart to hear them. And later in your book, your mom warned you to stop when that tornado was about to cross your path in Texas. Oh. Let's not forget what you said about playing your flute: *'Annie, it's weird, but I don't listen to the music while I play. I just close my eyes and let spirit guide my fingers.'"*

Jon David looked intently at his friend. "There's one more thing. The dream you had recently, where your parents appeared to you, pointing to the cabin—they were telling you to bring Danny there for his healing." He touched his friend's shoulder. "I hope you can see how Spirit has come to you often in the form of your parents or in the beautiful music you played with your flute."

"My God, you're right about Spirit talking to me. My God." In awe, Colt looked at his friend. "So, what do I do now? Tell me what I should do."

Jon David smiled. "Again, you're asking me to be your guru. I can't."

"Well, then tell me what you did after being touched by something holy. I mean, the proverbial genie is out of the bottle. Knowing what I now know, I can't go back to the way my life was."

Jon David laughed. "At the cabin, I asked what happens after you've found enlightenment. The silver one replied with a wry smile, *'Before enlightenment, chopping wood, carrying water; after enlightenment, chopping wood, carrying water.'* He was right. Just because you 'know' doesn't mean your life has to change radically, especially if you're already leading a life filled with honor and integrity."

Colt looked disappointed. Jon David knew he was expecting more. He decided to rise to the challenge.

"Okay, if you indulge me, I'll tell you how I came to terms with my new awareness."

Colt nodded in reply.

"At the cabin, the gold figure whispered one last thing to me as he left. It was a simple word. *'Be.'* It took me a long while to understand the enormity of that simple, two-letter word. I invite you to contemplate the meaning of this word."

"I will."

"Regarding hearing the still, small voice within, in the Bible, Jesus said, *'Neither shall they say, Lo here! Or, lo there! For, behold, the kingdom of God is within you.'* Colt, to hear the voice, or Spirit, within you, you need to become open to it. Your dad told you this when he said they danced with joy when you opened your heart to hear them. Listening to your divine essence means turning yourself over to God and walking in Spirit."

Jon David finished the rest of the soda, crumpled the can, and put it back in the cooler.

"Okay, where was I? Oh, yeah. From the miracles that happened to Jamie and me at the cabin, I reasoned that God, or spirit people acting as God's emissaries, have appeared or spoken to certain people over the millennia. Some of those touched by Spirit include the Judaic, Christian, and Islamic prophets and mystics, Buddha, and the great Eastern philosophers such as Lao Tzu. I've studied the words of these people, which enabled me to grow closer to God. For example, Buddha said that *peace comes from within; do not seek it without.* The more I've studied their enlightened words, the more I've come to understand the Universal Truth, which is that we are all part of a oneness that binds everything together. *I am within God, and God is within me.* I've come to accept and embrace this concept, and it's now easy for me to hear my Higher Self guidance."

"I don't think it'll ever be easy for me," said Colt dejectedly.

"It will. Trust me. Meister Eckhart said nothing in all creation is so like God as stillness. You need to quiet your mind to hear. I love these words by Abraham Heschel: *To be is a blessing. To live is holy.* So, keep living your life with honor and integrity. That's a form of holiness."

"You know, given the hell we've both experienced in war, it's almost a miracle in itself that we're here, having this kind of conversation," said Colt. "I still struggle with coming to terms with all I've done and all I've been through."

"I know," said Jon David quietly. "The Buddha helped me come to terms with my suffering. May I tell you about what I've learned from him?"

"Sure."

"In the stillness, Spirit revealed to Buddha the Four Noble Truths about the human condition:

There is suffering
There is a cause for the suffering

There is the end of suffering

There is a path that leads to the end of all suffering

And then Spirit revealed to him the path, or way, to end all suffering. Buddha called it the Eightfold Path. Some say it's the guide for the attainment of enlightenment. The eight tenets are easy to remember. Following them is the eternal challenge. Here they are:

Right Understanding—knowing and accepting the Four Noble Truths

Right Intention—acting with love, goodwill, and kindness to all

Right Speech—using your words to promote truth and the higher good

Right Conduct—radiating honor and integrity in all your deeds

Right Livelihood—meeting your needs in harmony with Nature and others

Right Attitude—employing the power of pure and positive thinking

Right Mindfulness—balancing body, mind, and spirit in all actions

Right Concentration—bringing clarity with meditation."

Jon David looked at his friend. "Buddha was saying that suffering is inevitable for every human being, but overcoming suffering is possible by practicing the Eightfold Path. I do my best every day to follow these tenets, and I can tell you they've brought peace to me. Colt, Buddha isn't the only one speaking words like those in the Eightfold Path. I repeatedly find in my readings of the enlightened ones certain unifying themes. For example, Jesus said, *'You will know the truth, and the truth will make you free.'* Christ's words in the Bible are remarkably like Buddha's teachings. Meister Eckhart said, *'Spirituality is not to be learned by flight from the world, or by running away from things, or by turning solitary and going apart from the world. Rather, we must learn an inner solitude wherever or with whomsoever we may be. We must learn to penetrate things and find God there.'* Oh. With respect to Buddha, I'd add one more to his eight. I don't know who said it, but it's spot-on: *Never love anything that can't love you back.* Examples of what can't love you back include booze, drugs, and material things."

Colt smiled. "I'd add that one, too. Thanks, Jon David. It makes sense. I think, without knowing it, that I've always tried to follow the Eightfold Path. It's a reflection of the values my parents instilled in me."

"I agree. I saw it throughout your book. It's why I feel a kinship to you." He grinned. "You know, I could make a case for your Jekyll being a reincarnated enlightened master, given his penchant for having you read Zen to him every night."

"I think you're right," said Colt with a chuckle. "He was a very odd dog, but I loved him with all my heart."

Jon David nodded. "There's something else. Jamie told me this shortly before he died, and I think about it often."

"What's that?"

"He said when he was a soldier in Vietnam, he met a Buddhist monk who said, *'Knock on the sky and listen to the sound.'* Jamie remembered the words but could never figure out what they meant until his spiritual experience at the cabin."

"So, what does it mean?"

Jon David smiled. "The monk was telling him that to hear from Spirit, you first have to 'knock' to let Spirit know you're ready to listen. Jesus echoed this when he said, *'Ask, and it will be given you. Seek, and you will find. Knock, and it will be opened for you.'"*

"Wow, I see the universal truths."

"Yep. So, my friend, you need to look inside yourself to find the answers you're seeking. Just remember this: you can't hear the voice of Spirit until you find your silence. I suggest you take some time to be alone to meditate. When I follow the voice within me, I know I'm on the right path because I'm happy. When I'm not happy, I take the necessary steps to get back on the path. It's not always easy, but I stay with it. And the only path that brings happiness is the one that includes God. It's so comforting to know that God is always with me. I only have to take the time to listen. It's as simple as that, but most of us have a hundred thoughts in our head at any moment. I've learned I need to quiet my mind to hear. For my well-being, meditation has become as necessary as oxygen."

"You're a wise man, sir."

Jon David laughed. "God still needs to send down an occasional lightning bolt to my ass to get my attention. Colt, it's not all milk and cookies with everything rosy for my family or me." His cheerful demeanor changed. "Danny's healing has taken a toll on me. To convince you and Rachel to bring Danny to the cabin, I had to relive my past in graphic detail. Doing that awakened many unpleasant memories within me." He fixed his gaze on the valley for a few moments before looking at his friend. "My nightmares have returned."

His disclosure shocked Colt. "I'm so sorry, Jon David. The nightmares I used to have ravaged my soul. I don't have to imagine what you're going through. I know. Is there anything I can do to help you?"

Jon David shook his head. "Like I told Sara, I just need some time to reconnect with my divine essence, and then the nightmares will go away."

"I hope you're right. Jon David, I recognize the enormity of what you did for my family and me. I'm grateful beyond words." He paused. "As a sniper, I killed a lot of people—a lot of people. In my thoughts, I asked those I killed for their forgiveness. I also asked their families for forgiveness. You, uh, you might want to do the same."

"God, how I hate war," Jon David absently replied. With sad eyes, he looked at his friend. "You're right. I'll do it."

"Call me anytime, day or night if you ever need to talk. We're friends for life as far as I'm concerned."

"Thanks for your offer. I second your motion on being friends for life." He extended his hand to Colt, and they shook on it, sealing the pact.

Jon David smiled. "Let's have some chow. All this heavy talk has worked up my appetite."

"Um, I have one more thing," Colt said. He sighed. "We're heading back to California this Tuesday. As much as I love it here, the simple fact is our bills have piled up, and Rachel is out of family sick leave. We have to go back."

"Damn."

"I know. I wish we could stay here. If we did, I'd hound you mercilessly to take our boys and me to the cabin for some serious fishing."

"I'd like that, too. I'd probably be the one dogging you to go. One of us would have to get our pilot's license and a nice four-seat Cessna, but I'm getting into the weeds with those petty details."

Colt smiled. "I never fancied myself as a pilot, but anything is possible if salmon are involved." He turned serious. "The welcome mat in California is always out for you and your family."

"Same here. Let's keep in touch. Call or email me whenever you want."

"I will. I expect the same from you. Oh! Pat and Annie want to have a farewell bash at their place on Monday, so this is a formal invite for you and your family, including Penny. I asked Annie to make lasagna."

"I'm working that day, so if she doesn't mind us showing up around six, we'd love to come."

"That'll work just fine."

"Excellent. Now, toss me a sandwich, or I might turn cannibal."

29

SARA AND RACHEL WAVED goodbye as their husbands pulled out of the driveway, bound for Alpenglow. Kelly and Riley were excited to see Christa and Danny. They all bolted to the backyard to try out a new tire swing Jon David had rigged to a birch tree.

"Do you think the kids will be okay back there, unattended?" Rachel asked with concern.

"Sure. There's nothing for them to get into. We can sit on the deck and keep an eye on them if you want."

"That would be nice. Thanks for having us over. It's good to see you again."

"I'm so glad you came. Danny looks great. How's he doing?"

"He's fine. He has an insatiable appetite, which my mom is happily catering to. Anything he can think of, she'll make it for him."

Sara chuckled. "That's good to hear. Maybe later, if you don't mind, I'll give him a quick physical."

"Thank you."

"Come on, let's go through the house to get to the deck, and we can make a few snacks for everyone. Penny is spending the day with a friend in Wasilla. Hopefully, she'll be back in time to see all of you."

"That sounds good. How's Penny coping with the loss of Jamie?"

"Since the cabin, she's been on cloud nine. Danny's revelation that Jamie is one of the spirit people has brought so much joy to her."

Rachel frowned at what Sara said.

"Sara, I have to tell you, it's been hard for me to accept that a miracle occurred at the cabin. I mean, as a scientist, it defies all logic. In my work, I'd get drummed out of the business if I suggested something occurred because of a miracle. On the net, I've found articles discussing recovery from a coma. Maybe the change in altitude going to the cabin stimulated his brain, and that's what caused him to regain consciousness. You know, none of us saw any 'spirit people' or witnessed a miracle. Colt said when he looked up, Danny was awake and staring at him. That sounds like spontaneous recovery rather than a miracle to me."

Sara looked at her and sighed.

"Rachel, I understand how you're struggling to accept what happened, but statistics don't support your supposition of spontaneous recovery. Ninety percent of patients who are vegetative for a month or more will have severe disabilities if they regain consciousness. Danny is physically perfect, which is implausible given the severe trauma he experienced. You can't casually dismiss the miracle that occurred. As a medical professional, I'm convinced it happened."

"Well, your ninety percent statistic means that ten percent do recover without severe disabilities."

"Okay, fine, let's accept that as true. But, Rachel, scars don't spontaneously vanish when a person regains consciousness. No amount of science can explain that simple fact. What happened at the cabin is undeniable."

"I don't know. I guess I'll have to think about it some more."

The sliding glass door leading to the deck opened, and Riley stepped in. "Mom, Danny needs a Band-Aid. He scraped his knee on the tree when he fell off the swing."

Rachel gasped and raced out the door, almost knocking him over.

"How bad is it, Riley?"

"Not bad, just a little scrape."

"Okay, tell him to come in, and I'll wash it off." He nodded and went back out. Sara opened a cabinet in the kitchen and retrieved their first aid kit.

Riley ran back in. "Mom, you better come out. Rachel is crying, and she won't let Danny go."

Sara hurried out and was shocked to see Rachel wailing as she held Danny in her grasp.

"Rachel, let me see him," Sara said assertively. She wouldn't release her iron grip on her boy.

"Mom, I'm okay. Let me go! You're choking me!"

Sara touched Rachel. "Listen! He's fine. Let me have a look at him."

Only then did Rachel release her death grip.

"Geez, Mom, it's only a little cut."

"You have to be more careful, Danny! You're not well yet!"

"I am too well. Stop treating me like a baby."

"What happened, Danny?" asked Sara.

"I just hit the tree a little and fell off the swing. It's no big deal."

"Did you hit your head on anything?"

"No, my knee just hit the tree a little. It doesn't even hurt."

Sara looked at his knee and found nothing but a superficial scrape. She looked at Rachel. "It's minor. He won't need a Band-Aid. Danny, let's go inside, and I'll clean it off. After that, you can come out and play again."

"No! Playtime is over," Rachel barked. "I'm going to call your dad so we can all go home."

"Rachel, may I speak to you for a moment over there?" Sara pointed to the far side of the yard.

Rachel started to say something but clenched her jaw. She marched to where Sara had pointed.

The kids stood together, looking dejected. "Cheer up, everyone," said Sara. "Let me talk to her. I'll ask if we can go inside and play. We've got lots of computer games and movies. Danny, I'll tell your mom I'll give you a quick exam to sweeten the pot for you staying." He nodded and smiled.

She went to Rachel. "He's fine. I wish you'd stay. I told them I'd ask if they could play downstairs. We just rented a new movie, and we have plenty of computer games for them to play. Danny's willing to let me give him an exam if he can stay." She winked as she said it. Rachel eased her defensive stance and smiled slightly at the playful wink. "Okay. I'm sorry for overreacting. Sara, I need to talk to you. As you can see, I'm struggling."

Sara hugged her. "I know you are. You've gone through so much in the last few months. Tell you what—let's all have a snack, and then we can get the kids situated downstairs. After that, we can talk."

Sara and Danny joined the others downstairs after she cleaned his scrape and gave him a quick exam. Rachel sat with the girls, watching them play a computer game. Sara smiled and gave Rachel a 'thumbs up.' "Hey, kids," she said, "Rachel and I are going upstairs to chat. If you need anything, let us know." None of them paid any attention to her. They were deep in play.

"Let's sit at the table, and I'll make us some tea. Do you like peppermint?"

"I do. Thanks." Rachel sat, looking weary. Sara put a tea kettle on the stove and joined her. She took Rachel's hands in hers.

"From my cursory examination, Danny's in perfect health. But, if I were assessing you, I'd be less optimistic. You look exhausted, Rachel. What's going on?"

Her lips quivered. She squeezed Sara's hands. "I know you and Jon David say he's healed, but I'm terrified he'll slip back into a coma. I can't take my eyes off him. Neither can Colt. We aren't sleeping well at night. The urge to get up and check on him throughout the night is overwhelming. If I'm not looking in on him, Colt is. It's like we've replaced our coma vigil with a new one. Danny is miffed at us watching his every move, and he wants to play soccer again and go mountain climbing. We've said no to everything, which frustrates him to no end."

Sara smiled. "It sounds like you and Colt have joined the ranks of overprotective parents whose mantra is *We'll protect them from all forms of harm, hurt, and pain.'* Do you realize how fear is completely controlling your actions?"

Rachel dismissed the assertion with a question. "I'm wondering, should we get another CT scan done to ensure he's okay? The scan might show if there's any residual damage. I'd breathe a lot easier if the tests confirmed everything is fine."

"In my trade, what you're suggesting is called defensive medicine. Doctors often do CT scans and other tests to protect themselves from malpractice litigation. But there's a downside you need to consider carefully. CT scans expose the body to ionizing radiation, which can be up to 200 times greater than a standard X-ray. Children are more vulnerable to radiation than adults because they'll live longer. Many professionals in my field believe excessive testing may set children up for a higher cancer incidence ten to twenty years down the road."

"So, tell me what to do," she pleaded.

"I will, but before I do, I want to talk about you. It's evident to me that you have post-traumatic stress like what soldiers experience from the stresses of war. And it's not just you. Jon David is having nightmares again, and I've been obsessed for days with calling you guys every hour for a status report. Colt, I'm sure, is experiencing PTSD as well."

"You might be right, but that doesn't answer my question about what to do regarding Danny medically."

"That's an easy question to answer. God healed him. So, I'd treat him as if he's never been injured. I know you're struggling to wrap your mind around what happened because it's not explainable by natural or scientific laws. But, I believe a miracle happened with all my heart, and so should you."

Sara paused for a moment to let her words resonate. "Rachel, if you continue to overprotect him, he'll end up being afraid to try new things, and his lack of life experiences will likely result in him being socially inept and neurotic. One of the joys of life is discovering new things, climbing mountains, or soaring through the air with the greatest of ease. Every time you let him reach and grow, to have new adventures—even though he may skin his knee—

you're empowering him, and that's what life's all about. Don't give him the fear-filled life that you're now experiencing. God touched and blessed him. Let him soar and give thanks for every skinned knee or bruise because it'll mean he's living."

A tear rolled down Rachel's cheek. "I wanted him to come to Alaska this summer for what you just described. But now, I just can't."

The kettle started to whistle. Sara jumped up and turned off the burner. She poured the hot water into a couple of large cups and brought them to the table, along with a box of tea. "You're in for a treat. This is Bigelow peppermint herbal tea, my favorite. I like mine strong." She took a sip after letting the tea bags steep. "Ah, that's nice. Give it a try."

Rachel cautiously took a sip. "Mmmm, this is good." Hesitantly, she looked at Sara. "If you could indulge me, there's something else I'd like to talk about."

Sara blew on the hot liquid and took another sip. "Sure."

"It's about Colt."

"Go on. We're friends, Rachel. You can tell me anything in total confidence."

"Well, um, I don't quite know how to say this." She paused a moment before continuing. "Colt was a Ranger, and from all I know, he was fearless as a soldier. He won a Silver Star for bravery in Afghanistan. Then, when that man kidnapped my sister, he rescued her by killing the guy with his bare hands. I always thought I was safe with Colt being there, knowing he would protect our family and me. But he didn't protect Danny from getting hurt, and when Danny was in the coma, Colt didn't do anything but cry a lot. He was helpless and—I hate to say this—but I've come to resent him for being so pitiful. I always thought he was somehow invincible, but he's proven to be quite fallible. I don't know if I feel the same about him as I once did."

Sara sighed. "Rachel, he cried because his little boy was grievously injured. Those are qualities to be admired rather than pitied. My husband suffered more than any of us could imagine, to the point of trying to take his life to end his pain. I don't think any less of him for it; in fact, I respect him so much because of what he's overcome in his life. He's not a god, perfect in every way. He's fallible, just like Colt. But seeing Jon David's determination to face and defeat his challenges is what endears him to me. I love him beyond words. I'm sure I'd be quite bored being married to a perfect god."

"I guess, for me, it's easier to love a god. That's how much I esteemed Colt for all the time we've been together—since before the accident, I should say. I suppose I have high expectations."

"Rachel, if that's how you viewed Colt, this was bound to happen one day. No one could live up to such high expectations. You might want to think of this as a learning experience. Let your husband be human. He's an incredible guy and a wonderful father."

She sighed. "My feelings have affected our intimacy. I have no desire for sex. None."

"Rachel, look what you've been through. You're exhausted from it and your constant vigil of Danny. No one would be in the mood for sex with the stress you're both under. Trust me; it's time for you to see a counselor."

"Maybe so," she said dejectedly. "We're leaving for California this Tuesday. After things settle down there, I might talk to someone." She looked at Sara, and her eyes welled with tears.

"I have one more thing—and this is the big one."

Sara smiled in empathy. "Okay. Talk to me."

Rachel wiped her eyes. "This is hard to say. I look at Danny now and even Christa and wish I could give them away." She started crying.

Sara got up and hugged her. "It's okay. It's okay."

"No, it's not okay! I just don't want to be a mother anymore. There's too much to lose. It's more than I can take."

"Rachel, the thoughts you're having are normal for anyone going through what you've gone through. You need to talk to a counselor. Until then, be gentle with yourself. It's okay to have these conflicted feelings."

Rachel shook her head as if knowing her troubling feelings regarding her children would never go away.

30

Two years later ...

RACHEL STORMED OUT OF the bathroom. Colt was half-awake in bed, feeling no urge to get up since it was early Saturday morning. Her abrupt entrance startled him, and he cringed when the bright bathroom lights assaulted his eyes. She leveled an icy stare at him. "Well, I hope you're happy. I'm now thirty pounds heavier than I was a year ago, and it's all because of the stupid antidepressants you insisted I take. As of today, no more pills and no more counseling. All the pills do is make me fat, and I'm tired of humoring you by going to that idiot marriage counselor who's as worthless as the pills. I'm going to get my hair cut. Have fun with your kids."

She charged out of the bedroom, slamming the door behind her before he could say a thing. "You two get your own breakfasts! I'm not your slave!" she yelled at the kids on her way out.

Colt pulled the covers over his head to shield himself from the harsh lights. "Damn," he whispered. A minute later, with a frown, he tossed off the covers, got up, and turned off the bathroom lights, which he knew she left on to spite him. Though further sleep was now futile, he plopped back down on their bed after cracking open the curtains.

He looked at the ceiling and sighed. He seemed to be spending a lot of time lying in bed alone, looking at the ceiling, lamenting. By now, he knew every subtle nuance of the sprayed-on ceiling texture. Some of the blobs reminded him of balloons floating in the sky;

others resembled flowers. He sighed again. Rachel was right; he was the one who pestered her into seeing a marriage counselor, and he eagerly endorsed her doctor's recommendation that she take an antidepressant. A year of this regime only seemed to escalate her anger toward him and, more disturbingly, toward their children. He studied the ceiling texture again, letting his thoughts drift. When was the last time they made love, he wondered? Last year? No. It was six months ago, a week before his birthday. She accommodated him but admonished him to make it quick. He sighed again.

Well, enough reminiscing, he eventually declared. It was time to get on with the day. He tried his best to muster some enthusiasm—the children deserved at least one cheerful and loving parent. He looked upward. "Hey, Mom and Dad, please give me the strength to be a good parent today." He tried out a smile. Yeah, he could do it. With that, he unleashed a yell. "Hey, kids, come on in!"

A moment later, the door burst open, and soon two squiggly masses enveloped him, one on each side. He laughed and hugged them. His dark thoughts vanished. He marveled at how effortlessly his kids could whisk away his sadness with their love. "Thanks for the hugs, you two."

"Why's Mom in a bad mood again, Dad?" asked Danny. "She's always mad."

"She never wants to play," added Christa.

"I know," said Colt. "We need to be patient with her. She's under a lot of stress at work."

Although the excuse sounded plausible, he knew it wasn't the reason for her 'moods.' The truth was that she didn't seem to like her family anymore. Colt could tolerate her surliness toward him, but it broke his heart to see the same behavior focused on the sweet souls of their children. How a mother could cease loving her children stretched the limit of his comprehension. He mentally shooed the sad realization away and shifted to something more pleasant. "Hey, I have an idea. After breakfast, let's pack a lunch and go to Hermosa Beach."

"Yes!" said Danny. "I love bodyboarding."

"Can we make sandcastles, Daddy?"

"We sure can, sweetheart."

"Can we go to Paciugo's for dessert?"

Colt laughed. "Yeah, Danny, I suppose we could drop by for a gelato." Close to the beach, Paciugo's was "the" place to go for handmade gelato in LA. "Okay, how about you two go have some cereal while I get ready."

They bounded out of the room, happy and eager to get on with the day. Colt smiled at how easily their moods could change. He thought about waiting until Rachel returned and inviting her to join them but grimaced as soon as the idea came to him. The truth was that she'd love coming home to an empty house. Another reality was that they'd be happier spending the day without her. Two years ago, before the accident, such thoughts would've been inconceivable. Rachel was such a joy to be around back then. It now seemed like an eternity ago.

They got back from the beach late in the afternoon. To Colt's surprise, Rachel wasn't there. On the back of the note he left her, she wrote that she was going to work and didn't know when she'd return. He frowned. The woman practically lived at JPL. Sixty-hour workweeks were now the norm.

"Where's Mom?" asked Danny.

"She's at work, son. Let's shower off the sea salt, and then I'll grill some hot dogs for dinner."

After eating, they watched a movie. A family tradition called for Saturday evening movies to be accompanied by Colt's stovetop-cooked popcorn with real butter. He didn't let them down. They munched away and wiped their buttery fingers on a dishtowel. He was glad they didn't protest going to bed following the movie. It had been a long and happy day together.

Around eight-thirty, Rachel walked in. She ignored Colt, who was reading a book in the living room, and went to the fridge. After pouring a glass of orange juice, Rachel stepped onto the patio and sat on the porch swing. She didn't turn on the light even though it was dark.

Colt watched her through the window and debated whether to join her. Odds were good that he'd encounter her ire if he went out.

He sighed—this time, the sigh registered in his awareness. He hated how he seemed to sigh all the time. It had to end. He got up and went to the patio.

"May I join you?"

She looked at him. In the moonlight, he could see the exasperation on her face. "What do you want, Colt?"

"I want to talk. I'm concerned about you."

"I'm tired. All I wanted was to sit here for a few minutes in peace."

"Rachel, you seem so unhappy."

She looked at him. "I am unhappy. The only good thing in my life is my job."

He sighed. *Damn,* he thought. *Another sigh.* "Rachel, how can you say that? We have a wonderful family. I love you, and the kids love you."

"Well, maybe love isn't enough."

"Okay, then, why not tell me what you need or want from us."

She laughed cynically. "I want you to turn the hands of time backward and make things like they were before the accident. You've changed, Colt. You're no longer the man I married. Danny's accident changed everything. The kids have changed, too."

"I'm the same man I've always been, and the kids are simply growing up."

That drew another disparaging chortle from her. "You live in a dream world, Colt."

"And why is that?"

"Let's start with all the cabin nonsense. A miracle didn't heal Danny. Wake up. *Get on the net and look!*" She shouted the words in a voice laced with contempt. "There's article after article about spontaneous recovery for coma victims. But let's not stop there. Jon David reeled you into his cult. You talk to him constantly—it's quite a bromance between you and Swami Luke, your guru. And then there's all that tai chi crap you do every day, and let's not forget you meditating every morning in the backyard. I hope our neighbors don't ever see the embarrassment of you in your lotus position. It makes me sick to see how you've been brainwashed by zealots pretending to be 'normal' people. I won't be surprised if you change your name to Starlight Fairyland. It would be the perfect name for you."

Colt winced at her rant. He took a deep breath to tamp down his anger.

"First of all, Jon David is not my guru; he's my good friend. I talk to him because I spend most of my time with our children. It's nice to converse with an adult. I'd be happy to talk to you instead, but you're never here anymore. Regarding tai chi, *look on the net* as you say, and you'll see it's been practiced for millennia for its health benefits. I teach tai chi classes at the local VA to help veterans cope with various physical and mental problems, the chief of which is post-traumatic stress. I so wish you'd practice it with me to discover the benefits it provides.

"Regarding meditation, there's nothing 'cultish' about it. Yes, it's good for my spiritual health, but the physical benefits derived from it are also well-documented by scientific analysis. As for our neighbors, I'm starting a tai chi class here in our backyard next week, and half of them are planning to come. And, regarding the miracle at the cabin, it happened, Rachel, and even though you ardently deny it, it happened."

The cabin assertion drew a sarcastic snort from her.

"Rachel, our family has been touched and blessed by something holy. It should be such a source of joy and celebration for us, yet somehow, it's fractured our relationship. My 'festering spirituality,' as you often call it, has brought wonderful peace and insights to me. I wish you'd open yourself to the joys that come with walking a spiritual path." He paused a few moments before going on. "You know, none of your complaints about me explains your behavior toward our children. It's one thing to be mad at me, but how you treat them breaks my heart. I wish we could find a way for you to love them again."

"Oh, yes, I see. It's all about me and what I'm doing wrong because you and the kids are perfect. You, of course, get a pass on everything because you're following 'God's will.' I'm so tired of it. By the way, I'm going to Chile again for the rest of the summer.

They were kind enough to offer me the assignment again because of my aborted first attempt there. I hope this time you can manage to not put one of the kids in a coma again."

He shuddered at her cruel words and fought the urge to explode in anger.

"How could you say something so ugly? You were once such a sweet person. I can't believe how you've changed."

"I've changed? Take a good look in the mirror, Colt. You used to be a warrior. Now, you're some sort of spiritual gadfly, tossing daisies to everyone you meet. I find you to be rather pathetic."

"So, what do you want, Rachel?"

"I already told you. I want to get away from everyone. Going to Chile will do me good."

"Okay, fine. I suggest we jointly tell the kids tomorrow."

"Fine."

"Rachel ..."

"What, Colt?"

"I still love you."

"Well, I'm not sure I feel the same about you."

"I know. I made a promise when we married to love and honor you. I intend to be faithful to my vow."

"Is that supposed to make me giddy with delight?"

"No. I just wanted you to know that I'll work hard to preserve our union. Maybe we could try more marriage counseling when you get back."

She ignored his suggestion and finished her glass of orange juice. "I'm going to bed." She got up and left.

Colt sat in the dark for the rest of the evening, lost in sadness.

31

Three years later …

AFTER CHECKING IN TO their room at the Westin Hotel in Pasadena, the Lukes spent some time unpacking and getting comfortable. The journey from frigid Anchorage to the land of palm trees and sun started nine hours earlier. They were all tired but excited to be in warm weather again. Riley looked out the window, and his weariness disappeared. "Look, they've got a big pool here! Can we go swimming?"

"Maybe later," said Jon David. "The Mercers are coming in a bit to take us to dinner. Colt says we're going to a place that serves the best burgers in the country." Riley nodded in reply. His growling stomach let him know that eating was a better option than swimming.

Sara kissed her husband. "Are you nervous about the book signing tour with Colt tomorrow?"

He shrugged his shoulders. "A little, I suppose. Imagine me, a coauthor of a book. It's exciting."

"I hope it sells well. With Colt's track record, you two might end up on the bestseller list."

"Thanks. But remember, we didn't do this for ourselves. We did it to help people who are struggling with life."

"It's a noble cause. I'm proud of you for taking the time to do it. Between the video chats, phone calls, and emailing back and forth, you and Colt have been joined at the proverbial hip. I'm amazed that you still like each other."

"I know, but the funny thing is, rather than growing tired of him, our conversations always energize me. He's become a true friend if ever there was one. I smile when remembering how he came to me after Danny's healing, asking for spiritual advice. Now, he's the one I turn to for spiritual fellowship."

"He's come far, that's for sure," said Sara. "I'm so proud of him for becoming a certified tai chi master instructor."

"I know. When I congratulated Colt for becoming a Master, he smiled and said he'd never master tai chi, meaning there's always something more for him to learn. I'll bet the counselor who recommended Colt take a tai chi class never would've guessed that one day he'd become a master."

"Isn't it interesting how innocent encounters can change your life?"

"It is. I hope our book will do the equivalent for those who are struggling."

Someone knocked on their door. Jon David looked at his watch. "I'll bet it's the Mercers."

Riley ran to the door and opened it. Colt, Danny, and Christa were there, smiling. Colt held a package wrapped with gift paper.

"Come in!" Jon David yelled with a sweeping arm gesture.

Colt made a beeline to his friend and hugged him. Then, he did the same with Sara and their kids. "Welcome to Pasadena, you all. Rachel got called to a last-minute meeting at work, so the three of us are the welcoming committee."

"That's okay," said Sara. "I know she's busy." Deftly, she changed the subject. "Wow, it's warm here. When I'm in Anchorage in the dead of winter, I just assume it's cold everywhere."

Colt laughed. "You've got to get out more, Sara."

"Yeah, I know, but we love the winters. We have season passes at Alyeska in Girdwood, and Riley's become an accomplished alpine skier. Jon David dazzles me with his fearlessness on the slopes."

Jon David chuckled and patted his prosthesis. "My fake leg never gets cold like my real one."

"Well, there won't be any skiing in the week I've laid out for you, but I think you all will be happy with the beach, Disneyland, and Six Flags. Plus, Rachel plans to give you a tour of JPL. Trust me; you'll be amazed at what they're doing there."

"It sounds like fun," said Sara.

Colt held up the package. "I have something for you two." He handed it to Jon David. "I think you'll like this."

His friend took the package and shook it next to his ear. "Well, nothing is rattling around in it. I wonder what it could be."

Colt laughed. "You know what it is. Open it."

Jon David smiled and removed the gift wrap. It was a book. His face conveyed delight in seeing the professionally designed cover featuring a Purple Heart medal sitting on an American flag with a faint picture of him in the background. He put his finger on the title and read the words aloud: *After the Purple Heart.* I guess I'm a genuine author now—or should I say, co-author?"

"That you are," Colt beamed, "and you have the very first copy of our book, hot off the press. Open the cover and see what I wrote."

Jon David opened the cover and read the words. Tears welled up in his eyes. He handed the book to Sara, who read the words aloud.

Dear Jon David and Sara—

I've yet to fathom the depth of my love for you. Its enormity is beyond the reach of words. Every day when I hug my son, I close my eyes and say a silent prayer of thanks to you and God. With all my heart, I hope our book will touch others as you've touched me. Fair winds, sweet days. Colt

Sara hugged him. "It's beautiful, Colt."

"I second that," said Jon David. "I can easily imagine Jamie smiling somewhere in heaven, pleased with what we've done."

"Me, too," said Colt. "And he'd be pleased that we changed the story enough to protect the cabin's location."

"Dad, we're hungry," said Danny from across the room. "When are we going to eat?"

Colt laughed. "We can leave now if everyone's ready."

"We are," said Sara.

"To preserve your sanity, we can all go in my minivan if you want."

Jon David eagerly agreed. "That sounds like a plan. So, where are you taking us?"

"It's called Slater's 50/50, and their burgers are the absolute best. Their patties are fifty percent ground bacon and fifty percent ground beef. Trust me; these burgers rate a fifteen on a scale of one to ten. And if you like bacon, you're in for another treat. Their bacon milkshakes and bacon brownies are terrific."

"Well, sir," said Jon David, "your love of hamburgers is legendary, so if you're recommending the place, that's good enough for us."

A half-hour later, they were scanning the menu at the eatery.

Colt put his menu down and looked at his guests. "My favorite is the Hawaiian burger, but you can't go wrong with anything here. Oh! The beer-battered jalapeños with cilantro-lime sour cream is an amazing appetizer."

"You picked a good place," said Jon David. "I think I'll have a Flamin' Hot burger with onion rings."

"The World's Greatest Turkey Burger with smoked gouda looks good to me," said Sara. "That and sweet potato fries. Kids, what about you?"

"May I have the Peanut Butter & Jellousy burger, Mom?"

"Sure, Riley."

"My favorite is the Fritos Crunch," said Danny. "It's messy."

The girls opted for twice-grilled cheese fingers.

As they feasted on some of Southern California's finest food offerings, there was a lot to catch up on for both the adults and kids.

Jon David wiped his mouth, put the napkin on his plate, and gazed at Colt with a satisfied smile. "Whew—I'm stuffed. This is, without doubt, the best burger I've ever eaten. If I lived here, I'd gain a hundred pounds from eating here every day."

"It's wonderful," said Sara. "The sweet potato fries are fantastic, and the pumpkin sauce is sublime." She took another sip of her bacon milkshake and smiled. "I'll remember this shake in my dreams."

Colt delighted in their comments. "A national TV program featured Slaters; they're that good."

Jon David touched his friend's arm. "While we have a moment, I've got some good news to share regarding my sweet lady."

Colt smiled. "Good news is always welcome. What's up?"

"Sara is starting her own practice next month, focusing on holistic medicine. We just signed a lease for office space in Midtown."

"Wow. That is good news. Congratulations, Sara. So, what's holistic medicine?"

Sara beamed. "What I experienced at the cabin has profoundly changed me. I now believe in a body, mind, and spirit-based approach to healing. In a nutshell, a holistic doctor addresses normal medical needs while also encouraging alternative healing methods such as acupuncture, yoga, meditation, and tai chi to enhance the quality of life. I'd love for you to teach a few tai chi classes the next time you visit us."

Jon David smiled at Sara and then winked at Colt. "I'll sweeten the pot for you to see us. Sara and I are now licensed pilots. We bought a four-seat Cessna to fly out to the cabin."

"And why is this the first time I've heard about all of this?"

"We wanted to surprise you," said Sara. "From the look on your face, I think we were successful."

"Congrats to both of you. Teaching tai chi and fishing is an offer I can't refuse. I hope your practice thrives, Sara, and more importantly, I hope your soul will resonate with this new endeavor."

"Thanks. I'm excited about it." She dabbed her lips with her napkin. "I'm sorry Rachel couldn't be here. I wanted to tell her our news, too."

Colt frowned. "I apologize for her not being here. She practically lives at work. Eighty-hour workweeks are her norm. I feel like I'm married to a stranger, and I can't begin to tell you how much it disturbs me not having your family staying at our home."

"Don't worry about it," Sara replied. "We understand. So, did she completely give up on counseling?"

Colt nodded. "She gave up on that and antidepressants years ago."

"Are you two doing any better?" asked Jon David.

Colt eyed the kids to see if they were eavesdropping. They were fully engaged in conversation. He leaned toward his friends and spoke quietly. "I suppose it depends on who you ask. She'd probably say everything is fine and no doubt would gloss over how lonely the kids and I feel."

"Maybe you should consider couples therapy again," said Jon David.

"I've suggested it countless times. Her standard reply is it would be an extravagant waste of her precious time."

"I'll talk to her," said Sara. "Sometimes, you don't realize how myopic your life can become. In today's times, it's easy to get tunnel vision."

"Trust me; if you do that, you'll incur her immediate ire. Our fragile peace demands separation from each other and limited conversation. I'm amazed how I can upset her just by saying hello. We just exist. Our lack of intimacy dates back to Danny's accident." He looked at the rest of his meal, frowned, and pushed his plate away. "I just lost my appetite."

"I feel for you, my friend," Jon David said with empathy. "I hate to say this, but sometimes the best course is leaving a relationship if all means to recover the union have been exhausted."

"I'll never abandon her. I take my vows seriously."

Sara put her hand on his. "We both know how hard you've tried, and we'll respect any decision you make. Jon David and I know the lack of intimacy has taken its toll on you. Above all else, just know we wish a happy life for you."

"Thanks." He sighed. "Let's switch to more pleasant matters. Can I go over the schedule tomorrow?"

"Please do," said Jon David. "You know I'm quite naïve when it comes to promoting a book, so I'll take my cues from you."

Colt smiled. "Just dazzle them with your smile and remember that tomorrow is not the day to be impatient or intolerant of other people."

"I guess I can do that. Shoot an elbow into my ribs if I start getting rowdy."

"I will. I'll be at your hotel at 0700 tomorrow. After breakfast with our publisher, we'll do two television interviews and, following that, three radio shows. Then, we'll spend the rest of the day at bookstores throughout the metro LA area. Sara, while we're doing that, I recommend you and the kids spend the day at Old Pasadena. There are lots of shops along with places to eat and movie theaters. It's an easy drive from here. I can draw you a map if you want."

"Thanks. It sounds good. I hope you guys have a fun time."

The following days passed quickly. The book promotion went well and was far less painful than Jon David imagined. Amazingly, he thought it was fun. Disneyland, Six Flags, and a day at the beach came and went. They all had a blast. Rachel was absent from all the activities. "Pressing" work matters demanded her attention. On Friday, she called Sara, inviting her to lunch with her at work with a tour of JPL afterward. There was no mention of Jon David coming as well. Sara let the snub pass and cheerfully accepted the invite. She wanted to see for herself how Rachel was doing.

"I'm so glad you could join me here today, Sara. Sorry for not being there with you guys, but this week has been crazy. I don't know if Colt told you, but I'm now the project scientist for MIRI."

"No, he didn't. What's MIRI?"

"Sorry, we speak in acronyms around here. MIRI is short for Mid-Infrared Instrument. It's one of the instrument clusters on the James Webb Space Telescope. MIRI has both a camera and a spectrograph to see light in the mid-infrared region of the electromagnetic spectrum. MIRI is so sensitive that we'll be able to see the redshifted light of distant galaxies, newly forming stars, comets, and even objects in the Kuiper Belt. Sara, I'm still pinching myself for being selected as the project scientist for this."

"Congratulations. So, why do you use infrared over visible light?"

"Good question. When the earliest stars and galaxies formed in the universe billions of years ago, they began emitting electromagnetic radiation, including visible and ultraviolet light. As this light energy traveled through space, the universe's expansion caused it to be 'stretched' into longer wavelengths that appear to us as infrared. This is called redshifting. Unlike visible light, infrared light will allow us to see through gas and space dust to view warmer objects, like stars in distant galaxies that formed over 13.5 billion years ago. We'll also be able to explore for Earth-like planets orbiting around stars like our sun."

"Is this telescope in Chile?"

Rachel chuckled. "No, the Webb will be an orbiting observatory that'll greatly extend the discoveries made by the Hubble telescope. Think of it as Hubble on steroids, with longer wavelength coverage and unimaginably improved sensitivity. The instruments on Webb are so sensitive that we could detect the heat signature of a bumblebee on Earth from the moon. It'll have a segmented primary mirror, beryllium optics, and four instrument packs within the ISIM—sorry—within the Integrated Science Instrument Module. The Webb is a multinational endeavor involving over a thousand people from seventeen countries. If everything goes right, it'll be launched on a European Space Agency Ariane 5 rocket in about seven years. I'll be there to view the launch at the European Spaceport in French Guiana. How cool is that?"

"It sounds fascinating."

"It is. The Webb will allow us to observe how galaxies form or when, for that matter. Or if black holes cause galaxies to form or vice versa. And get this—we'll be able to view incredible details of Earth-like planets and see if they have oceans that would make them conducive to supporting life. This may all sound boring to laypeople, but to me, it's as addictive as crack cocaine. Seeing how our universe formed is the ultimate thrill."

"I'm sure it is."

Rachel's cell phone buzzed. She read a text message and frowned. "Ugh. I'm sorry, Sara, but I'm going to have to cancel the tour. We're having a multi-disciplinary team meeting right after lunch to brainstorm a problem with the spectrograph. It's always something around here."

Sara touched her hand. "I know you're busy, but we may not see each other again since we're leaving tomorrow, so please, may I bring something up for your consideration?"

"Sure. What's up?"

"Rachel, Colt said you're routinely putting in eighty-hour workweeks. Since being here on this visit, it's been obvious to Jon David and me how much he and your family miss you. Are you aware of how your long hours at work are affecting everyone? I'm saying this to you as your friend."

Rachel tightened her jaw and glanced at her watch. "Sara, it wasn't that long ago in our society when the husband worked long hours, and the wife stayed home and ran the household. Take your family, for example. Your father was off fighting in wars for long periods, and your mom was left to run the show. No one said anything about that. Now that the roles are often reversed, why can a man say, 'oh, boohoo, woe is me,' and everyone runs in symphony to his aid? I love what I do and have received international recognition for my efforts. So, am I supposed to feel guilty for poor little Colt? Well, my response is 'screw my sniveling husband.' I'm sorry for being blunt, but the truth is that I work a hundred times harder than he does as a writer. Our kids are in school now, so aside from making dinner, he can pretty much sit on the couch eating cookies and ice cream all day. So, forgive me if I'm intolerant of his whimpering."

Sara flinched at her terse response. She sighed. "Rachel, I think all Colt was trying to say is that he loves you and misses spending time with you."

Rachel stood, indicating the discussion was over. "Well, Sara, I'm sure he'd love for me to be the naïve little girl I once was when we first met, catering to his every need, but those days are long gone. I make good money and don't need to be a housewife, hero-worshipping a man for providing a roof over my head. What perverse societal brainwashing women have had to endure over the ages. I need to go. Any further discussion about Colt and me is off the table. It's a personal matter between us."

Sara was shocked by the bluntness of her words. She stood and struggled a moment to compose herself. "Thanks for lunch, Rachel. Please forgive me if I offended you."

That night in bed, Sara snuggled in with her husband and sighed. "Rachel has changed so much. She's become cold and surly. When I mentioned how her long work hours were affecting her family, she nearly took my head off. I feel sorry for Colt. She's torturing him with her lack of love and attention."

Jon David sighed. "I'm no psychiatrist, but I have a gut feeling that she's afraid to love again. Danny's accident showed how easily something you love can be stripped from you. To protect herself, she detached from those she loved and uses work as a refuge where she doesn't have to deal with her emotions."

"I agree. After all these years, I don't see Rachel ever getting help. How long Colt can endure it is the only real question."

"Colt was an exceptional sniper. The patience of people in that profession is legendary. Couple that with his honor and integrity, and it's easy to see how he'll die an old man before he abandons her."

"I can't imagine a life devoid of love and intimacy. I hope he finds love again one day before it's too late."

"Yep. He tries to hide his sadness, but I feel it."

"I know. I feel it, too. What about us, Jon David? Are we doing okay?"

He kissed his wife. "You are and shall ever remain the love of my life."

"I feel the same way." She smiled and kissed him again, this time with passion. "Let me show you how much I still crave you."

32

Seven years later ...

COLT CALLED HIS WIFE at work. "Rachel, we got a letter from the school district today. It says: *'Due to your child's continuing truancy, your child has now been declared chronically or habitually truant. As a result, your child has been referred to the District Attorney's Office for truancy mediation. You should expect to be contacted by the District Attorney's Office shortly regarding this situation.'* Well, 'shortly' arrived an hour after I got this letter. They want to see us ASAP."

"Darn it, Colt. You know I can't do anything this week or next. We're about to get our first high-resolution images from MIRI. I need to be here. Why can't you handle him? Next, we'll be hearing that he knocked up his girlfriend again. But I suppose it doesn't matter because she'll just get another abortion. It's their method of birth control."

He ignored her comment. "I called his school. Besides truancy, they want to expel him for not reaching his potential academically. So, we'll need to explore a private school. They might be able to better deal with him. Also, the letter says that according to the California Vehicle Code, his driver's license can be revoked for truancy. We have a lot to deal with, Rachel."

"Just handle it, Colt. You're home all day, and you haven't written anything in months, so you have more than enough time. Maybe you should try a little harder at being a parent."

"How can you possibly say that? You've been non-existent as a parent for years. Hell, you even missed his sixteenth birthday and weren't there when we had to put Harley to sleep. Rachel, he told me last night he wants to quit school, get his GED, and join the Army."

"Great. The military was good to my father, so fine, let him enlist."

"He needs a parent's permission to join. There's no way I'll give it."

"Well, then I'll be the one to give permission."

"You do that, and it's over between us. I mean it, Rachel."

"It's been over between us for a long time."

"What are you saying?"

"I'm saying I want out. I'm sure you'll be fair, so draw up the divorce paperwork, and I'll sign it. You can have full custody of the kids. All I want is out."

"Rachel, do you understand what you just said?"

"Pardon the pun, but I do. What you've become disgusts me."

"What happened to us, Rachel? You used to love me so much."

"I grew up. I need things you can't provide."

"Are you having an affair?"

She laughed sarcastically. "Yeah, right. Like I could fit that into my ninety-hour workweek. The reason for us parting is nothing so dramatic. I simply don't love you anymore."

"Fine, Rachel, you win. But don't expect me to stay rooted here. Maybe a change of location would be in the best interest of our children and me."

"You do what you think is best. I have no doubt what you're obliquely saying is that you're moving back to your beloved Alaska. I'm sure my parents will welcome you with open arms. They always sided with you, so fine, I'll be the villain. You can blame our divorce on me. As I said, I'll sign the paperwork if the settlement is fair." She ended the call abruptly.

Colt stared into space. He felt like having a drink and glanced at the clock. Christa would be arriving home soon, so he let the temptation go. He took a deep breath and made another call.

"Hey, Scotty, it's me. Well, Rachel just told me she wants out. She said I don't give her what she needs. Hell, if I had a few billion bucks lying around and bought her a space-based telescope, I suppose everything would be hunky-dory. Scotty, she loves her damn work more than the kids and me. What the hell do I do now?"

"Easy. Get a divorce and move back here. You're still part of our family, and Maggie and I will support you one hundred percent."

"Thanks. Alaska sounds great right now. Oh. There's more. Danny's about to be expelled from school. The DA contacted me today. They want to nail my ass to a tree for his truant behavior. Damn, Scotty, my life has become an unrelenting nightmare."

"C'mon, Colt. You knew this shit with Rachel was coming, and it should be no surprise that your poor relationship with her has affected your kids. We've spoken for years about how unhappy you've been. She's been an absentee wife and mother. Maggie and I are astonished you've put up with it for so long. It's time for a new start. Call the Brennans and tell them what's going on. Pat and I ran into each other at the commissary last week, and we talked about you. They know you've gone through hell with Rachel, and they won't be surprised by your news. Call them, Colt."

"I will. Scotty, where did I go wrong? My parents loved each other to the day they died. Where did I go wrong?"

"Colt, listen to me. You've been damn-near a saint, supporting her and raising a family by yourself without complaint. Any relationship requires both participants to be engaged; otherwise, it's doomed. No matter how much you wanted things to work, she checked out a long time ago. It's a damn shame, but it is what it is. My advice is to move on."

"You're right. Hey, I need to go. Christa will be here any minute, and I need to make dinner. Thanks for being there for me."

"We're family, you and me. Don't ever forget that. Colt, you're in for a few tough months, but then it'll get better. Call the Brennan's tonight. You need their support, too."

"I will. Take care, brother."

"You, too. Adios."

Later that night, Colt went to the patio. To warm up before talking to the Brennans, he decided to call Jon David and Sara.

"Hey, Jon David, it's me. I've got some news to share, and it's not good."

"Uh-oh. What's up?"

"Rachel said today that it's over between us. She wants a divorce. And Danny's about to get kicked out of school for truancy. Other than those two things, everything's rosy."

"Oh, man, it sounds like the sky is falling on you. I'm truly sorry. I wish I could say I'm shocked, but Sara and I knew it was coming. That it's taken so long is the only surprise. I know this must sound insensitive, but I'm happy for you. Rachel has put you through hell for years. Hold on a second—let me get Sara. I know she'll want to talk to you."

A moment later, Sara was on the phone. "Hey, Colt, what's up?"

Colt sighed. "I just told Jon David that I'm getting a divorce."

"Oh. My. Divorce is never easy. I know that from firsthand experience. I'm sorry, Colt. You know we'll do anything to help you. The sad truth is Rachel was traumatized by Danny's accident, and she never recovered from those unseen wounds. We saw it years ago, as did you. I so wished she would've sought help."

"Me, too. I wish you could've known her before the accident. She was such a kind and loving person. I'll never speak unkindly of her as long as those thoughts remain in me."

"You're a good man," said Jon David. "So, what now?"

"I'm thinking about moving back to Alaska."

"Well, if you choose to move back, the welcome mat is out for you and the kids," said Sara. "We have plenty of room here, so you'll have a place to stay for as long as you need."

"I echo what Sara said. Consider our house yours."

"Thanks to both of you. Please pray for me because I'm going to need it. After this call, I have to break the news to the Brennans."

"They had us over for dinner a couple of weeks ago and voiced their concern about you," said Jon David. "Your news won't take them by surprise. They know how hard you've struggled."

"That's good to know. Well, I'll let you go. I'm not good company right now."

"Call me anytime, buddy."

"Thanks. I love you both. See you soon."

Colt got up, grabbed a beer from the fridge, and downed it in a few gulps. With a sigh, he dialed the Brennans. Annie answered the phone. "Hey, Annie, it's me. I have some sad news to share. Pat needs to hear it, too."

"Hang on; he's here. I'm putting you on speaker. Go ahead."

"Hello, Pat. Rachel told me today she wants a divorce. She doesn't want marital counseling, and she doesn't want the kids. I'm so sorry."

There was a brief silence.

"Colt, Annie and I knew this was coming. She's our daughter, and we'll always love her, but she hasn't been right since Danny's accident. Maybe her innocence was stripped from her back then. I don't know."

"Pat's right," said Annie. "For years, he, Katie, and I begged Rachel to seek counseling, and she steadfastly refused. As a psychiatrist, Katie says Rachel never got over the post-traumatic stress from Danny's accident. We'll continue to support her, and maybe someday, she'll be able to address and deal with her emotions. But, after all these years, I'm not optimistic. What will you do with the kids?"

Colt sighed. "Danny is about to be expelled from school for truancy. He wants to join the Army. I said hell no, but Rachel said she'll give her permission for him to enlist since he's underage. I don't think they'll take him without a high school diploma, but who knows."

"She actually said she'd sign him over to the military?" said Pat. "What the hell is she thinking?"

"She did. As to what's she thinking, I just don't know."

"Do you want me to call her?"

"Maybe, if Danny's joining the Army becomes more than talk. I'm also calling you guys to say I realize that blood is thicker than water, so I'll understand if you want to distance yourself from me."

"She's our daughter, but you're our son. We'll never abandon you."

"Pat's right. Colt, it so pains me to say this, but Rachel failed to meet her obligations as a wife and mother. Danny's accident left her damaged. We know how much you loved her and how desperately you struggled to keep your marriage afloat. Our hope is you'll find love again one day. You didn't fail us, and you didn't fail her. We love you all the more for all you've done."

"Thanks, Annie. I love you two as well."

"What do you want, Colt? I mean, for yourself?" asked Annie.

"I've missed Alaska more than you'll ever know. I talked to Scotty earlier. He thinks I should move back. Maybe a change would be good for the kids and me."

"I agree with Scott," said Pat.

"Me, too," said Annie. "I suggest this: School there will end in a month, so let Danny and Christa finish and then send them here to be with us. In the meantime, find a lawyer and do what you need to do. After the divorce paperwork is submitted and you divide things up and sell your house, move up here. You all can stay with us for as long as it takes to get reestablished."

"Thanks, Annie. But I doubt I can persuade Danny to do that. And I don't think his school will allow him to complete the year. He has the grades to pass all his classes, but as I said, I think they will expel him for his truancy."

"Colt, if you want, I'll fly down," said Pat. "We can try to convince the school officials to let Danny stay. I'll explain how hard the family situation has been on him. Plus, I'll talk to Danny. He trusts me. I propose you let me tell him that if he finishes school with no more truancy and spends the summer here, then if he still wants to join the Army in the fall, we'll let him. That'll give Annie and me some time to help him find his way."

"It sounds okay to me, but with one caveat. Danny needs to get his GED, or even the Army won't take him. If you want to come down, you'd better get here soon. His school wants to see me ASAP."

"Wait a minute, you two. I'm a high school counselor. I should be the one talking to the people at his school about letting him stay. Do you want me to come down, too?"

"You'd be welcome, Annie. But, if you're coming mostly to see Rachel, don't waste your time. Her MIRI instrument cluster just began producing hi-res images, so she's practically living at JPL."

"I'd be coming for Danny," said Annie.

"When are you going to tell the kids about the divorce?"

"I don't know, sir. Rachel and I should tell them together, but I doubt I can get her to come home to deliver the news."

"I'll call her and ask what she wants to do," said Annie. "If she won't participate, then you, me, and Pat can discuss the divorce with them. I'll call her right away and get back with you."

"Okay. Thanks for your support, you guys."

"Colt, there's one more thing I want to ask you," said Annie.

"What's that?"

"Are you still looking in the mirror every morning and saying your mantra?"

"Yes, ma'am. *I choose happiness.*' Since Dallas, not a day goes by without me saying it."

"Good. It's important that you continue doing it, especially now."

"I know. Thanks, Annie."

"I'll hang up now and call Rachel."

Annie dialed her daughter. "Hello, Rach—"

"Mom, I'm swamped. Can you call me back in a few days?"

"No. I need five minutes of your time. It's urgent."

"What is it? I assume Colt called, right?"

"Of course he called. But it wasn't just to speak of the divorce. He's frantic about Danny getting expelled from school."

She ignored her mother's mention of her son. "Look, Mom, save any speeches you have about trying harder or seeing a marriage counselor. I don't love him anymore, and I want out."

"Rachel, I'm not calling to do any of that. Divorcing him is your choice; if it's what you want, then so be it. I'm calling to say how critical it is to salvage Danny's education. Your dad and I offered to fly down and help Colt negotiate with the school officials to allow him to finish the school year. Danny needs you right now, too. Also, we offered to have the kids stay with us this summer. It'll give you and Colt time to focus on the divorce, and coming here will help the kids adjust to their new reality."

"Boy, it didn't take long for you and Dad to help Colt pirate the kids away to Alaska. Did the three of you have this plan in place, ready to go at a moment's notice?"

"No, Rachel. Until a few minutes ago, we never spoke of anything related to a divorce."

"Whatever. Mom, I've got to go."

"You didn't answer my question. Do you want your dad and me to fly down and help Colt with Danny?"

"Mom, I really don't care. If you want to rescue Colt yet again, fine—I shake my head at how you two coddle him. He's pathetic, you know. At least I can stand on my own two feet."

"It's not about Colt; it's about your son. You really should be there to talk to the school officials, too."

"Mom, how many times do I have to say I don't have the time!"

"Okay, fine. We'll fly down and be there for our grandson. Rachel, with or without you, we will tell them about the divorce. They need to know we all care about them, including you. They need such comfort and security."

"They'll be fine hearing it from the three of you. I'm sure the kids will be thrilled to hear that I'll soon be out of their lives."

"Goodbye, Rachel. I love you." Annie hung up. Pat was listening on the other line and came to her, stunned.

"My God, Annie, what became of our kind, sensitive little girl?"

The next day, the kids were shocked when they arrived home from school to find their grandparents sitting in the living room with their father. Colt offered no reason for them being there and hustled everyone to a local In-N-Out Burger for dinner.

When they returned home, he got down to business. "Christa and Danny, I've asked Nana and Grandpa to be here today because I have something to say regarding your mother and me. We've both been unhappy for a long time and believe we could be happier apart. I'm sorry to tell you this, but we're getting a divorce."

The news brought no gasps or shock of any kind. They sat silent for a while.

"Will we have to live with her?"

"No, Christa. You both will be living with me."

"Maybe *she* will, but not me," said Danny. "As I said, I want to join the Army."

"Let's table that topic for a bit, Danny," said Pat. "I'd like to talk to you about it later."

"There's nothing to talk about, Grandpa. School is stupid. It's a waste of time."

Annie put her hand on him. "Danny, please let your grandpa speak to you. I think you'll like what he has to say." Danny's jaw tightened, but he nodded a silent okay.

"Would you and Mom stay together if I tried harder to be good?" Christa blurted out.

Colt hugged her. "Honey, our getting a divorce has nothing to do with you or Danny. We both love you."

"C'mon, Dad, get real. Mom doesn't love us. She loves her job."

Colt glanced at Annie. She knew what he was thinking—*How do I spin this when we all know Danny's right?* To his relief, she jumped in. "Danny, your mother has struggled with dark feelings within her for years. One day, when you're older, we can talk more about it, but just know that she does love you and Christa. It's hard for her to show you her love."

Christa looked at her father. "You should've tried harder to love her, Dad. Maybe she'll change if you love her more."

Annie looked at her granddaughter. "Sweetie, your grandpa and I can honestly tell you that your father has given it his best. But sometimes, even your best isn't good enough. It's no one's fault."

"Dad, are you seeing someone else? Is that why you want out? Is she nice?"

"Oh, baby, I'm not seeing anyone else. I've always been faithful to your mother as she's been to me. But, if I ever find someone in the future, her being nice will be a must. Honestly, I doubt I'll ever marry again."

"So, why isn't our mother here tonight to tell us this news?" said Danny. "Oh, wait, that's right, it's like my last birthday. Her work is more important. I so want out of this family."

"If that's your lead-in to saying you want to live at your girlfriend's house, you can forget it."

"Don't worry, Dad. We broke up after I told her I might lose my license. It appears the transportation I provided was the chief reason for her love. She has already found my replacement. Women. I'd be better off being a hermit."

"I'm sorry to hear you broke up." Colt forced himself to say the words.

"Danny, after we're done here, let's talk about that, too."

"It looks like we'll have a lot to talk about, Grandpa."

Christa jumped back into the conversation. "Will we have to move, Dad?"

"I don't know, baby. I haven't figured everything out yet. To help me, Nana and Grandpa want you to spend the summer with them in Alaska. I'll stay here to sort things out with your mom regarding how we'll split our property."

There was more silence.

Colt looked at his children. "Do you have any other questions?"

They shook their heads.

"Well, just know that Nana and Grandpa will be here for us, helping in any way they can. I'm grateful for their help. You can talk to them anytime if you have questions I can't answer."

On the patio, Pat spent the next hour talking to Danny. They reached an agreement. If he finished the school year with no more truancy and spent the summer in Alaska, where he would get his GED, then he could join the Army in the fall. Pat called Colt out and went over the deal he reached with Danny. After listening to his son's assurances that he would honor the agreement, Colt shook Danny's hand to seal the pact. In the coming days, he hoped Pat would be equally persuasive in talking him out of joining the Army.

The next day, with the able assistance of his parents-in-law, Colt convinced the school district to allow Danny to finish the school year under the proviso of no more truancy. With this nailed down, they convinced the DA not to revoke his driver's license.

Danny fulfilled his promise to finish the rest of the school year without skipping classes, and his elevated grades reflected his determination. He continued to honor the deal by traveling to Alaska with his sister. He didn't do any of it to please his father or grandparents. His efforts were strictly self-serving. The Army was his ticket to freedom, and a GED was what they required to board the Freedom Express.

For Colt, the month after school ended went by in a blur. He got a lawyer and got the divorce paperwork completed. Rachel agreed that his proposed property division was fair, and they signed a Marital Settlement Agreement. Colt's attorney submitted it and the other required documents to the court and told him the final divorce decree would take months. Colt found a realtor and listed their home. During this process, Rachel slept in the guest bedroom and did her best to ignore him.

33

WHEN DANNY PULLED OUT of the driveway in his grandmother's car, the sense of freedom kicked in. A smile came to his face. He was "free," if only for a few hours. He grabbed his cell phone and called his friend.

"Hey, Riley, it's Danny. My grandma let me use her car today, so do you want to hang out?"

"Sure. That would be great. Would you be up for a movie? The latest Star Wars is playing at the Bear Tooth. You can eat in the theater while you watch the show. They make killer nachos."

"Sounds good. What time should I pick you up?"

"You can come over now. We need to get there early to beat the crowd."

Within minutes, Danny knocked on their door. Riley greeted him. "It's good to see you again. Come on up; Mom and Dad want to say hello."

"Danny! Welcome back to Alaska. You remember our daughter, Kelly, right?"

"Hello, Uncle Jon David. Yes, I remember Kelly." He gave the pretty girl a look that only a hormone-infused teenager could render, the kind of look that said, *"It could happen."*

Sara interrupted his ogling, oblivious to his silent advances on her daughter. "Danny, let me have a look at you. You've grown into a handsome young man, tall like your father."

"Thanks. Well, we better get going; Riley says there will be a long line. Kelly, you're welcome to join us."

"Thanks, but Momma and I are going for a swim today."

"Come back any time to visit," said Jon David. "You're welcome here." Danny nodded and said goodbye.

Back in the car, he headed with Riley down the hillside toward town.

"Dude, your sister is hot. I'm so horny right now. You've got to fix me up with her."

Riley looked at him, dumbfounded. "Fix you up to have sex with my sister? Yeah, like that's going to happen. She's hands-off to you, Danny, and I mean it. I'll kick your ass if I see you making even the tiniest of moves on her."

"Geez, Riley, calm down. I was just messing with you. Besides, she's a bit young for me. Maybe your girlfriend knows someone to hook me up with. We could all hang out and smoke some weed. You do have a girlfriend, right?"

"Yeah, but trust me, she'd never 'hook you up.' She's not like that. And, just so you know, she and I don't do drugs."

"Next, you'll tell me she's not putting out."

"No, she isn't, and it's okay with me. Besides, my focus is on school right now. I hope to go to Stanford, like my mom. I'm taking a couple of classes at UAA this summer to get a jumpstart on college."

Danny shook his head, amazed that his once best friend had become a small-town, goody-two-shoes yokel.

"I have no time for high school. It sucks. I almost got expelled for truancy. My grandma gave them a big song-and-dance about how hard it was on me with my parents divorcing, and they bought her crap. I plan on getting a GED and joining the Army in a couple of months. Until then, I'm going to party and get stoned a lot."

"I'm sorry to hear about the divorce, Danny. Regarding the Army, my dad had it hard as a soldier. You know he lost his leg in Iraq, right?"

"Yeah, I know. I guess he zigged when he should have zagged."

"It's pretty hard to dodge an exploding grenade."

"You're not much for humor, are you?"

"There's no humor in my dad's leg getting blown off. You should talk to him about the Army. I think he'd try to discourage you from joining."

"My dad already had that talk with me. He was a sergeant in the Army, and my grandpa was a colonel in the Air Force, so the military is our family's business."

"I know what you mean about the family business. I want to be a doctor, like my mom and dad. That's our line of work."

"I'll bet they're making some tall green as doctors."

"I'm sure they are. They're great people, Danny. I'm glad they're my parents."

"Well, my dad's okay, I suppose, but my mom is a real loser. All of us mean nothing to her. We're annoyances that she had to endure. I'm so glad she's out of my life. I hate the bitch."

Riley winced at Danny's words. "I'm sorry you feel that way about your mom. Maybe someday you can mend fences with her."

Danny laughed. "All she does is work. To mend fences, I'd have to make an appointment to get ten minutes of her time. Let's drop it, okay? Trust me, she's a heartless bitch and always will be."

Riley let it go as requested. An awkward silence ensued, which lasted for the rest of the evening.

34

THE FOURTH OF JULY weekend was approaching. During his morning tai chi routine, Colt thought about heading to Yosemite. Dana Meadows—on the eastern edge of the park—was his favorite place to hike. After performing a graceful move known as "the white crane spreads its wings," it occurred to him that hordes of urbanites would be swarming that weekend, infesting not only Yosemite but every other place off the beaten path. So much for serenity, he mused. He frowned and reluctantly opted for weenies on his grill. *Yeah,* he thought, *I'll be living large.*

His cell phone rang.

"Hey, Colt, it's Katie. How are you doing?"

"Well, hello there, my dear sister-in-law. It's good to hear from you. Right now, things aren't so good as I'm sure you can imagine."

"I know, and that's why I'm calling. I'm inviting you to come up for the long weekend. Portland has lots of fun things to do."

"Thanks for the invite, but I'm not good company. Besides, wouldn't it be a clear breach of your sisterly solidarity to see me?"

She laughed. "Hey, you were my friend before Rachel ever met you. Consider the invite as me fulfilling the promise we made back then to care for and support each other. Colt, you're soon off to Alaska, and who knows when we'll see each other again. Come see me. I'll treat you to the finest burger in Portland."

"A burger, eh? Well, I can't refuse an offer as tempting as that. When do you want me to come?"

"I'll send you flight numbers and departure times on Southwest that I've already researched. Call me back once you've booked a flight, and I'll pick you up at the airport."

"Great. I look forward to seeing you. Katie, thanks for caring."

"You're welcome. Don't delay booking your tickets. Seats are being snapped up quickly."

"Yes, ma'am. I'll book a flight as soon as I hang up and send you the info."

Friday came, and Colt took a noon flight out of LAX. After landing in Portland, he headed to the baggage area. Katie was waiting outside the security area and lit up when she saw him. "Colt, over here!" He waved in reply and smiled at her enthusiasm. She dashed his way and engulfed him in a big hug. "Welcome to Portland! It's so good to see you."

He returned her hug and laughed. "You sure know how to make a guy feel welcome. Thanks again for inviting me."

She kissed his cheek and beamed with an infectious smile. "I've been busy thinking about all the fun things we can do."

"Cool. You look great, Katie."

"Thanks. Maybe my time at the fitness center is paying off. You're looking good, too."

"I've been running a lot lately. That and tai chi do wonders for relieving stress."

"Do you have a checked bag?"

"I do."

"Baggage claim is right over there," she said, pointing. "Have you had lunch yet?"

Colt shook his head. "No, and I'm starved."

"I figured you'd be hungry when you got here. Are you up for that burger?"

"I'm always up for a burger," he said with a smile.

After claiming his bag, they headed to her car. She touched his arm as they walked. "It's good to see you. I mean it."

"Thanks, Katie. I've missed seeing you, too."

"The metallic-blue car over there is mine. It's a Subaru WRX, and it's wicked fast."

"If I'm nice, will you let me drive it?"

"Only if you're extra nice," she said with a chuckle. "There's a winding mountain road not far from my house that's fun to drive. Maybe we can do it tomorrow."

"I'd like that."

She ran a few steps ahead and opened the trunk of her car. He noted again how good she looked. Compared to the eternal glumness of her sister, the happiness Katie radiated was intoxicating. He liked being around someone so cheerful.

Katie smiled. "Foster Burgers is about a half-hour away if traffic cooperates."

"I can't wait."

She put the car in gear. "I'll hurry as fast as I can."

She expertly maneuvered through the airport maze and got on I-205. Several southbound miles later, she exited the freeway and pulled into a burger joint.

"Welcome to Fosters. It's my favorite place to indulge. Nothing fancy, but oh so good." They walked in, and she pointed to the menu written with colored chalk on a blackboard. "Dinner's on me. Do you mind eating out on the patio?"

"The patio's fine, and thanks for treating me. What do you recommend?"

"For you, it's a no-brainer: The Foster Burger with a large side of Black & White Fries. I'll have the Mini-Foster Burger and a few of your fries if you don't mind."

"Sounds good." He looked at the long list of locally crafted beers and shook his head. "I'll leave it to you to select a nice lager for me."

"I know the perfect one for you."

They found a sunny spot to sit on the patio. Katie looked up and admired the sky. "You picked a good day to come. We Portlanders call the rains here *the Portland mist*. That's because it seems to mist more than it rains, which is ideal if you're a gardener."

"I've gotten used to the eternal sunshine in arid SoCal. The greenery here is beautiful. I love the conifer trees."

"I hardly seem to notice the rainy weather anymore. Like everyone else here, I've learned to adapt."

She handed him a massive burger from their tray and smiled. "I hope you like it."

"Thanks." He took a bite and rolled his eyes with delight. "My, oh my, this is good." He downed a few fries and tasted the beer. "You hit a home run here, Katie."

"I knew you'd like it." She took a bite of her burger and swooned. "This will cost me another two hours at the gym, but it's so worth it."

"I expected you to pick me up with a boyfriend."

She laughed. "Nah. I've been too busy at work to be dating."

He cringed when she said that. The thought of Rachel's marathon workweeks danced in his head. "Becoming a psychiatrist was no easy endeavor, and I'm proud of what you accomplished. My only hope is you don't get buried in your work."

She touched his hand. "Colt, trust me, after seeing what happened with Rachel, I'll never be a workaholic."

"I'm glad. Hey, enough oblique talk of Rachel. Do you like being a doctor?"

"I do. The Oregon Health & Science University is perfect for me. It provides leading-edge patient care as well as research opportunities. I feel I'm making a difference in many children's lives."

"That's good to hear."

"How about you? Are you writing again? I loved both *Howling Across Bridges* and *After the Purple Heart.*"

"I'm glad you liked them. No, I haven't been writing. My mind isn't in the right place for that."

"Once you get reestablished, I'm sure you'll tickle the keyboard again. So, are you excited about moving back to Alaska?"

"I am. Of course, I'll be a single dad, but your parents will be there if I need help. Speaking of that, Pat and Danny have been hanging out. Hopefully, he can straighten Danny out."

"Being a teenager is hard. Peer pressure is brutal."

"Yeah, I know. By the way, the kids think we're heading back to Pasadena after the summer. I haven't broken the news yet to them."

"Well, as you said, Mom and Dad will be there to help you with that. Just take it one day at a time."

They finished their meal and drove to her condo.

She opened the door and motioned for him to go in. "Welcome to my humble abode. Let me give you the grand tour, which won't take long," she said with a chuckle. "It's a two-bedroom unit."

Colt looked around. "I'm impressed with how tastefully you decorated the living room."

"Thanks. Come see the kitchen and bedrooms."

After the tour, Colt picked up his bag. "Do you mind if I take a quick shower? I feel a bit grimy from the flight."

"Not at all. The blue towels in the bathroom are for you."

"Great." He brought his bag to the guest bedroom, got out his shower essentials, and headed to the bathroom. "I'll make it quick, Katie. Thanks again for inviting me. I'm having a good time."

"I'm glad you came. Oh! I have a German Riesling that I've been dying to try. Would you like a glass after you shower?"

"I would. Riesling is my favorite wine, especially an Auslese from the Rheingau region."

"I think this is a Spätlese, which isn't as sweet as an Auslese. Don't worry, though; the sweetness of my personality will enhance its taste."

He nodded and chuckled as he closed the bathroom door.

While Colt showered, Katie changed into a simple, powder blue halter neck jumpsuit that perfectly complimented her trim figure.

Colt emerged from the bathroom, looking refreshed. He smiled at Katie, who was in the kitchen. "That felt good. I see you've changed, too. You look beautiful in that outfit."

"Ah," she said, delighted by his compliment. "Thanks. Have a seat on the couch. I'll be out with the wine in a sec."

He sat and looked around, admiring her decorating style. "You have a nice place, Katie. It suits you."

"It does. I like things to be simple with a touch of color here and there." She gave him a glass and sat next to him. "Here's to better times ahead," she said, raising her glass.

"Amen to that." He touched his glass to hers and then took a sip. "Mmmm, this is good." He took another sip and looked at her. His mood turned serious. "Tell me straight up, Katie. Could I have done anything else to make my marriage work?"

She sipped her wine and pondered his question.

"Sadly, no," she said with a sigh. "I can't begin to tell you how many times I've pleaded with her to seek counseling after Danny's accident, but she always refused. She nixed my repeated urgings for marital counseling, too. Mom and Dad also tried, to no avail. Colt, we all have protective mechanisms built into us, and with Rachel, after the accident, they shut down her ability to love. I won't go into the fancy medical words for it, but she essentially put herself in a cocoon that no one could penetrate and cause her pain. The irony is that after doing it, she lost all who were dear to her. As her sister, it breaks my heart."

"As her husband, it broke mine, too." He swirled his wine glass and watched the liquid whirl. He looked at her sadly. "Forgive me. This weekend is supposed to be about having fun, and here I am crying in my wine."

"You did everything you could, Colt. I know how hard it's been on you. You've been love-starved for years. Years. She once loved you, and then she took it away. I can't imagine the sadness you must've experienced."

"The kids experienced the same thing. But, as they say, hope springs eternal, so maybe love will find me again someday."

She brought her legs up and rested her chin on her knees, looking at him attentively. He couldn't help but notice how beautiful she looked with the dusting of freckles on her face.

"I'm confident you'll find love again. After what they've been through, the kids deserve a good stepmother as well."

"Speaking of love, what about you? You're a gorgeous woman. I've always wondered why you never met your Prince Charming. What's up with that?"

Katie paused a few moments and sipped her wine. He could tell she was searching for the right words and gave her time. She returned her gaze to him with sadness. "I—I met my Prince Charming a long time ago, but it didn't work out."

"Was it in med school?"

"No, it was earlier than that. Hey, do you mind if we drop the subject? It's still painful for me."

"Sure. Forgive me, but it sounds like you and Rachel have both closed down to love."

She sighed. "No, Colt, Rachel and I are nothing alike. I still love this man with all my heart."

"Did you leave him or vice versa?"

"Boy, you're persistent on this, aren't you?"

"I care for you, Katie. That's why I'm asking."

"Do you want to hear my little tale of woe?"

"I do. We have all night to talk if you want."

She finished her wine, set the glass down, and gazed at him before speaking.

"I've been in love since I was a teenager. The man I love is the kindest and most caring person I've ever known. No one has come close to him, and that's why I never date. I'll love him until the day I die."

"You never told me about this guy. So, what happened? Talk to me, Katie. What happened?"

Her face reflected her inner heartache. Colt saw how difficult it was for her to go on.

"One day," she said, her voice soft as a whisper, "like a bolt out of the blue, I found out he was in love with my sister. She asked for my permission to marry him since she knew I had feelings for him. I couldn't say no if he loved her, which he obviously did. So, I said yes to her. My heart broke into a thousand pieces and has never recovered. It's you, Colt. It's always been you."

His mouth dropped open in shock. "Katie, I knew you liked me, but I was almost ten years older than you. I thought yours was only normal puppy love. Being in a relationship with you was out of the question. You were a child, for God's sake."

"Colt, even girls are capable of love. Yes, you were always the perfect gentleman, the perfect 'big brother.' But I loved you. And then Rachel told me how she met you in Maine, how she knew you were going to be there, and how she went there to win your heart. I cried for weeks after your wedding. In fact, I've never stopped crying. The years of witnessing how poorly she's treated you have taken their toll on me as well. I so wanted to wrap my arms around you and comfort you."

She stood. "I need another glass of wine. How about you?"

He stood, too. "Katie, I'm so sorry to have brought you pain. My God, I never had a clue."

"Yes, you did. Remember when Jen told you that I planned on marrying you?"

He paused for a moment and thought back. "Yeah, I do. We were sitting on the couch at your parents' house. I remember bringing my lips over my teeth and acting like a toothless old man, saying I'd be using a walker by the time you were old enough to marry me. I also remember you saying that you wouldn't care. Katie, honest to God, I thought it was just a teenage infatuation on your part."

"When I was a little girl, my mom told me that one day I'd meet a man who would sweep me off my feet, and we'd have a wonderful life together. I always remembered what she said, so when I became a teenager, I was already waiting for my knight in shining armor to arrive. You were that knight, Colt. Do you want some more wine? I really need some more wine."

He halted her escape with a hand on her arm. "Rachel—"

In tears, she looked into his eyes. "No, Colt. I'm Katie."

He gasped at what he'd said. "I'm sorry. I—"

She kissed him. "I'm Katie." She kissed him again, deeply, breathless and urgent, leaving no doubt about who she was. Her first kiss startled him. The second one didn't. He responded in kind, wrapping his arms around her, pulling her close, kissing her with passion and need. They stumbled into her bedroom, losing clothes along the way. The night brought unmitigated bliss.

"Are you up for breakfast?" she asked with a smile as the first rays of morning sunshine bathed the bedroom.

He matched her smile and slid his hand over her silky-smooth body. "I am, but not just yet. Stay with me a little longer."

She snuggled against him, intertwining her legs with his. "I love you, Colt."

"God, this is going to be complicated."

Her lips feather-touched his. "Let's not talk about it, at least for today." He nodded and moved his body atop hers. Breakfast would have to wait.

35

TRY AS HE MIGHT, Colt couldn't banish the grin from his face. Such was his return flight to LA. He exited the plane looking a thousand percent cheerier than when he left for Portland. He was in love, and it showed. Lost in thoughts of Katie, he didn't remember the drive home. After tossing his bag on the couch, he texted Katie at work, telling her he had arrived safely. She responded, saying how much she missed him. He read and reread her words. Love felt good. It was as if he'd found an oasis in the desert after years of futile wandering.

He got a beer and went to the patio. After taking a swig, he surveyed the yard and made a mental note to mow the grass. A wave of sadness rolled through him. He was back at his house, the place of darkness, the black hole that sucked away all happiness. An overwhelming urge to rid himself of the place of sadness and gloom gripped him. He went to the garage, pulled out the mower, and went to work. Without realizing it, he began running, cutting the grass with wild abandon. His subconscious was now in control, screaming at him to make the yard and house look flawless so it would sell faster.

Days passed. Rachel came and went at odd hours. When she was home, Colt often would leave to jog or do tai chi in the backyard. Spending evenings with Katie, talking on the phone for hours, felt like heaven. By Thursday, their time apart became too much. He got on a plane the next day for Portland.

On Saturday morning, Katie came from the kitchen with breakfast on a tray. She retook her place in bed next to him. They quickly consumed the simple meal of yogurt and sliced fruit.

She put the tray aside and kissed him. "I love you so much, Colt. I hope you feel it."

"I do. My face hurts from smiling so much."

"Am I a good lover, Colt? Are you happy with me in that regard?"

He sighed. "This is a new relationship, so can we agree to be honest with each other, even if the other won't like what we say?"

She looked at him intently. "Of course. I wouldn't want it any other way."

"Good. Correct me if I'm wrong, but you're indirectly asking if Rachel is better in bed than you."

"Yes, I suppose I am."

"Your sister was a wonderful lover until things changed. It's just as special with you, and I can't even begin to tell you how well our parts fit together. I could spend the rest of my days with you and want for nothing in bed. I only hope you're as physically happy with me as I am with you."

She kissed him. "I am, and you answered my question beautifully."

"Since sexual history appears to be the topic du jour, may I ask you some questions in that regard?"

"Ask away."

"Dare you comment on my fanciful assumption of me being the one who claimed your virginity?"

She laughed. "Sorry, stud, but your conjecture is off the mark by a factor of three. But fear not—my trysts were devoid of fireworks. I lost my virginity when I was nineteen in college. The whole clumsy event lasted maybe twelve seconds. He was immature and so unlike you. He wasn't my knight, and I ended the relationship a few days later.

"My next experience came during med school. I thought he was cute, but in bed, he was an arrogant jerk with a penchant for rough sex. I didn't know much, but I sure knew I didn't want that. Then, there was the guy you and Rachel met when we came down to see you three or four years ago. That relationship lasted less than four months. What I remember about sex with him was doing homework in my head while he did his thing. That should tell you how much I got out of it."

She took a sip of orange juice. "Would you like some?" Colt shook his head. She put the glass back on the tray. "As for dating, I got my black belt in jujutsu last year, and that required most of my free time. So, the total of my sexual adventures is rather pathetic. By the way, congrats again for becoming a tai chi master. We'll have to show each other our skills someday."

"Thanks. That sounds like fun. I'm not sure if you know it, but tai chi began as a martial art for self-defense, but now it emphasizes movements to improve both your physical and mental health. Back to sex, are you mentally elsewhere in your head when we make love?"

She kissed him. "We're being honest, right?"

"Yeah, we are."

"For years, I've imagined us making love. Taking a bubble bath with thoughts of you was my favorite pastime. When the real thing finally happened, it was far better than my fantasies."

Colt smiled and then looked absently at the ceiling.

"It won't last, you know," he almost whispered.

She looked at him quizzically. "What won't last?"

"This. The fire. The sizzle. The passion. The fire always subsides. The question is, what will remain after the heat fades. For many, it never develops into deep love."

She smiled and touched his cheek. "Passion shoots for the stars; love is already there. In response to what you just said, for me, at least, it's pretty simple regarding you. I've had a deep, abiding love for you for half of my life. I'll have it until the day I die. So, yes, the sizzle may fade, but if you keep making sweet love to me, I'll never tire of it. As far as I'm concerned, that kind of love will last forever. Anyway, that's how I feel."

"My parents had what you describe. They loved each other in a way that still leaves me in awe. What they had is all I've ever wanted. I thought I had it with Rachel, but it proved to be an illusion."

"You'll have that kind of love with me. I can promise you that."

Colt sighed. "If anyone analyzed me, they'd say I'm having a rebound relationship, and I'm using you to help mend my heart. Honestly, being with you has given me a reprieve from all the hurt and emotional pain that's dogged me for years. I've been lonely for so long that I never realized how numb I'd become. I don't want to hurt you, Katie."

"I'm a big girl now, Colt. I understand what a rebound relationship is, and if you were a stranger, it would never have gotten this far. But I know you. You're everything I want in a man, and I have no doubt about my love for you. But, if you're unable to give me your heart, if there's still an ember that burns within you for Rachel, then I'll understand and let you go."

"There are no embers. They faded away long ago. The woman I loved no longer exists. But I need to know if what we have is genuine love or merely another illusion. I have a lot of work to do regarding that."

"To help sort out your feelings, I recommend seeing a counselor. I've waited years for you. I can wait longer if you'd like."

"Katie, I'm not the same guy you knew as a teenager. I've changed so much."

"You're exactly how I remember you. In what way do you think you've changed?"

He looked at her, astonished by what she said. If she thought he hadn't changed, she was living in a dream world. A feeling swept over him that this affair was a gigantic mistake. He felt the urge to get up and run away.

She saw his discomfort but was undaunted.

"C'mon, humor me. We have all day. How do you think you've changed?"

He bit his lip, debating whether to flee or confront her for being nuts.

She tried to kiss him, but he turned away.

She sat up, looking sad. "For this relationship to work, we must have the courage to let our souls speak. I'm offering you a respite from the storm. Please don't run away."

He didn't respond.

She playfully poked him in the ribs. "Speak to me."

Her lightheartedness didn't ease his apprehension. He looked her in the eye. "If you don't think I've changed, no offense, but I seriously question your psychiatric prowess."

His tone, devoid of pleasantness, did not intimidate her. She grinned. "No offense taken. You're stalling. I'm listening."

He moved to the foot of the bed and sat, facing her. The tautness of his body and the scars he bore from war were on full display. He seemed unaware of his nakedness. The scowl on his face conveyed a willingness to engage in a verbal brawl.

"Colt, take a breath. Just tell me how you think you've changed. That's all I'm asking."

He buried his face in his hands. She let him be, knowing he was trying to reclaim his calm.

When he raised his head and looked at her, the scowl was gone.

"To explain how I've changed would require me to tell you my story. Do you really want to hear it?"

"I do. As I said, we have all day."

"Okay. Fine. Here goes: You know how messed up I was when you first met me. I was lost and aimlessly drifting, with no clue of how to get on a solid course. My transformation began with Jekyll. That little dog taught me what it was like to be loved purely and unconditionally. He became my confidant. I talked to him about anything and everything, and he never tired of listening. He comforted me through all my tears and the many war-related nightmares I had back then. No offense again, but he was the finest therapist who ever lived. I've yet to find the words to describe my love for him. I know one day he'll be there, welcoming me into heaven, assuming, of course, I ever make it there given all I've done as a sniper in Iraq and Afghanistan."

Katie smiled. "No offense taken again. We all loved Jekyll. I'll never forget after you rescued me from that kidnapper how Jekyll stayed by my side and loved me. So did you."

Colt nodded his understanding before continuing his story.

"Your parents befriended me in those dark times and have loved me in countless ways ever since. They so remind me of my parents, and, like Jekyll, I'll love them until my last breath."

"My parents are special people. Just know that you've brought much joy to them as well. Dad talks about you all the time, and Momma long ago adopted you as one of her own. You're their son. And don't forget that you've given them two wonderful grandchildren for which they'll be eternally grateful."

"I'd do anything for them. Anyway, I thought my life could get no better after marrying Rachel and having our children. She and I were so in love, and being a father agreed with me. But my perfect world ended with a thud and my son flying through the air, near-fatally injured. I felt so helpless sitting next to him day after day at the hospital. I never cried so much or prayed so hard in my life. But no matter what I did, Danny didn't get better. As the months rolled by, my despair grew. I decided to end my life if he died. I couldn't live without him." A tear rolled down his cheek. He wiped it away.

"It was Jon David and Sara who threw my family a lifeline. He told us his story and how the spirit people could heal Danny too if we took him to the cabin. Never have I had to summon the faith it took to make such an audacious decision."

Colt looked her in the eye. "Danny's healing at the cabin was a miracle. Rachel has always tried to dismiss it, claiming his return to awareness was a spontaneous recovery that can happen to those in a coma, but that's bunk. It was a miracle. If you can't accept this, then our relationship has no hope of working. I'm sorry for my bluntness, but that singular event has shaped the way I am today. I believe in God with such conviction now that I'm intolerant of naysayers."

Katie noted the anger returning to his voice. She opted for silence to give him time to calm down.

"You said you read *After the Purple Heart*. Well, just know that I've wholeheartedly embraced what the spirit people shared with Jon David at the cabin. My life has changed so much by following a path that includes God. I'm sorry, Katie—I thought I could mask from you how I feel like I did with Rachel. But I can't do it anymore. It didn't work with her, and it won't work with you or anyone else. Please forgive me for not seeing the folly of this relationship. My loneliness clouded my reasoning. I hope, one day, you'll forgive me. I'll get dressed and be on my way."

She looked at him with empathy. "Hey, come here. Come to me." He didn't budge. She moved over and touched him. "I need you to listen to me for a few moments, and then if you want to leave forever, please do so with my blessing. Can you agree to that?"

"Yes."

"Good. I know more about Danny than you're aware of. After his healing, Mom and Dad flew to see me after you all flew back to California. They had to speak to someone, and I was the only one they could trust. They told me in confidence what happened at the cabin and made me swear never to discuss it with anyone, including you. Colt, my dad is the most logic-driven person on the planet, and for him to state with such conviction that a miracle occurred astounded me. But Momma was right there, confirming everything he said.

"After they returned to Alaska, I asked my neurology professor what the chances were for a patient in a coma for months from severe brain trauma to have a spontaneous recovery with no residual disabilities. He said it was next to impossible. I visited you and Rachel and took a good, hard look at Danny. He had no scars, none. In the hospital, I saw his head wounds. Those kinds of wounds don't go away without a trace. You and Rachel told me he recovered after receiving an experimental drug, but I knew it was part of your cover story to keep the cabin from becoming a healing mecca. Anyway, unbeknownst to you, on that day at your home, I accepted as truth what my parents had told me."

"I'm glad you chose to believe that the miracle occurred because it's the absolute, unquestionable truth."

"I did more than just believe. I started taking classes in transpersonal psychology. In a nutshell, this field of study seeks to integrate psychology with spirituality to promote authentic power, healing, and well-being. Pioneers in the field include Carl Jung,

Stanislav Grof, and Victor Frankl, to name a few. Anyway, after taking the first course, I was hooked. As a practicing psychiatrist, I've found that children are very receptive to transpersonal counseling techniques such as guided imagery, expressive arts, and meditation because they haven't lived long enough to become jaded by societal biases."

She touched his cheek to emphasize what she was about to say. "Jon David got a crash course in transpersonal psychology that night in the cabin when he was visited by what he calls the spirit people. I believe that he and Danny were able to connect to their divine essence. It's as if they 'phoned home' and asked God for help. I think one day, we, as a species, may evolve into 'enlightened' beings, where we all can connect to God at will."

Colt looked at her, wide-eyed. "Damn, Katie."

She laughed. "You're a little anemic on eloquence with that utterance."

He didn't respond, so she pressed on.

"I wanted to speak to you countless times about what happened to Danny and what I was learning in transpersonal psychology, but I felt bound by my promise to my parents to keep quiet. Plus, Rachel would've regarded any talk of Spirit to you as treasonous."

He stared at her, unable to string together a coherent set of words.

She kissed his forehead. "If you permit me, since you appear to be a bit short on words, I'd like to clarify what I said about you being exactly how I remembered you."

He nodded.

"The essence of who you are hasn't changed. I'm talking about your honor, integrity, kindness, bravery, and just plain goodness. It's all there, just the same as it was when I first met you. But you've added something to your noble mix. Do you want me to tell you what it is?"

He nodded again.

"You added soulfulness." She kissed him gently and looked into his eyes. "It makes me love you all the more."

He drew her close and held her.

"Hey," she whispered. "There's one more thing. Rachel used to harp about you doing tai chi and meditating. It was nonsense to her, but I knew what you were doing. They're your way of connecting to your spiritual essence. My connection comes through yoga and jujutsu."

"I love you, Katie."

She laughed. "Whew, I think that means you might be staying for a while. I love you, too."

A peaceful silence ensued. Katie curled into the curve of his body. The reverie didn't last as long as she'd hoped.

"This relationship faces enormous obstacles. So many that it makes my head spin."

"You know, normally, I'd prescribe sex with me to boost your optimism, but you've already exceeded the daily recommended dose for that. I'm starting to think you may need more fiber in your diet."

His deep sigh crushed her attempt at humor.

"Okay, Colt, let's talk about the obstacles. You appear to be drowning in them, so tell me what you think they are."

"Okay. Here are a few, and I stress a few. Do you even want to be a stepmom? What would my kids think? I mean, you're their aunt. What will your parents think? Where will we live? I keep getting derailed in my quest to live in Alaska. If the kids and I moved here, this condo would be too small for a family. Would our being together destroy your relationship with Rachel? And what about your job—maybe you're a workaholic and don't even realize it. I won't be my partner's afterthought anymore, period. At least I know that much about myself. God, my head is whirling." He sat up and moved to the edge of the bed, burying his face in his hands again. "It's too much, Katie. It's just too much."

"Hey, come back here," she said softly. She ran her fingers gently down his back. "Come back." He did as she requested, heavy with sadness. "Look at me, Colt." She waited for his eyes to meet hers. "I'll address your concerns in order of importance, starting with the kids. I love them and would be honored to mother them. They like me, so my guess is we'll get their blessing. Now, my parents. I'll be the one who'll tell them. They already know how much I love you. I'm just kicking that love up a notch. After the shock subsides, I'm confident they'll accept the new reality.

"Okay, on to location: I hope you'll let me make a case for Portland, but the choice of where we will live is yours to make. You've earned this right after all the years you spent in California for Rachel. Now, on to her. You became irrelevant to her long ago, and I don't rate much higher. As a formality, I'll tell her about us, and if she gets surly, well, our relationship is more important than her love. Oh! Me being a workaholic. Not a chance. I've known loneliness, too, and have prayed for a loving husband and a family. I never prayed for more work. It will never become an issue because I'd quit before it did. You have my guarantee on that. There. All done. See, no worries."

"It won't be that easy, Katie. This relationship could cause carnage in three generations of our family."

"We'll find a way to make it work."

"And why are you so sure?"

"Because, like you, I've added spirituality to my core essences. The higher power within me sanctioned our togetherness long ago."

They lay in silence.

"Colt, if I were your therapist, I know what I'd say to you."

"I'd prefer to hear what you'd say if you were my partner."

"The advice would be the same. I would say it's time to live your authentic life, your truth. It's time to come out of the shadows and shine in the light of God, fully embracing your spirituality with no apologies or concealment. I'd like to be there as your partner, living in my authentic self, learning, growing, and loving with you along the way."

"That sounds great."

"I'd also say, take some time to sort through your feelings. Listen to what your higher self has to say. I'll be here when you come to your senses. In the meantime," she said with a mischievous smile, "I believe there are a few things I can do to ease your troubles."

36

BACK IN CALIFORNIA, JUST after Colt got home from jogging, his realtor called. "Colt, we got a full-price offer today, contingent on a satisfactory inspection and getting the house cleaned by pros. Their finances are impeccable, so I urge you to accept the deal."

"Excellent! How soon will we have to vacate the house?"

"It'll take about six weeks to close. If you want, I can run the paperwork over for you and Rachel to sign."

"Thanks, but she's working. If you bring the documents here, I'll drive to JPL and have her sign them."

"I can meet you at JPL if you like."

"Sure. How about two o'clock? I'll call you back to confirm if it's doable for Rachel."

The logistics worked, and they signed the papers on the hood of the realtor's car. Colt fought the urge to leap in the air and shout, "Yes!" as he watched Rachel ink her name on the various documents. She was signing his emancipation papers. He tried to suppress an ear-to-ear grin and felt insensitive when the effort failed. She appeared a bit melancholy as she signed the papers. He wondered why she wasn't the one sporting a grin, given how all this was her desire.

The impromptu meeting ended with handshakes to the happy realtor and Colt offering a polite nod to Rachel. As he opened the car door to leave, he glanced at her walking back to the building. It sparked a curious irony. He flashed to the day in Prescott, where she surprised him by flying there from Yale and asking him to marry her. The elation he felt on that day was seared into his memory. And now, as she walked away, his joy was just as intense.

He got in his car and texted Katie. *Accepted full-price offer on the house. Call me.* He smiled, wondering if his unassuming message would elicit the same euphoria in her that he was feeling. A wave of fear swept through him. *Katie. What to do about Katie?* Decisions soon needed to be made, decisions with far-reaching consequences.

Despite his many meditations, the still, small voice within had yet to endorse the relationship. It troubled him. Up to now, secrecy had made their liaison easy. What would happen when their relationship became known? He could lose her. That thought generated another wave of fear. He left the parking lot rattled.

Back home, Colt found it hard to shake the dark thoughts. He tried to meditate, but the lightning storm in his head made it impossible. He cracked open a beer and went to the patio. On the porch swing, he took a long swig and flashed on Rachel, signing the papers today, looking so sad. This was supposed to be her moment of triumph, so why the long face? Maybe she was sad because she didn't want to let him go. God. "Damn it, Colt, get real!" he shouted. "You're like an annoying insect that she wishes would go away. You tried to make it work. Get over it!" He gulped down the beer and got another.

Back on the patio, his thoughts turned to the work required to vacate the house. A decade's worth of belongings crammed every nook and cranny. After getting what she wanted, Rachel no doubt would dump the task of clearing the place out on him. He tried to quench the anger by downing the second beer all at once. It didn't work. He crumpled the can and then glanced at his watch, hoping Katie would call soon.

He got up and tossed the can into the kitchen's recycle bin. From behind the kitchen counter, he surveyed the living room. Damn, there was a lot of stuff to get rid of. He glanced at the folder on the counter that his realtor had given him. Absently, he opened it and glanced at the summary page, which was jam-packed with numbers—realtor fees, title company fees, escrow fees, HOA transfer fees, the home warranty cost, etc. He didn't have the patience to sort through them and dropped to the bottom line. After the vultures got their respective bites, the net to him and Rachel would be $2,710,000. He mentally divided the number in half to reflect his share. It brought a smile to his face. It was more than enough to buy a decent home in Anchorage. Or Portland. He sighed at the thought of that. He flashed to when he first met Jekyll in Alaska; those were the hard days. His net worth back then was about a thousand bucks if you threw in his ancient Honda. Fortune had smiled upon him in the years since. A similar kindness failed to prevail in his marriage. He closed the folder and pulled a pizza from the freezer. Dinner tonight would not be noteworthy.

After eating, it seemed like forever waiting for Katie to call. Oddly, staring at the wall clock for a half-hour, watching each second pass, did little to lessen his stress. He decided tai chi would be a better way to burn time. He kicked off his sandals in the backyard and felt the grass with his bare feet. He took a deep breath, closed his eyes, and raised his hands slowly. Then, he started swaying back and forth like a tree moving in a breeze. *Back and forth, back and forth, breathe in,* he told himself, *breathe out, be one with the breeze.* Minutes began melting away; his precise movements looked like a sensual dance in slow motion. He felt his peace returning.

The phone ringing yanked him back to awareness. He raced to answer it.

"Hello," he said, panting.

"Hey, it's me. Are you out of breath?"

"Sorry, I was doing tai chi and had to run to the phone."

"I can call back if you want."

He laughed. "I almost went crazy waiting for you to call, so, in desperation, I resorted to tai chi to preserve my sanity."

"Sorry. I wanted to eat before calling so we could talk uninterrupted. Congrats on the house offer."

"Thanks. It's contingent on passing a home inspection, but I've kept up with maintenance, so I know it'll do fine."

"You seem less excited than I thought you'd be."

"My elation lasted about five minutes, and then reality set in."

"Do you want to talk about it?"

"Well, I have a decade's worth of belongings to deal with."

"I hear you. I'd love to fly down and help you, but that might not be a good idea."

"Yeah, it wouldn't go over well. I guess I'll take it one room at a time and get a dumpster delivered so I can toss out the junk. In six short weeks, I'll be a vagabond. I haven't a clue what I'll do with the stuff I want to keep. I guess I'll put it in storage for a while."

"You're welcome to stay here. I'll help you in any way I can."

"Thanks. I suppose I can't do a thing until Rachel claims what she wants."

"You might want to buy some colored dots to mark whatever each of you wants."

"Good idea. Rachel looked sad today as she signed the papers. I thought she'd be gloating and yelling, *Free at last, free at last!* but she seemed subdued."

"Well, who knows what's going on with her? For all you know, it could be work-related. I wouldn't read much into it."

"I suppose."

"So, here we are."

"Yeah."

There were a few moments of silence.

"Colt, what's up? I was hoping the sale of your house would precipitate talk of us, but you're painfully quiet on that front."

More silence …

"Colt, I can almost feel you shriveling up. Please talk to me."

"You said Spirit long ago sanctioned our togetherness, but try as I might, I hear nothing. I can't make any decision about us without receiving a clear direction. I hope you understand."

"I do."

Another round of silence followed.

"Katie?"

"What?" Her voice sounded shaky.

"Are you crying?"

"Don't worry about it. Go to Anchorage and be with your children. You can rent a place there until you figure out what you want to do. Colt, I need to go."

"Wait. Now you're the one shriveling up. Please talk to me … Katie, are you there?"

"You act perturbed for waiting a few hours for me to call. Try waiting since you were a teenager, and you'll know how I feel. Here's a newsflash: Spirit has already spoken to you."

She had an edge to her voice.

"Uh-oh. I believe I've aroused your Irish ire."

"You're damn right you have."

"Katie …"

"What?"

"How do you know Spirit has spoken to me?"

"This isn't a good time to talk about it. I should go so I can cool down. Goodnight. I'll call you tomorrow."

"Please don't hang up. Take a breath. I really need to hear what you have to say."

Silence …

After what seemed an eternity, she spoke.

"When you last made love to me, you looked at me so tenderly, and I knew, I knew right then. Your soul was making love to my soul. It was the most profound thing I've ever experienced."

Now he was the silent one.

"You're … you're right. I felt it, too, in the same way you described. I'm sorry, Katie. The message from Spirit couldn't have been any clearer, and I was oblivious to it."

"Then wake the hell up and do something about it!"

He laughed. "Yes, ma'am. I think I will."

She couldn't help but laugh, too. "I love you desperately. I ache for you."

"I can fly up tomorrow if you want."

"I'd love that."

"While I'm there, you could give me a tour of Portland and show me what the town and area have to offer. Let's drive that fine car of yours up to the mountains and explore. We can even look at homes if you want. Maybe I can find a way to thrive there."

"Do you mean it?"

"Yes, but I offer no promises other than to be open-minded."

"Colt, do you think I'll make a good stepmom? Talk to me about them."

"I think you'll make a wonderful stepmom. The bar for the mothering they've had hasn't been set very high. Christa melts my heart. She has the same personality that Rachel had before Danny's accident. She's kind and sweet and quiet in a good way. She still has an innocence about her that I find so appealing. Although she's beautiful, she doesn't date. I think she's terrified that all relationships will end up like what Rachel and I have. I love her so much. It's been hard watching her try so hard to seek her mother's affections only to get rebuffed time after time. She never complains, but I see the hurt in her eyes, and it tears me up inside. I've tried to love her extra hard—to be a mother to her as well as a father."

"I've seen it every time I visit—how you always have an arm around her, how you hug her hello or goodbye, how you are kind and considerate when you talk to her, and how many times you say 'I love you.' I love how you taught her tai chi and do it together every day. She's quite skilled at it." Anger rose in her voice. "So many times I've wanted to shake my sister and scream, *Wake up! You have a beautiful child who needs your love.*' Christa loves you so much, Colt. Thank God at least one of her parents never let her down."

"I can't thank you enough for letting her fly up to be with you for a week each summer. She always came home elated. You've been a wonderful aunt to her."

"I looked forward to our times together as much as she did. I love her, Colt. After she'd leave to go back, I'd sit staring at my phone, fighting the urge to call you, asking if I could adopt her. I've been concerned that one day she might seek a substitute for her mother's love from either boys or drugs, but you've done a good job keeping her centered."

"Thanks. I wish I could say I've been as successful with Danny."

"Tell me about him—beyond the current trouble he's in and his girlfriend issues."

Colt sighed. "The story is especially tragic with Danny. He was old enough to remember his mother's love before the accident. She loved him so much, and they were inseparable. After the accident, her love for him withered and died. To experience that is heartbreaking to a little boy. I could see his sadness slowly turning into anger, and by the time puberty hit, he had a rage inside of him, like the rage I felt toward that drunk driver who killed my parents.

"I tried as hard with Danny as I did with Chris, but I couldn't fill the void. Eventually, he sought a substitute for her mother's love, and I suppose the girl he was dating was a shining example of that. I tried getting him counseling, but Danny is so intelligent that he just toyed with therapists. Now, he wants to join the Army as his way of escaping. The thought of him experiencing what I've gone through frightens me."

"I hope Dad will be able to influence him this summer. But I think he's pretty determined to join the Army this—"

"Hold on." In the background, Katie heard a muffled "Hello, Rachel, what do you need?" Colt got back on. "Sorry. Can I call you back? Rachel said she wants to talk."

"Uh, sure. Unless it's something major, call me tomorrow because it's late and I have an early patient appointment in the morning. If you decide to fly up, any time after three will work."

"Okay, I'll see you."

"I'll say I love you for both of us."

"Thanks. Bye."

He walked into the house. Rachel was sitting on the couch, looking at him. "Who was on the phone?" she asked.

"A friend. What's up?"

"Could we talk for a few minutes?"

Her voice didn't have the typical sarcastic edge.

He sat on the other side of the couch. "Sure. Are you okay?"

"I'm fine. Colt, today in the parking lot, signing those papers, it hit me that we really are separating."

He nodded.

"I, uh, I was wondering, could we, uh, you know, could we give it more consideration?"

"Give what more consideration? Selling the house?"

"Us, Colt. I mean, us. Could we give us some consideration?"

"I'm sorry, Rachel. I don't know what you mean."

"I think I made a mistake saying I want a divorce. I was just angry. There's so much going on at work."

He felt sucker punched.

"The ship has already sailed on that, Rachel. I need much more than you're able to give."

"What if I say I'll be open to marriage counseling?"

"Counseling won't work if you aren't willing to change."

She looked at him, her lips quivering. "I think I can be open to it."

He looked at her, stunned.

"Rachel, I'm done battling. You've been an absentee wife and mother. I say this not to provoke you. I've had my heart trampled for years, and I can't do it anymore."

"I still love you."

He shook his head. "No, your love for me ended with Danny's accident."

"No, it didn't. The way I treated you changed."

"I loved you so much back then. I've missed those days more than you can imagine."

"I know. I've missed them, too."

"If you're trying to tell me that you'll change and become the person you used to be, well, sorry, that's a leap of faith far greater than I'm capable of making."

She looked at him with sad eyes. "I'm asking you, my husband, not to abandon me. I'm asking you to consider loving me again. I told them today that I'm dropping my hours at work. I'll consider a leave of absence if you want so that we can work on our relationship."

"Why are you having this sudden change, Rachel? This is so out of character for you."

"I don't want to die alone."

"Here's something to consider. You can be with someone and still die alone if it's a loveless relationship. I know what I'm talking about. It's been that way with you."

"I know. We had it good once. I'll work hard to get to that place again."

"There's more to it than that, Rachel. I've changed so much since Danny's healing at the cabin. I believe in God with all my heart. I'm no longer the man you knew when we were happy together, and I can't pretend that God is irrelevant to me. For you, a miracle at the cabin didn't occur. For me, the hand of God touched our son. That sums up the gulf between us."

"I've seen how believing in God has changed you. I got mad at you for doing tai chi and meditating because I couldn't find the calm you found. Maybe you could teach me tai chi someday."

"I thank you for saying that, but, again, our son was healed by a miracle. We can't bridge that split in our thinking."

"I'll be more open to hearing what you have to say about it. Honestly, I could never explain how Danny's scars disappeared or how we had the same dream about taking Danny to the cabin."

"We can't back out of selling the house. I hope you know that. The buyers want this house badly and will sue us for backing out. We signed a contract today."

"The house doesn't matter. It's just a house."

Inside, Colt reeled. *Dear God,* he thought. ...

Rachel spoke again. "I don't need an answer from you tonight. All I ask is for you to think about it. I'll try, Colt. I promise you I'll try."

He looked at her without responding.

"Well, it's getting late. I need to go to bed." She smiled, stood, and went to the guestroom.

Alone in the living room, Colt's life turned topsy-turvy.

37

SLEEP DIDN'T COME EASY that night for Colt. He was in shock. Rachel acting polite was shock enough but saying she was willing to change raised his level of astonishment exponentially higher. Her words echoed in his head. They all sounded good and contrite, but were they too good? Or was he questioning her genuineness to support his romantic dalliance with Katie? *God.* He wanted to call Katie, but this was news she wouldn't want to hear. Besides, he had already brought tears to her when they talked. He felt awful about that. Should he still go on the proposed trip to see her? *God.* He fell asleep with those troubling thoughts.

Colt loved the dream he was having of Katie and him making love. It felt so good, so familiar.

"I love you, Colt."

His eyes shot wide open. It wasn't a dream, and it wasn't Katie. It was Rachel! She was on top of him, naked, and he was in her. He gasped and pushed her off.

"I can't do this!"

"It's okay, Colt. I want to." She touched his manhood. He gasped again and leaped out of bed, panting. "I can't do this!"

"Colt, it felt so good making love again. Come back to me."

"I'm seeing someone."

She sat up. This time, it was her turn to be shocked. Her eyes met his. "Do I know her?"

"Yes. I mean, God. Rachel, you demanded a divorce."

"How long has it been going on?"

"It happened after you said you wanted out."

"What's her name? Is she pretty? You were talking to her last night, weren't you?"

"Her name is none of your business. And, yes, I was talking to her last night. I love her, Rachel."

"I see."

She got up, put on her bathrobe, and left.

Colt fell back on his bed, shaking from what happened. *Oh my God,* he thought, *what will Katie do if she finds out? Should I tell her?*

Several minutes later, he heard the garage door open and then close. Rachel must've left. Good. Her going was good. He wouldn't have to face her in the morning. He smelled her perfume on him. A shower now became a must. The water, as hot as he could stand it, didn't wash away the guilt gripping him. Back in bed, sleep was impossible. He looked at the alarm clock: 4:20. His mind raced. He decided to call Katie. She had to know. He looked at the clock again: 4:25. It was too early. He'd wait until six. The home phone rang.

"Hello."

"Did you make love to Rachel?" It was Katie. She was crying.

"Yes, but not in the way you're thinking. Let me explain."

"What a fool I've been. Goodbye forever, Colt."

The phone went dead. He hit the redial button. She didn't answer.

He raced to the kitchen for his cell phone. He'd text her and beg her to call him back. His eyes squinted when he flipped on the light. The cell phone wasn't on the charger. Rachel must've taken it! She must've looked at his call log and saw that he was talking to Katie. He sat on a dining room chair, shaking, his mind racing through possibilities. *Oh my God, what if Rachel tells the kids! What if she tells Pat and Annie?* As if on cue, the phone rang again. He looked at the caller ID. It was the Brennans.

"Hello."

"What in the *hell* is going on down there? Rachel just called ranting like a maniac." It was Pat.

"Please, sir, let me explain."

"Shut the hell up. I have one question. Are you having an affair with Katie?"

"Pat, please, let me explain."

"Answer the damn question, Colt."

"I am."

"Dear God in heaven!"

The call ended with those words.

Colt ran to his laptop and booked a flight to Portland. He got dressed and drove like a madman to the airport. Aboard the plane, he prayed the whole way not to lose the woman he loved. After landing, he raced down the concourse and rented a car. He looked at the car's clock. It was 10:30. "Please, God, let her be home."

At her condo, she didn't answer his repeated doorbell rings. An older woman walking by saw him. "Sir, Katie already left for work."

"Thanks for letting me know, ma'am." His mind raced. *What's her workplace called again? Oregon University? Damn. Think.*

He ran back to his car and punched the university name into the navigation system. *Damn!* There was an Oregon State University, but that was in Corvallis. He queried universities in Portland. There it was: the Oregon Health & Science University. He punched it in and followed the directions.

He frowned when he got there. It was a big place. Should he go in and try to find Katie or cruise around and find her car? If he went in, she'd likely refuse to see him. If he found her car, he could wait until she showed up. She'd have to talk to him then. He opted to find her car. He drove to the staff parking lot and soon spotted it. He found a place to park and ran back to her car. Now, the waiting would begin. He glanced at his watch, hoping she'd use her car to go to lunch; otherwise, he was in for a long wait. It didn't matter. He had to see her.

Less than an hour later, he saw her walking out. She stopped dead in her tracks when she saw him. He quickly closed the distance between them.

"Go away, Colt!" Her eyes were bloodshot, no doubt from crying. She did an about-face and hurried back to the building.

"Wait! You'll know I didn't cheat on you when you hear what happened. You know I wouldn't be here if I did anything dishonorable."

She stopped and faced him. "You'll have to have the best excuse in the universe for me to believe you."

"I was sound asleep. I thought I was dreaming about making love to you. When I woke and saw it was Rachel, I pushed her off and jumped out of bed. I told her I was in love with someone else." Tears poured down his cheeks. "You *know* me. It's the truth."

Her lips quivered. "I find it hard to believe you could make love to someone while you're sleeping."

"It's the God's honest truth. I would never hurt you like that. Please, Katie. Please don't walk away from us." He looked into her eyes and pleaded. "Please."

"They all know. Momma called me. Rachel told everyone, including the kids."

"I don't care. If they all hate me, I don't care. You're all that matters. Don't leave me. I'm begging you."

Her demeanor softened.

"Please." He mouthed the word to her.

She nodded. He hugged her with all his might. "You're all that matters now." He kissed her. "I love you so much."

"What will we do now?" she stammered.

"We'll figure it out. We can fly to Alaska and tell them our story." He kissed her again. "Can we go to your home and be together? I need you so much."

"I was going home. I've been a mess today."

"I'll follow you there." He hugged her again. "I love you so much."

When they arrived at her home, Katie motioned for him to sit on her couch. She brought a chair from the dining room, put it in front of him, and sat. He felt the distance. "Okay," she said, "tell me what happened, and I mean *all* that happened, starting from when she interrupted our call."

He nodded.

"When I came in from the patio, she asked if we could talk. The pleasantness in her voice immediately caught me off guard. It was the first time in years that she wasn't cross with me. She said when she was signing the real estate papers, it suddenly dawned on her that we were parting. She said she thought it might be a big mistake and …"

He looked at her.

"What, Colt?"

"This all sounds surreal—as if I just woke up from a nightmare."

"I need to hear what happened. Keep talking."

"She said she was willing to go to marriage counseling, but I said it was too late for that. She then said she was paring her workweek down, and she'd take a leave of absence to work on our relationship if that's what I wanted."

Katie winced at that disclosure.

"I told her that I believed in God with all my heart, and I couldn't be with her because I believed that a miracle happened to Danny, and she didn't. I said we could never bridge that chasm."

"What did she say?"

"She said she couldn't explain how Danny's scars disappeared, and she'd be open to discussing what happened there more with me. She also said she saw how my belief in God had changed me and that she got mad at me for doing tai chi and meditating because she couldn't find the calm I had found. She said her work didn't give her that kind of peace, so she was jealous. She asked me to teach her tai chi."

"And what did you say?"

"I didn't say anything, so she said, please think about it. She said she really wanted to try to make it work."

A tear rolled down Katie's cheek. "So, you must've been swayed by what she said."

He took her hand. "Quite the opposite. All I could think about during the conversation was what you said about my soul making love to yours. I wanted to tell her about us and how much I loved you, but you said you wanted to tell her about us. So, I got up and went to bed."

Katie nodded. "Then what happened?"

"I tossed and turned, debating whether to call you or not. It was late, so I decided to call you the next day as you asked. I was so tired, mentally and physically. I finally fell into a deep sleep. That's when I dreamed of you making love to me." He looked her in the eye. "Of *you* making love to me, Katie. Then I heard *'I love you, Colt,'* and it slammed me into awareness. I gasped and jumped out of bed. I said, *'I can't do this! I'm in love with someone else.'* Rachel asked who it was, and I said it was none of her business. She asked if I was talking to my lover on the patio when she came out, and I said yes.

"She left the bedroom, and a short while later, I heard her leave. I had to call you, but when I looked at the clock, it was way too early, so I decided to wait until six, when I knew you'd be up. But you beat me to it with your call. Rachel took my cell phone and obviously looked at the call log. That's how she knew it was you. Pat called just after you and went ballistic."

He looked at her but said nothing more.

She sighed. "So, are you telling me that nothing she said touched you? Come on, Colt, I know you're not that insensitive."

He frowned. "If Rachel had said those words a few months ago, I would've been doing cartwheels in the street. But, the more I thought about it, there was something in her words that didn't ring true. When two parties disagree, the art of compromise dictates that both will grant concessions to reach an amicable agreement. But she was conceding everything and demanding nothing of me in return. It was as if I could've said there are no stars in the sky, and she would've readily agreed. There's something else, and it's even more important."

"Go on."

"After making love to you for the first time, I mentally divorced Rachel. I didn't need a court decree to tell me it was over. My heart became yours. Even if all she said was true, I couldn't go back to her, not after what's happened with us. My place is with you. Our last conversation sealed the deal. You were right—our souls are linked, and we can't untangle them."

Her lips quivered. "I know."

A few moments passed in silence.

"What you dreaded has now happened," she said. "This relationship has caused carnage in three generations of our family."

He sighed. "I know. I think we should fly to Alaska and tell them our story. Katie, no matter what happens—even if that means my kids will never speak to me again—I can't live without you. The connection I have with you is too powerful to ignore."

She looked at him in dismay. "You said it was going to be complicated after we first made love."

He smiled. "You replied by saying, let's not talk about it, at least for today." He took her into his arms.

38

LATER THAT DAY, KATIE called her mother. It was a brief conversation. She hung up in tears.

"What happened?" asked Colt.

"Mom's in Seattle, on her way to see Rachel. She said she's beyond angry with me. She said, don't even think about the two of us coming to see them or the kids. Colt, she's never treated me so coldly."

"I'm sorry, Katie. Maybe she'll cool down once the shock wears off."

"I know what they're all thinking. Katie, the homewrecker, stealing away her sister's husband."

"That's not the truth, and we both know it."

"I'm going to miss my parents. I love them so much."

"They'll never abandon you. Me, probably, but not you. Did Annie say anything more about my kids?"

Katie nodded. "She said under no circumstances are you or me to call Christa and Danny until the dust settles." She plopped on the couch, lost in melancholy.

Colt was silent for a few moments.

"This is going to stop, right here and now."

She looked at him with sad eyes. "What?"

"This. We're acting like we got caught red-handed doing something wrong. Well, it's not wrong. It's a beautiful love story about a woman who's loved a man with all her heart for years and a man who was in a loveless emotional wasteland. By the grace of God, they found each other. Instead of sitting around feeling guilty, we're going to celebrate our good fortune. This is an epic love story. I won't apologize to anyone for our relationship, and I damn sure won't feel guilty about it."

"Colt, I feel as if I've fallen into a bottomless pit, and I'll never again see the light of day."

"There's an old saying: *All the darkness in the world cannot overcome the light of the most humble candle.* I'm your light in this darkness, and you're mine. And right now, I'm brightly shining for you to see."

She smiled. "I'll be a light for you, too."

"Good." He kissed her. "Now, I'd like to take you out to dinner. Oh. There's one other thing. I'm moving to Portland."

"What?"

"We're going to be challenged by a tsunami of changes in the months ahead, so it's critical to minimize the changes wherever we can. By staying here, you won't have to get reestablished somewhere else with your work. That alone will be a huge stress reduction."

"Colt, I can't be that selfish. I already accepted that I'd be moving back to Alaska if we become a couple."

"I know, and for that, I'm grateful. But you said the choice of where to live is mine to make. Well, I've made a choice. I'm moving here. Oregon has lots of mountains and beaches. I can easily picture us cruising to the coast, walking on the beach, and having a blast."

She hugged him. "Thank you so much. I love it here and know you will, too."

"Can you humor me for one last thing?"

"Sure."

He smiled and dropped to one knee. "Katie Brennan, will you marry me? I promise I will always be faithful to you and love you for the rest of my days."

"Oh my God. Colt! It's too soon to be asking me. Plus, you might change your mind once our family's anger descends on us."

He stood and cupped her face in his hands. "When things are at their worst, here I am, looking into your eyes, telling you that I love you and want to be with you forever. I love you, Katie Brennan. Will you marry me?"

She choked up. "Yes. I've been waiting my whole adult life for this moment."

He kissed her. "I'll bet if we hurry, we can find a place to buy you an engagement ring."

"I'd love that."

"Your ring will have to be rather humble. A large expense isn't possible until after my divorce."

She smiled. "Well, you're off the hook on that one. I've thought about this for many years. All I want for a wedding ring is a simple gold band. I love the understated elegance of it."

"You really are special; do you know that?"

She kissed him. "So are you, my man."

Two hours later, they found a jeweler who had what she wanted. The comfort-fit gold band looked perfect on her hand. Katie beamed as she gazed at the ring, looking as proud as a lady sporting a three-carat diamond.

"So, can I tell Jen and my other friends I'm engaged?"

"Sure. Tell Jen it just took a little longer than you planned."

"She was the first person I told about wanting to marry you when I was seventeen, so she should be the first person I'll tell that we're engaged. I wonder if she'll be surprised."

He laughed. "I think that's a given."

Katie turned serious. "You know that old saying, *Hell hath no fury as a woman scorned?* Well, if Rachel wants, she could derail the divorce process to spite us."

"Are you already saying you want to return the ring? Man, that was fast."

"No, no, that's not what I'm saying. I just think Rachel could draw the whole thing out."

"The courts can't tell me where to live or who to be with. If Rachel draws it out, I'll still be with you. That's all that matters."

"I agree."

Katie looked at her watch and frowned. "Do you mind if we get fast food tonight? I'm exhausted."

"That's fine."

After returning home, while Colt took a shower, Katie called Jen. For the first time, her friend since childhood was speechless. Following that, she called her supervisor and told her what had happened.

She joined Colt in bed. "I got tomorrow off. My boss was worried about me after my behavior today. When I told her everything was fine and we got engaged, well, let's just say she was more than a bit surprised. I told her about you, and she's happy for us. So is Jen."

"I'm glad we'll have a long weekend together."

"Me, too. I know it's late, but could we talk a bit more? Everything has happened so fast today that I missed a few critical points we should've discussed before I said yes to your proposal— you know—what I need from you as my partner."

"Okay. I have expectations, too. Can we discuss mine as well?"

She nodded.

"Do you want to start?" he asked.

"I do, I say, tongue in cheek."

"Shoot."

She turned off the light. Telling him in the dark must've seemed safer. She snuggled next to him.

"Well, here is what I must have."

"You've given this some thought, I see."

"Yep. So, buckle your seatbelt, mister, because here I go."

"Lay it on me."

"I understand that we'll have to wait for the courts to marry, but I expect you to act after your divorce. I won't play house with you, Colt. If you can't fully commit to this relationship, we can stop right now."

"Ring through my nose; got it. Next?"

"Love me even when I'm not lovable."

"I have a track record to prove I can do that."

"You do. Next, keep having sex with me like you're doing now. I need your gentle, tender lovemaking. I can't even begin to describe how it soothes my soul."

"That's good to hear, Katie. I, too, savor how we make love to each other."

"Speaking of sex, be faithful to me. It would simply crush my heart if you cheated. You saw that today."

"That's easy. I feel the same. What else?"

"Respect me. My feelings, thoughts, opinions, and desires should carry equal weight with yours."

"No problem. Katie, this is pretty basic stuff."

"Basic, yes, but it's the glue that will keep us together. Do you want me to go on?"

"Sure."

"Be the man, which means protecting me and caring for our family. I'm simply asking you to keep doing what you've always done."

"I know what you're saying."

"Okay, drum roll, last but not least. Give me attention. Play with me, laugh with me, cry with me, and support me. I suppose all I'm asking is for you to be my friend."

"I can easily agree with all your requirements."

"Oh! There's one more. Love me when my father's Irish ire stirs within me."

"Ah yes, the demon within that makes you a fiery redhead. Hmmm, that might be a tough one."

"I have a slow fuse, Colt, but I do have a fire within me. Just know that when I'm mad, I'm never cruel. I know how words said in anger can bounce around in your head forever. So, even if I'm angry with you, your heart will be safe with me."

"I understand what you're saying, Katie. Your heart is much bigger than your temper and always has been. So, is it my turn now?"

"It is. Speak to me."

"We already talked about the importance of Spirit in my life, but I'd like to clarify it more from the perspective of us as a couple."

"Okay. I can tell that you also have given this some thought."

"I have. Katie, with all my heart, I hope we'll commit to something higher. By that, I mean having a relationship that rises above a physical, emotional, and financial union where Spirit is woven into the fabric of our existence. In Genesis, God said, *'Let there be light, and there was light. God saw the light, and saw that it was good.'* Beyond the literal interpretation of these words, I believe God was putting a spiritual light into each of us so that we may see and become 'enlightened.' When we talked about Danny's healing, you said you thought that one day we might evolve into 'enlightened' beings. I think you were saying what I'm trying to say now. Does this make any sense?"

"It makes perfect sense. Nothing would make me happier than us being on an 'enlightened quest' together, where we learn and grow to widen and deepen our lives in Spirit."

"An 'enlightened quest.' I like the sound of it. Katie, when I got mad when you said I hadn't changed, it dawned on me how I could no longer mask what I believe. For so long, I hid my authentic self to create some semblance of harmony in my marriage. But pleasing Rachel and others required putting my spirit in an invisible cage. Jon David told me that one of the spirit people whispered something to him before leaving the cabin. It was one word: *Be.* Well, for me to be, I need to strip away the mask I've been wearing for so many years. To live my life authentically, I need to stay true to myself and speak my truth. I hope you'll provide a safe harbor for me to be me. I promise I'll do the same with you."

"I'll always be your safe harbor. Colt, ever since I've known you, you've been that safe harbor for me. Do you remember how terrified I was after being kidnapped? You said, 'call me anytime, and I will come.' I called you at two in the morning, and you came, spending the night comforting me. I felt so safe with you there. I still carry that feeling within me, and when we talk like we are now, that feeling resonates inside me. I so love being with you."

He hugged her a little tighter. "I feel safe with you, too. Katie, I wanted to go back to Alaska because when I'm out in nature, it amplifies my spiritual strength. Being outdoors for me is like being in church. I feel connected to the divine, and it fills me with positive energy. I remember how I loved playing my flute at sunrise.

It made me feel like I was welcoming God to be with me for the day. I hope you'll share my love of the outdoors for these reasons."

"I love to hike, but I have to tell you, this girl likes her daily shower."

He chuckled. "I'm not talking about being in the bush for weeks. A simple hike away from the hordes of people is all I need. I can do that here in Oregon just fine."

"That I can do."

"Great. One last thing on leading an authentic life, and that's to be of service to others. Before Danny's accident, I did a lot of things to help veterans, but after his healing, I felt compelled to do more as my way of saying thanks to God for my son's healing. I've taught tai chi for years now and find pleasure in helping others to use it as a way of connecting to their divine essence. Authoring the book with Jon David is another example of that. As a couple, I'd love for us to help others in some noble way."

"I try to do this with my patients. You cannot imagine what cruelty and abuse some children face every day. Whenever I see them, I close my eyes and imagine putting them in a bubble where they are safe from harm. I ask God to protect them. Maybe someday we could do something together to help. You could teach them tai chi, and I could teach them yoga."

"I'd like that. Do you want me to go on, or is this too much?"

"Please go on. It's exciting to hear."

"Okay, this is the nuts and bolts of a relationship." He took a deep breath and exhaled. "I'd need from you rock-solid trust, honesty, and integrity; I consider them to be the cornerstone of any relationship."

"Me, too. What else?"

"We need to listen to each other and speak in such a way that our thoughts and feelings are heard with empathy and responded to with respect. And, from that, we'll always strive for a win-win situation instead of a win-lose."

"Wow, I should've let you go first. You're nailing it right on the head. Please continue."

"I need to know, especially with the obstacles we face, that if the going gets tough, you won't run. In other words, I'll require more than a fair-weather relationship."

"Yep. That goes both ways."

"Okay, here's a big one. Having quality time together. After what I've been through, not having it would kill me."

"I know, Colt. I agree."

"Here's another, and it won't sound very manly. I need to be touched and touched often. You spoke of sex, but I need more than that. I need affection. I need to have my cheek kissed, my hand held, and my body caressed. There's nothing more soothing than simple human touch."

"You're melting my heart, do you know that? That's what I was trying to say when I mentioned sex. You said it better. We both need affection. Providing you with that type of love will be effortless for me."

"I need to hear, every day, how special I am to you and that you love me. I'll treasure hearing those words, and they'll do wonders to soothe my soul. And I'll need liberal doses of compassion and patience. Mostly patience. I've been through a lot in my life, and sometimes my past can resurface just like your Irish temper."

"I understand. Anything else?"

"Yes. I thought I finished talking about Spirit, but these words just came to me regarding the turmoil we're going through now. I want us to celebrate our relationship as a direct gift from God. We'll never apologize for what our spirits have sanctioned. And, we'll share our joy with others to promote a higher good."

She kissed him. "I love you so much."

"I love you, too. I have one more, and this could be troubling."

"What's that?"

"Family. Do you want to have children with me?"

She turned the question around. "Do you want us to have a child?"

"No. Katie, I'm not a young buck anymore, and being a parent is all-encompassing."

"I'm past my prime as well, and I'll love your children as my own. So, we can pass on making babies."

"We've covered a lot of territory tonight."

"We have, but I'm so glad we had this talk."

"Hey, I propose we spend this weekend free of worry and speculation. There'll be plenty of time to sort things out later. We need to focus on us."

"Do you mind if we do just one more thing?"

"What's that?"

She kissed him. "Please make love to me."

39

COLT AND KATIE SPENT Friday and Saturday staying close to her condo, loving, talking, and going for walks around the neighborhood. At the local park, he practiced tai chi while she did yoga. Their agreement to spend their weekend free of worry and speculation was paying dividends. A sense of peace returned to them. Confidence in their relationship once again blossomed. Sunday morning came, and they planned to go on a drive in the mountains. Katie wanted to show him a bit of wild Oregon, and Colt was eager to test the capability of her car. Just as they were about to head out, there was a knock on the door. Katie opened it and was shocked to see her mother.

"Hello, Katie. May I come in?" Annie looked at Colt but didn't acknowledge him with a greeting.

"Of course you may come in." She motioned to the armchair. "Please have a seat. Can I get you anything?"

"No, thanks." Annie sat, looking tense.

Colt and Katie sat on the couch, facing her.

"I see you're wearing a ring. That's a bit premature."

"It's an engagement ring, Mother."

Annie paid no attention to the response and put a withering stare on Colt. "I just left your wife in California. Congratulations on the job you did to destroy her. Or, should I say congratulations to the two of you for your handiwork?"

"Annie, I—"

Katie put her hand on him. "Pardon me, Colt, but I need to talk to my mother alone." The expression on her face let him know this request wasn't open for debate.

"Uh, sure. I'll go to the park." He squeezed her hand and left without saying another word.

Alone with her mother, Katie spoke first.

"I had planned on flying up to tell you and Dad after I got permission from Rachel to marry Colt."

"Suffice it to say that approval from Rachel will not be forthcoming. Katie, I forced myself to come to see you today, given that the urge to disown you is overwhelming."

"I'm glad you came. Please do me the honor of hearing what I have to say, and then you and Dad can do whatever you want."

Her mother nodded.

Katie bowed her head and said nothing for a while. She then looked at her mother. A tear fell down her cheek.

"I told my supervisor about being engaged, and she asked me to describe my fiancé. I said I've known Colt for a long time and, from a distance, have loved him with all my heart. I told her that's why I never dated much because no one could measure up to him. I told her it was unrequited love until recently, and he's the most kind, loving, and caring man I've ever known. That's what I think about Colt."

"Did you also tell her that Colt's your sister's husband!"

"Do you want to listen to me or just shout?"

Annie responded with a tightened jaw.

"I've been in love with Colt since I was a teenager. He's always been the perfect gentleman and never made romantic gestures toward me. I invited him to come to see me during the Fourth of July weekend, way after Rachel told him she wanted a divorce, and that's when I told him of my feelings for him. I love him. I always have loved him. I always will love him."

"My God, Katie. How can you be so selfish? Think about Rachel. She was trying to put their marriage back together. And the kids—they're beside themselves."

"Rachel hasn't wanted anything to do with Colt for years. And now, she magically changed? Get real, Mom. Colt said something didn't quite ring true with her words of wanting to mend fences, and I'm sure his intuition was correct."

"Okay, fine. Look at it from a different perspective. How could you be so blind to Colt's reaction when you said you loved him? He's in emotional turmoil and has suffered through years of neglect. What man in that state wouldn't jump on a pretty woman offering him her love and her body? You could very well have nothing when the passion subsides. Darn it; you're a psychiatrist. You know how vulnerable he is. You should've given him time to reestablish his life."

"You're right, Mom. I'm a board-certified psychiatrist. I think that qualifies me to render an assessment of Colt's mental and emotional state and to be able to ask proper and pertinent questions. We've spent hours—days, for that matter—talking. But, let's talk just about me." Her Irish temper was rising, confirmed by her flushed face and edgy voice. "When Rachel called from Maine saying what she'd done to win Colt's affections and how she made a mess of things, you and Dad hopped on a plane and roared off to be with her. You never once considered me and how I was feeling. I stepped back when Rachel asked me for my permission to marry him partly because she loved him but, more importantly, because Colt loved her.

"I cried myself to sleep for months after their wedding. Can you even imagine the anguish I felt being the bridesmaid and watching the man I loved marry my sister? Everyone felt because I was young that I was incapable of love. No one ever knew how badly my heart had broken. I never, in any way, interfered with their relationship. I watched as she treated him horribly for years, and it broke my heart again. When Rachel finally discarded him, I stepped in. Now, it's my time for happiness, *and I'll be damned* if I let him go again."

The conviction in her daughter's voice shocked Annie. "Okay, Katie, I accept what you just said, and I'm sorry for the pain you've experienced. I do remember your melancholy after their wedding, but obviously, your dad and I didn't understand its cause or depth. I also remember when Colt got the news of Scotty going to a bad place in Afghanistan how you comforted him through the night. Yes, in retrospect, your love for him was plain to see."

"Thanks for accepting at least that, Mom."

"While I can accept your deep love for him, it's his love for you that I question."

"Do you remember when you and Dad came to see me and told me about the miracle at the cabin?"

Annie nodded.

"It affected me more deeply than you could've imagined. Your conviction of what happened touched me so much that I couldn't let it go. I did a lot of research and flew down to see Danny for myself. To make a long story short, I agreed that a miracle healing must've occurred. I started taking classes in transpersonal psychology, which integrates psychology with spirituality, and found myself being drawn more and more toward God. Then Colt and Jon David wrote their book, and the words in it have changed me forever. I learned how to connect with my spiritual essence. Colt does it through tai chi and meditating, and my connection comes through yoga and jujutsu. I can say, with confidence, that I know when Spirit speaks to me."

Her eyes bore into her mother. "Regarding Colt, the higher power within me has long ago sanctioned our togetherness. Spirit has spoken to Colt as well and blessed our union."

Annie sat rigidly, unable or unwilling to convey her thoughts. Finally, she broke her silence.

"You know we love Colt. We've witnessed the hurts he has suffered in his marriage, and our hearts go out to him. But he's just running to the safety of your arms."

"If he is, I'll give him the comfort he wants for the rest of his days and die a happy woman."

"Katie—"

She raised her hand and stopped her mother. "Mom, forgive me for interrupting you, but with or without your concurrence, I will marry the man I love. My happiness has been subordinate to my sister for my entire adult life. No more. If marrying Colt means being estranged from my family, so be it. I have a deep, abiding love for him, and this time, I will *not* yield my feelings to comply with the wishes or dictates of others."

Katie stood. "I'm going to be with my man." She opened the front door and turned around. "Your daughter is standing before you, asking for your blessing, asking for a chance to experience happiness. Colt will not let me down." She walked away in tears.

Annie sat dumbfounded, lost in her daughter's words. ...

She gathered herself and called Pat to tell him what had happened.

"Dear God in heaven. She pirates away her sister's husband and shows no trace of guilt? What else can happen to this family?"

"Pat, on the face of it, yes, it sounds bad what the two of them have done, but somehow, everything Katie said makes some sort of sense. You should've seen her talking to me. God, how she loves him. She's loved him like that since she was a girl."

Pat said something, but Annie didn't hear him. She was thinking. Suddenly, everything became ... clear.

"Annie, are you there? Annie?"

"I'm here." Tears poured down her cheeks. "Pat—"

"Annie, what's wrong?"

"I've, I've been so blind."

"What do you mean?"

"Katie's right. She's loved Colt for years, just as she said. I've been a fool for never seeing it. That's why she hardly dated. It makes such perfect sense now. What man could match Colt in her eyes? She's right about something else. Colt will love her as no one else can. I see it so clearly." She paused for a moment. "I'm going to support Katie and bless their love."

"Damn it, Annie, how can you condone this? What about Rachel? What about the kids? Katie's their aunt, for God's sake."

Annie sighed and wiped her eyes. "At first, I believed Rachel's crocodile tears. But then, like Colt told Katie, her words didn't ring true. It didn't take long for her to get bored talking to me, and she went back to work. That's hardly the behavior of a destroyed woman. What she really loves is Colt being there to pay the bills, watch the kids, and do all the maintenance around the house. Now, she'll have to fend for herself, and it scares her. It's not about love; it's about convenience.

"As for the children, Katie and Christa have always loved each other. It scares me how Christa could end up cold like her mother. Katie could show her a mother's kind of love, and it's something Christa desperately needs. I can think of no one better than Katie to raise her. You can't argue that. Danny already has one foot out the door, so we'll have to see. Should he elect to be with them, Katie would love him, too."

"Annie, for Colt, it's a rebound romance that could destroy another daughter. We talked about this."

"Pat, you need to listen to your heart regarding Colt. He's honorable and has demonstrated what a good man and father he is countless times since we've known him. When I told Katie she would be in for a massive hurt, she spoke of the spirit within her blessing their union. She and Colt are more deeply connected to God than we ever knew. Somehow, I know this relationship won't end badly."

"I think this is nothing but madness, Annie."

"Pat, as soon as my heart weighed in, I knew it was wrong to think that way. I know Colt wouldn't ask for her hand if he thought he'd hurt her. We're talking about the man who nearly sacrificed his life to save her from that abductor. Please search your heart, and you'll know what I'm saying is true. Katie has a chance for love. She's waited years for him. He has the chance to be with a woman who adores him and will take care of him for the rest of his days. It'll be a happy union. It's clear to me now." Her lips quivered. "I've never demanded anything from you in all our years, but I'm begging you to bless their union."

"Do you truly believe what you're saying?"

"Yes. Do you remember Jon David telling us to listen to the still, small voice for the answers we seek? Well, that voice has spoken to them, and it's speaking to me now. Pat, your blessing will be the greatest gift you'll ever give to Katie. Nothing else will come close."

"And what about Rachel? One daughter will be hurt with either choice we make."

"To me, the answer is easy. Let's side with love. Colt and Katie will have a union filled with love. All Colt would have with Rachel is more of the same wretched existence. I vote for love."

"If ... if your feelings are that strong, then I'll accept what you're saying."

A while later, Annie heard faint sounds coming from the back deck. She looked through the sliding glass door window. Katie was sitting with her face buried in her hands, crying. Colt had his arm around her. He looked so sad. She opened the door and went to them. Katie wiped her eyes in a weak attempt to hide her anguish. Annie leaned in and kissed her cheek. "You chose a good man, my dear daughter. You and Colt will have the full support and blessing of your father and me."

Katie looked at her, shocked. Annie nodded that she had heard her right. She hugged her mother. "Thank you, Momma."

"Please forgive me. I've been so blind." She looked at Colt. "I'm excited for you two. You both deserve the chance for love."

Annie had an evening flight and spent the rest of the day brainstorming options with them. Colt's decision to move to Portland surprised her, but she agreed the choice made sense, given all the changes that were about to happen. Plus, Annie suggested leaving the kids alone for a while. She'd call when the time was right for them to fly up and speak together as a family and announce their engagement. Katie couldn't help hugging her mother throughout the day.

Colt spent the rest of the week with Katie. Pat called, and he and Colt had a good talk. It killed Colt not to talk to the kids, but he knew Annie was probably right to have her and Pat clear the way for him and Katie. He also called Jon David, who offered his support after getting over the shock of what happened. He and Sara spoke to Katie to welcome her into their extended family. Scotty offered to fly down and help him clear out the house. Things were shaping up.

40

KATIE BEAMED. "Now you see what Portland has to offer." She spread a blanket in an open area with sweeping views of the city and mountains.

Colt used his hand like a visor to shield his eyes from the bright sun. "This is nice. What's the name of this trail again?"

"It's called the Marquam Trail, and this is Council Crest. It's about eleven hundred feet in elevation and is one of the highest points in Portland. See those four mountains—they're extinct volcanoes. And over there is Portland proper. Cities like Beaverton and Lake Oswego surround it.

"Are we still within the Portland city limits?"

"Yep."

"Wow, this is a decent elevation rise within a city. It's a nice little hike."

"There are lots of trails in and around Portland. Sit with me, and let's have our sandwiches."

He joined her and smiled. "The cool breeze up here feels good after the hike."

"I love coming here in the summer. I bring a book and enjoy reading while listening to the singing birds. For being only fifteen minutes away from my home, you can't beat it."

"You picked a great way to spend Saturday morning." He took a bite from the club sandwich. "This is good. Can you hand me a drink?"

She got out a soda and passed it to him. "I packed some chips, too."

"No, thanks. I've never cared for them."

She took a bite of her sandwich and looked at him. "I wish you didn't have to go back."

"I know, but I've got to get the house done. There's a firm deadline for me to be out of it."

"I hope everything goes well, if you know what I mean."

"Trust me; I'll do my best to avoid Rachel. I might even move the dresser in front of the bedroom door to stop any nocturnal visits."

She frowned.

"I'm sorry. That was a poor attempt at humor."

"It's okay. Actually, I love your sense of humor."

"I have a sense of humor?"

She laughed. "Don't think I've forgotten how you messed with me when I was a teenager. I fell for that dry wit of yours every time."

"I have no idea what you're talking about," he said with the faint beginnings of a smile.

"Well, let me refresh your memory. You'd look at me and say something in a calm and composed voice, and I'd eat it up."

He shrugged his shoulders. Katie poked him in the ribs. "You're doing it again."

"Doing what?"

"Messing with me. Do you remember telling Jen and me how you were stranded in the Iraqi desert for twenty-one days and barely managed to survive by using your emergency supply of powdered water? Or when you called Army food the spoils of war?"

He grinned. "No, I don't recall that."

"Or when my abductor tried to shoot you, you said you were able to dodge the bullet because it was a heavy caliber?"

"Oh," he said with a sheepish grin, "I do remember that one."

"Let's not stop there. Remember, after having dinner at our house, you would flip a coin with me to see who would do the dishes? I began to wonder why I always lost and why Dad snickered afterward. Then one night, I finally figured it out. *Heads, I win; tails, you lose.*' You always looked so innocent when you said it, and I fell for it every time." She rolled her eyes at how gullible she was to the wordplay that made it impossible for her to win. "And do you remember telling me how you counted to infinity twice when you were twelve years old?"

Colt chuckled. "I hope you're not mad about this morning."

She laughed. *"Say, do you know the freckles on your belly form an elephant?* I can't believe I handed you the pen and said, connect the dots and show me. Now, when I see my belly button, I'll picture that not-so-flattering focal point."

"Hey, that elephant had a cute rear end."

She smiled at their lighthearted banter. "I'll have you know that I cracked the code for your humor. I'm just a little rusty at spotting your devilishness."

"And just how did you crack the code?"

She tried to suppress a giggle and touched the left corner of his mouth. "Your lip upturns here in the slightest way; that gives you away. Sometimes, your face will flash a hint of irony. It's like your mind is dancing with delight, and some of it slips through despite your best efforts to tamp it down. You're quite good at your craft, but the many hours I spent observing you paid off."

Her revelation brought a mischievous grin to his face. "Did you really watch me that closely?"

"Colt, I was head-over-heels in love and couldn't take my eyes off you. I'm glad to see your sense of humor returning. I love your wit and how it keeps me on my toes. Your humor is one of your most endearing qualities."

He smiled. "My dad and mom always had humor-filled play. I think it's one of the reasons they loved each other so much."

She hugged and kissed him. "I have no doubt we'll be lovers and best friends. Call it a package deal."

"That sounds good. Hey, while we have some time, do you want to talk about options for living here?"

She looked at him, surprised. "Wow. That's an abrupt change of subject. What's on your mind?"

"Well, regarding a house, after Pasadena, I'd prefer being out of the city and maybe have a place with some land."

"The public transportation here is great, so I can commute to town from the outlying areas. The lease on my condo is up in three months, so I'll be free to move after that. Besides having some elbow room, can you give me some more thoughts about what you want in a house?"

"We haven't discussed our collective finances, so do you want to start there?"

"Sure."

They spent the next half-hour discussing their respective assets and debts.

"So, we could easily afford a million-dollar home."

"I suppose we could, but I don't want a mansion. Paying cash for a less expensive place and having no mortgage appeals to me."

She ate a potato chip and pondered. "After living in my small condo, any house will seem huge, so I can agree to that. But, if both kids come to live with us, we'll need a place with four bedrooms. That'll give us a spare bedroom for guests. A house meeting those needs would be about twenty-five hundred square feet. Also, with the rain here, a three-car garage would be nice."

"Good points. I'd love to have three or more acres where I could have a four-season gazebo for writing, but if acreage requires a long commute for you, it won't work. Oh. I don't want an old house. They usually come with a thousand things that need fixing, and they aren't energy efficient. Something less than ten years old is the way to go."

"Now we have a starting point. This is exciting. Do you want to head home and plug our criteria into the computer and see what turns up?"

"Yeah, that would be fun."

They finished their meal and hiked back to her car. Back home, Katie brought her laptop to the table. After feeding in what they wanted, six places popped up with three or more acres. "Look at this," said Katie. *"Custom home on eighteen acres, unobstructed views in every direction, master on the main floor, and terraced lawns with a garden."* She looked at pictures of the place. "Oh my God, this house is nice. Look at the views! Let's check out the school rating." She clicked on another window. "Lincoln High School is the one for this area, and it's rated at ten, which is the highest possible."

Colt shared her enthusiasm. "Excellent. Hey, look at the small barn. Maybe it could be turned into a writing retreat. Try plugging in the address in Google Maps and your work address to see how long the commute will take."

She did as he asked with a few keystrokes. "Thirty minutes. That's doable. Let's go see it, Colt."

"It sounds great, but it's $900K and 4100 square feet. Are you sure you want to live in such a big home? We could also look for places closer to your work on normal-sized lots."

"Sure, we can see other homes, but let's see this one today, just for fun."

He nodded. "Okay. Try calling the realtor."

An hour later, they pulled into the driveway and saw a middle-aged woman waving and smiling. "Well, that must be the realtor," said Colt, "or maybe she's a very lonely homeowner."

"Hello, Mr. and Mrs. Brennan. I'm Margie."

Colt shook her hand. "Please call me Colt. And, my last name is Mercer, not Brennan. That's my fiancée's last name. I plan on moving here from California. This is the first house we're seeing."

"Congratulations. May I ask how you plan on financing your home?"

"Most likely an all-cash offer."

"Cash is always the easiest way to purchase a home. What do you two do for a living?"

"I'm a medical doctor," said Katie, "and Colt is a writer."

"Both of your jobs sound interesting. Are you ready to tour the home?"

"Yes," said Colt, "but we'd prefer touring the home alone so we can talk candidly to each other."

"Okay, go ahead. I'll walk around to the patio, and you can meet me there when you're finished."

"Thanks." He took Katie's hand and opened the front door. "Wow, this is nice," he said, gazing around. "Real nice. Look at the views through the living room windows." The hexagonal-shaped living room allowed views in multiple directions.

Katie squeezed his hand. "I could easily picture us in a hammock, out on the deck, enjoying these views."

He admired a telescope sitting on a tripod and smiled after looking through it. Katie moved to the kitchen. "I love the solid surface countertops and stainless-steel appliances. Momma would love this professional gas cooktop. And there's plenty of storage space."

After walking through the rest of the home, they joined Margie and headed to the small barn. She waited outside while they went in. Colt beamed at what he saw. "This would be perfect for me. It wouldn't take much to convert it to a writer's retreat."

"This could be our life, Colt. Look at my arms—I have goosebumps."

He smiled. "This beats anything Anchorage could offer for the price. Let's have Margie show us the property boundaries."

"So, what do you think?" the realtor asked after pointing out the four corners of the property.

"We're impressed," said Colt. "Is the market such that this place will sell soon? Please don't give me the standard realtor answer of 'oh, yes, anytime.'"

She chuckled. "Okay, here's my honest assessment. Sales for properties like this can be fickle. With the down economy, anything over $800,000 typically sits for a while. For every additional hundred thousand over $800K, the time on the market increases. Plus, rural properties sell slower than those in town. The owners just dropped the price by $20K to stimulate interest."

"The earliest we could make an offer is three months from now," said Katie. "With that in mind, is there any hope of us getting it?"

"Well, you never know. It's been on the market for a while, so it could still be available."

Colt nodded. "Thanks for your time. This house has our attention."

"Here's my card. Let's keep in touch, and you're welcome to call me if you have any questions or want to see more homes." Colt nodded as he took her card.

In the car, Katie glowed. "For me, this place is nirvana. Do you agree?"

"I do. I think Spirit spoke to both of us, saying this is the place, but we shouldn't get our hopes up. Three months is a long time. It could take even longer if the courts don't get around to my divorce case or if Rachel gets rowdy."

She took his hand. "We could host daylong retreats here for abused kids. It would be a great way to be of service to others."

"I'd like that. We'd sure have the room to do it."

They drove home, talking about what they'd do if the house were theirs.

41

ON SUNDAY, COLT WAS in the bedroom packing for California. Katie brought her phone to him and put it on speaker. "Go ahead, Mom."

"Hello, Colt. Can you and Katie fly up? It's time for the family meeting."

He looked at Katie, and she nodded. "If we can book a flight, of course we will. Have they warmed up to the idea of us?"

"Christa has been quiet and melancholy since her mom called. I hear her crying in her room, but when I try to comfort her, she withdraws, just like her mother does. She looks frightened, and that's why I want you to come up. Pat and I think she needs your assurance that everything will be okay. Danny's mad about so many things, and Pat can't reach him. Maybe you can help. I think he's more determined than ever to join the Army."

Colt sighed. "That's my worst fear. Give us a few minutes to see if we can book a flight."

They got on the computer. There was a flight leaving at six in the morning with seats still available, but nothing on the way back until three days later. Katie called her supervisor and explained the situation. She granted her request for time off. They booked the flights and gave Annie the news.

They left the next day and arrived in Anchorage before noon. Pat and Annie were there to greet them. On the way home, Annie looked at them in the back seat. "When we get home, we can all meet in the living room and talk. Colt, please try to remain calm if Danny mouths off. He's struggling right now."

"I'll do my best."

Pat looked at him in the rearview mirror. "Danny's determined to join the Army and has been studying hard for the GED. Colt, we made a pact with Danny, and you need to honor it."

"I know, sir. I will. Maybe we can talk him into something other than infantry. I read that the Army is starting a cyber warfare command. So, ideally, Danny could defend the nation in cyberspace. It sure beats shooting people or getting shot at."

"I'll talk to a recruiter here and learn more about it."

"Thanks."

The kids greeted them warily, and their coolness troubled Colt. He glanced at Katie with eyes conveying unease. She gave him a feeble smile, silently agreeing with his concern.

Pat took the lead. "Let's sit in the living room. It's time to talk."

Colt and Katie put their bags in her childhood room and came back out. They sat on the loveseat. Without saying a word, the others took seats around them.

Colt looked at his children, who were sitting together. "Kids, we flew up here because there's a lot to discuss concerning the future. It's tragic how you found out about Katie and me. After you hear what actually happened, I hope you'll understand and bless our relationship. I've asked Katie to marry me, and she agreed."

The news of marriage surprised both children.

"Your grandpa and I support their decision," said Annie. "We wish them a happy and wonderful life together."

"Can you marry an aunt?" asked Christa.

Colt smiled. "Yes, marrying someone's sister after getting divorced is legal."

"What will happen to me? Will I have to live with mom?"

"I love you, Christa," said Katie. "My hope is you'll choose to live with us."

She looked relieved. "I love you, too, Aunt Katie, I mean, Katie, I mean, what should I call you now?"

Katie smiled. "You can call me anything you want." Katie turned her attention to Danny, who was sitting rigid and stone-faced.

"Danny, I hope you'll give us your blessing. We both would like you to live with us as well."

His eyes bored into hers. "Worthless as she is, she's my mother, and you're her sister. Am I supposed to be happy about you shagging her husband?"

"Danny, that's enough!" Colt replied, glaring at his son. "We never had a romantic interest in each other until after your mom asked for a divorce. That's what I wanted to tell you today."

"Danny," said Annie, "when your mom called in the middle of the night, telling us what she later told you, your grandfather and I were furious. I flew down to comfort her, and on the way back, I stopped in Portland with the intent of disowning Katie as my daughter. But, after talking to your mother and listening to Katie, I knew that Katie and your dad should be together. I blessed their union, and so did your grandfather when I told him what happened. There was absolutely nothing going on between them until after your mom demanded the divorce. For years, your father tried to make his marriage work, and he has suffered more than you and your sister will ever know. He deserves to be happy after so many years of sadness."

Danny ignored her words. "So, where are you two lovebirds going to play house?" he asked his father with disdain. "Let me guess. You're moving to Portland."

"You guessed right!" Colt thundered back, unable to contain himself. "That's what I want to talk about next."

"Don't bother. It'll be a cold day in hell before I move in with you and my aunt, oh, sorry, make that, what, my aunt-stepmother now. What a pathetic joke." He rocketed out the front door, shouting as he went. "I so want out of this farce of a family. Army, here I come."

Colt started to go after him, but Pat grabbed his arm. "Let him go. Give him time to cool down and think about it."

Colt glared at Christa. "Are you going to side with your brother and run out, too?"

His bluntness drove her to tears. She spoke with anguish. "After Mom called, I thought you would leave me for Aunt Katie. And when you didn't call, I knew it was true. You're the only parent who loved me, Dad. I thought, what will I do without you? I've been so scared."

Her disclosure shocked Colt. "Oh, baby girl, I would never leave you. I'm so sorry for putting you through such heartache. We thought it would be best for you to first talk about things with Nana and Grandpa." He went to her and cupped her face in his hands. "I love you so much. You'll always be my girl."

"I love you, too, Dad. I'm happy for you and Aunt Katie."

She looked at Katie, who was in tears. "Ever since I can remember, I always wished you were my mother. The truth is my mother doesn't love me or want me. Aunt Katie, you always made me feel special. I love you."

Katie moved to comfort her. "I've always felt the same as you. Since you were a little girl, I've wanted you to be my daughter so badly. My prayers have now come true."

Annie looked at Pat and beamed with joy. He nodded, knowing his wife was right—Katie would love their granddaughter like no other woman could.

"Do you think I'll like living in Portland, Aunt Katie?"

"C'mon, let's walk to the inlet. I'll tell you what your dad and I are thinking about doing there and see if it's okay with you."

She nodded and looked at her father. "You made a good choice, Dad. Katie will make you happy."

He smiled. "It means so much to me that you approve. Thanks, sweetheart." He walked them to the door and watched as they headed down the trail.

Alone with Pat and Annie, Colt sat next to them and sighed. "Well, at least one of my kids still likes me and thinks it's a good thing."

"Oh, Danny boy," said Pat. "I like your cyber idea. It could work."

"I guess the best I can hope for is him staying with you and finishing high school here."

"He'd be welcome here," said Annie, "but let's give him a chance to think about things. The shock from what you just told him is huge. Don't write him off yet. In the meantime, why not go out and do tai chi to calm down. If Danny comes back and wants to talk, your being calm would help a lot."

"That's a good idea. When Chris gets back, I'll ask her to join me."

At two o'clock, Jon David called and asked to speak to Colt. "Hey, buddy, Danny's here. Geez, he's wound tight. He's downstairs with Riley and doesn't know I'm calling you. He said you told him and Christa that you're marrying Katie and moving to Portland."

"We flew up to tell them in person. As you can see, it didn't go well."

"That's why I'm calling. I'd like to fly Danny to the cabin and tell him what happened there and how it affected his mother. He's old enough to know these things. I told him I'm flying to the cabin today and asked if he wanted to come along for the ride. He said sure."

Colt mulled it over. "Okay. Maybe you can talk some sense into him. He's fired up now to enlist in the Army."

"Yeah, he said that to me today. I plan to talk to him about that, too. Give me two days, maybe three, okay?"

"Yeah, that's fine, but we fly out in the evening three days from now."

"Roger that. I'll have him back well before you leave. Riley's the same size as Danny, so we'll outfit him here. You can come later and pick up your car. Bring Katie if you want; Sara can't wait to meet her."

"Sure. Jon David, go easy on him. No browbeating Army drill sergeant stuff, okay?"

Jon David laughed. "My ass-chewing Army days are long gone. I'm just going to talk with him. Sometimes, it's all a young man needs."

"Thanks. I mean it."

"Hey, Rangers take care of each other. I said that to you a long time ago."

"I know you did. You're a good friend. Sara is, too."

"Hey, congrats again regarding Katie. We seem to have a weakness for highly educated women."

Colt smiled. "Yeah, I suppose you're right."

"I'll bring him back in a few days. He'll be fine."

"Thanks again, buddy. Bye."

Colt looked at Pat and Annie. "Danny's with Jon David. He offered to fly Danny to the cabin and talk to him about what happened there. I think it's time for him to hear the truth."

"I agree," said Pat. "Maybe it'll help him understand how his accident affected his mother."

"Jon David said we could pick up your car at their house. I'd like to do that with Katie so she can meet Sara."

Annie nodded and hugged him. "It will all work out, Colt. We'll do whatever it takes for Danny. We're family."

Pat hugged him, too. "Go be with your ladies. Share your joy about marrying Katie with Christa. She needs Katie's love as much as you."

42

JON DAVID EASED THE plane down and made a gentle landing. Danny had an ear-to-ear grin on his face. "Thanks for letting me fly it some. Maybe someday I'll become a pilot, too."

"Yeah, flying these puddle-jumpers over the Alaska bush is fun. I have to fight your Aunt Sara over who gets control of the wheel. Honestly, she's a better pilot than me, but don't tell her I said that."

Danny laughed. "I'll bet she's already told you."

"When did you get to be so good at knowing women?"

"I've had some experience," he said with a sly smile.

Jon David changed the subject. "Hey, let's unload our stuff."

They secured the aircraft and hustled their gear several hundred feet to the cabin. Inside, they opened the windows to air it out and then walked down to the river to see if any fish were running. By the time they got back, it was dinnertime. Jon David opened the Igloo and looked in. "Sara made ham sandwiches, and there's macaroni salad in here too. Will that work for you?"

"Yeah, it's fine. Can we go fishing after eating?"

Jon David tossed him a sandwich and brought over the macaroni salad. "Here's a plastic spoon. Let's eat it straight from the tub, bachelor style. I hate cleaning dishes."

"I like how you think." With a smile, he took a big spoonful. "This is good," he said with his mouth full. "What about fishing? It would be nice to catch something before we head back."

Jon David looked at him. "We'll have plenty of time to slay a fish or two because we'll be here for two or three days. I brought you out here to talk to you. Among other things, I'm going to talk some sense into you regarding the Army."

Danny's buoyant mood soured. "You're not going to talk me out of anything, Jon David." He dropped the ceremonial 'Uncle' title from his reply. He stood. "I want to leave now."

"You're welcome to leave anytime you want." He pointed eastward. "Anchorage is that way. Tread lightly, though, because this is prime bear habitat. The inlet might be a tough swim, given its thirty-eight-degree waters."

"My dad put you up to this, didn't he? Damn, what a sucker I was. Did you two have this planned all along?"

"None of this was planned until you showed up at my house today. We're not that clever." He pointed to Danny's sandwich. "Eat up because what I have to say to you goes far beyond your Army aspirations. Something extraordinary happened to me and you in this cabin. That's the main reason why I flew you here today. After I tell you, if you want to fly back, I'll haul your skinny ass back in a heartbeat. Fair enough?"

"Yeah, that's fair. And I'll hold you to it. Deal?"

"Deal."

They finished eating in silence. Jon David grabbed two chairs and put them facing each other in the cabin's center. "Do you need to take a piss because this is going to take a while?"

"I'm fine."

"Good. Then have a seat. We're going to talk, man-to-man. I swear to you that all I have to say is the truth, so help me God."

Danny plopped on the chair, looking bored.

Jon David sat and looked at him without saying a word. After a while, the silence became uncomfortable. Danny squirmed in his chair.

His 'uncle' finally spoke. "Three miracles have occurred in this cabin. One happened to me. One happened to my friend, Jamie. The last one happened to you." A tear rolled down Jon David's cheek as he spoke. His sincerity got Danny's attention.

"What happened, Uncle?"

"Let me tell you my story first. It's long, so please be patient. And some of it isn't very pleasant."

Danny nodded.

"I'll begin by telling you a little about me when I was young. My dad was in the Army, just like yours. He was in the infantry and did two tours in Vietnam. We moved a lot because the Army transferred him to many different posts during his career. Because we moved so much, my mom never worked. She stayed home, and she did a great job raising me and my kid-brother. By the way, his name is Danny, too. When Dad retired, we moved to Roanoke, Virginia, and I spent my teenage years there. My parents still live there. They're good people; I think you would like them. Like your father, they taught my brother and me to live our lives with honor and integrity.

"I always wanted to be like my dad, so I went to West Point. I did well there, and after graduating, like my father, I chose infantry and became a Ranger. I was a good soldier, Danny. At least I thought I was until I lost several of my men in Iraq."

"What happened there, Uncle Jon David?"

He sighed and proceeded to tell him about that awful day in Iraq. Danny often winced as the grisly tale unfolded. After reliving the events, Jon David needed to take a break. They walked to the river, and there, he resumed the story.

"After returning from Iraq, my life became a living hell. I was tormented by what I'd experienced, and the only way to escape that and the unrelenting pain from my wounds was with painkillers and booze. When I no longer could tolerate my dreadful existence, I decided to end my life. I planned to make my death look like an accident. Suicide would've broken my parents' hearts. That's when I met Jamie, who was vacationing in DC. He invited me to visit him and his wife in Alaska."

Jon David paused and looked at his young friend. "C'mon, let's go back to the cabin. What happens next will amaze you."

For the next two hours, Jon David spoke in a calm, firm voice. He described in detail what happened at the cabin. It was still as fresh in his mind as if it had happened yesterday. He told Danny about the five spirit people with their auras and what they'd told him. He explained how they changed his mind about taking his own life, how he woke up the next morning to find his scars and the shrapnel in his legs gone, and how his life had changed since then. He told Danny about committing his life to peace and helping children, which was why he decided to become a doctor. He told him how the spirit people had visited Jamie, too, and then how he came to be with Sara.

Jon David looked at his young friend, who was sitting straight up in his chair. "We can take a break if you want, or I can now tell you about the miracle that happened to you."

"I don't need a break. What happened to me?"

"Okay. It happened when you were six. While your mom was in Chile working, you and Christa flew to Alaska with your dad for the summer. You and your dad joined a soccer team here. He was the coach, and you were one of the players. Riley was also on the team—that's how you two met. One day, after practice, you guys were messing around, and the ball got kicked out to the street. You chased it and got nailed by an SUV. It was horrible, Danny— fragments from your shattered skull jutted out of your scalp. The paramedics rushed you to the hospital, and Sara was the trauma surgeon who first saw you at the ER. She almost lost it when she saw you because she thought you were Riley.

"It wasn't just the brain trauma you suffered; you had broken ribs, a bruised lung, and multiple contusions. You were on death's door. Your mom flew up from Chile, and Sara said she never saw a mother so in anguish. I'll talk about that later.

"You remained in a coma for months. Your dad and mom never left your side. The doctors finally told them there was little hope of you recovering. You would likely be in a vegetative state for the rest of your life. That's when I came in. After the Army, I went to med school and became a pediatrician. I'm rather good at what I do, so Sara asked me to look at your records to see if the doctors missed anything that could help you get well. I combed through your charts and found nothing amiss. I, too, concluded that you'd probably be in a coma until you died."

"So, what happened?"

"I told your dad I needed more time to do research, and then I'd get back to him. He thought I was blowing him off and was devastated since I was his last hope. After seeing you, I prayed. Jamie had died recently, and I talked to him in heaven. I pleaded for his permission to take you to the cabin so you could be healed." Jon David noted how intently Danny was listening. He continued the story.

"If Jamie approved of me taking you to the cabin, I asked him to give me a sign. On the way home, I saw a beautiful double rainbow. I raced home and told Sara and Jamie's wife, Penny, that we had to get you to the cabin. Convincing your parents to pull an unconscious child out of the hospital and transport him to a remote cabin for a miracle healing was, well, let's just say it was going to be a challenge. I asked them to come to my home, where Sara, Penny, and I told them our stories, just like I'm doing with you. They made a courageous leap of faith and agreed to bring you here. Your grandparents came, too.

"We brought you here on a stretcher and placed you on the table that we moved to the center of the room where we're sitting now. We all put our hands on you, silently praying for the spirit people to come and heal you. The night passed. At four in the morning, your mom was desperate, and she broke the church-like silence. I'll remember her pleas for the rest of my life. *'Please, God, please. I'm begging you, please. Please, God. Please, God. Please, God …'*"

Tears poured down Danny's cheeks. Jon David pressed on.

"The first feeble rays of the morning sun began shining through the windows. A half-hour later, sunshine bathed the room. The night had passed. There was no miracle. Your mom's tears spread to all of us. I was devastated, knowing I'd let everyone down, especially you. 'I'm sorry,' I remember saying to them. 'I'm so very sorry.'

"We all left the cabin to give your mom and dad time to be with you. Your grandparents were heartbroken. I remember them standing by the river, holding each other, crying.

"Inside the cabin, your mom went up to the loft, exhausted. Your dad stayed with you, his head bowed. Then, he raised his head and looked at you. He said it looked like you were staring at him. He wiped the tears from his eyes, as if to somehow reset them, and looked at you again. You *were* staring at him. He whispered, *'Can you hear me, Danny?'*"

Danny interrupted Jon David. "I whispered back to him, *'I thought you were sleeping and didn't want to wake you.'* I asked him where we were. He said, *'We're in a holy place.'*"

Jon David was shocked. He nodded and hugged Danny. "You *do* remember."

"I remember Grandpa Jamie telling me it was time to wake up. He said my parents were missing me. He was glowing like a big, green neon light. They all were glowing but in different colors. I didn't want to leave them, but Grandpa Jamie said if I ever wanted to talk to them, all I had to do was knock on the sky and listen to the sound."

"Jamie told me that, too. You don't know this, but you gave my family and me a tremendous gift that morning at the cabin. Your dad said you told him about meeting 'Grandpa Jamie.' You let us know he's still alive and dancing through the heavens."

Danny wiped his tears away. "After we got back from the cabin, I tried to tell Mom and Dad what happened, but they said it was a dream. They said you gave me some experimental medicine, and that's what cured me."

"Danny, medicines can't remove scars. Your head had many of them from where your bones tore through your scalp, but look at your head now—it's perfect. I'm the reason they told you it was a dream. Imagine if word got out that a miracle cured you. There would be thousands of people here now, hoping for a miracle. Your parents and grandparents respected my wishes. But, you're now old enough to know what happened."

"Thanks for telling me. It makes a difference."

Jon David took a deep breath. "It's time now to talk about the anger in you, the anger you feel toward your mom."

"Can we drop the subject of her? I want nothing to do with her."

"No, we can't drop it. You need to hear this."

Danny nodded hesitantly.

"In wars, soldiers returning from combat may be without physical wounds, but many have scars from invisible wounds. Today, they call it post-traumatic stress. It can affect everyone. Think of a rape victim, or an abused child, or people who go through a natural disaster. Statistically, women are twice as likely as men to develop post-traumatic stress. Some never recover from these invisible wounds. I tried to commit suicide because of the damage to my soul. Can you accept that post-traumatic stress is real?

"Yes. My dad tried to tell me about how wars can destroy you emotionally. That's why he doesn't want me to join the Army."

"Good. Let's focus on your mom now. Danny, before the accident, she was a happy, loving wife and mother. Search your heart. Before the accident, you knew her love."

He nodded, his eyes welling in tears.

"After the accident, your mom stayed by your side in total anguish. She blamed herself for letting you come to Alaska for the summer. It was the first time she was ever away from you and Christa. I don't know how to say this, but something inside of her broke. A darker side soon trumped her joy at having her boy being healed. She watched you like a hawk, afraid to let you out of her sight. You rebelled at being on such a tight leash. She always feared you would lapse back into a coma. She begged Sara to give you a battery of tests to prove you were okay.

"As the months passed, her mind couldn't accept that a miracle had happened, and you were okay. Her fears tormented her day and night for days, then months, then years. Her only solace came when she was at work. There, she was able to concentrate on things other than you. It became the only relief from her demons. Every time she saw you, it was like fuel being thrown on her emotional bonfire.

"Your dad begged her to get help. Your grandparents did, too. So did Sara and me. She refused. For years, she refused, and by then, her demons were in complete control. Her fear morphed into anger, and she focused this rage on your dad. She made his life a living hell. You know that to be true. Yet, he stayed with her, and he would've stayed by her side forever, but she demanded a divorce. Danny, given what's happened to your mom, I ask you to search your heart and rid yourself of your anger, or it will grow and consume you, too."

"You're right. I understand what you're saying."

"Danny, never forget that your mother's pain is a testament to the enormity of her love for you. She never recovered from her wounds. We owe her our love, not our contempt."

"Why don't we bring her here, Jon David? Maybe the spirit people could cure her, too."

"It doesn't work that way. Since Jamie built this cabin, the spirit people have invited only two people to come here and be healed— me and you. During my healing, when I asked why bad things happen to people, they replied that all human beings are of equal importance in God's eyes, and we each have a job to do. They called it a divine contract. For some, their contract includes suffering or early death. With me, you, and Jamie, God chose to alter our contracts. For some reason, your mom must go through her ordeal. When we get to heaven, it will all be made clear to us. I've learned to accept this on faith."

"It's my fault for what happened to her. If I didn't run after the soccer ball, my mom would be fine right now."

"Danny, I played the same mind games as you. If I hadn't been on point during the patrol, I could've better led my men. If I didn't like kids, none of those Iraqi boys would've been near me, and they'd be alive now. If you're not careful, you can 'what if' yourself to death. I want to share a couple of things the spirit people told me. Give me a second. I need to think back so I get the story right."

Jon David leaned back in his chair and closed his eyes. A few moments passed before he opened his eyes and looked at Danny.

"Okay, here goes. Jamie loved to work jigsaw puzzles here at the cabin. He did them on the table. When the spirit people visited me, a half-finished puzzle was on the table. One of them said, *Do you see the puzzle? It's made of a thousand pieces, but each of the pieces is unique and can only fit in the one spot meant for it. The pieces have different colors, some light, some dark. When they all come together, they form the puzzle's beautiful picture. And so it is with life. A beautiful life can only come from a palette of darks and lights.'*

"They let me think about it for a while. Then, they said, *'Think of your life as a puzzle. Right now, you have too few pieces of the puzzle assembled for you to see the whole picture. But, over a lifetime, when all the pieces of love, hate, anger, good, evil, bad, dark, light—when they all gradually come together, there will be a beautiful picture, and it will be the picture of your life.* And, Jon David, they said to me, *there is one important thing to remember about the puzzle forming your life. Your puzzle, like the puzzle of every other human being, has one unique piece. That piece is called God. People try to put other pieces in where only the God piece goes—drugs, alcohol, and the like. But, in the end, the puzzle will never be completed, for you or anyone else, until the God piece is put into its proper position.'*

"So, Danny, like me, the puzzle of your life is still being put together. When it's completed, everything will make sense to you. Until then, I've learned to accept things and do my best to bring good into the world. Does this make sense?"

"Yeah. You're bringing good to the world by being a doctor. What should I do? I mean, if they saved me, they obviously expect something from me."

"I asked them that very thing regarding me. They said all answers I seek could be found within me. They said God is there. When I asked them what my divine purpose was, they said I should listen to the still, small voice within me. That's what I'm telling you now. Find a quiet spot and listen to what your heart says. It will never let you down."

Danny nodded.

"Let me get back to the story of the puzzle, the part that mentions the one special piece and how people try to put other pieces in where only the God piece goes—sex, drugs, alcohol, and stuff like that. Riley spoke to me about you. It's pretty clear you've tried to put all those vices where the God piece goes, right?"

"Yes."

"Well, as you now know, they don't work. I haven't had a drop of liquor or painkillers in years, and I'm happier now than I've ever been. I listen to the still, small voice within me. It's never let me down. And, by the way, a true friend would never give you drugs, booze, or anything that could harm you. Riley was being your friend when he tried to stop you from doing those things."

"I know. I'll thank him when we get back."

Jon David hugged his young friend. "Well, there you have it. Something holy touched you and me. Because of that, we have a special bond. It's like the bond Jamie had with me."

"I understand. Thanks for telling me, Uncle. I love you."

"I love you, too. I've got one more thing for you to do while we're here. After you do it, I'll fly you home. Can you agree to that?"

"Sure."

Jon David got up and went to his backpack. He came back and handed Danny a book.

"I want you to read this while you're here. It's your dad's book. You need to know what an extraordinary man he is."

Danny took the book. "Okay, I'll read it."

Jon David smiled. "Good man. Tomorrow, if you need a reading break, we'll catch a few fish."

43

DANNY STAYED UP ALL night, reading his father's book by candlelight. When Jon David descended from the loft in the morning, Danny greeted him with a sigh. "My dad's going through some hard times right now. He's traveling with Jekyll across the country to meet the families of his soldier friends who were killed in action. He's on his way to Spokane after his friend's mom threw him out of her house in Wenatchee. She blamed Dad for her son's death, saying if Dad didn't urge him to become a Ranger, he wouldn't have died in Afghanistan. I remember Jekyll when I was a kid and how he loved carrots."

Jon David smiled. "Yeah, Jekyll sure was an odd dog. Let's take a break and eat breakfast."

"Do you mind if I read while I eat?"

"No. I'll bring you something."

Hours passed. Jon David brought lunch to Danny and then dinner. By ten that night, Danny, in tears, closed the book.

Jon David came over and kissed the top of his head. "Now, you know what your father has endured in his life and how much he loved your mother."

"I do. You're right. My father is an extraordinary man."

"I hope you'll find it in your heart to bless his union with Katie. He deserves some love and happiness in his life."

"I will. Uncle Jon David, I heard a voice last night. It said I should forgive my mom. I want to see her in person and tell her I love her."

Jon David choked up. "I think that's a fine thing to do, Danny. A fine thing to do." He put a hand on him and looked into his eyes. "Your mother is a brilliant astrophysicist, and your father has a sky-high IQ. You're their son and no doubt have the same intellectual prowess as they do. I'm saying this because you can do anything you want if you have the hunger to do it. Until your heart speaks to you, I ask that you not join the Army. If the still, small voice within you says joining the Army is what you should do, then so be it. I'll support you, and your father will too."

"Okay. It makes sense what you're saying."

"Let's hit the sack. Tomorrow morning, we'll get up early, catch some fish, and fly home. Want to bet who gets the first one?"

Danny laughed. "Dad calls you the fish whisperer, so it wouldn't be a smart bet for me to make."

Jon David smiled slyly. "Your father is a wise man."

The next day, they caught their limit of salmon and brought their gear to the plane. Jon David let Danny fly the plane again on the way back. They landed at the Merrill Field airport in Anchorage and, after securing the aircraft, drove to the Brennan's home. Jon David called to let them know they were coming, and Colt and Katie were waiting outside as they pulled into the driveway. Colt looked apprehensive. Jon David smiled at him through the car's windshield.

Danny got out and hugged his father. "I love you, Dad. Thanks for being such a good father to Chris and me."

"I love you, too, son."

Danny then hugged Katie. "You've been a great aunt; now you'll be a great stepmom. Welcome to the Mercer family."

She hugged him. "I love you, Danny, and promise I'll love your dad for the rest of my life."

Jon David waited a few moments before joining them.

"Hello, Katie, I'm Jon David. Congratulations on your impending marriage."

She hugged him. "I'm so pleased to meet you. Thank you for all you've done for this family."

"We had a good talk," he whispered. "Tell Colt Danny took everything well." She nodded and kissed his cheek.

Jon David looked at Danny. "Hey, young man, let's get your share of our salmon."

"I caught three reds," Danny said to his father, "and Uncle Jon David let me fly his plane on the way back, which was way cool."

"I envy you. Hey, Jon David, I'll talk to Annie about having you all over for a salmon dinner. Her blackened salmon with roasted vegetables would have many chefs in town blushing with envy."

Jon David smiled. "I'd like that. Well, I've got to run home. Tomorrow's a workday."

"Call me when you get a chance," said Colt. He mouthed the words, "thank you."

"I will. Goodbye, Danny."

Danny hugged him. "Goodbye, Uncle Jon David. I love you."

"I love you, too. Remember what I said about us."

"I will."

In the house, Danny looked at everyone. "If it's okay, I'd like to resume the family meeting." He hugged each of them before they sat.

"Uncle Jon David told me what happened at the cabin. Dad, when he told me about you looking at me in the morning, I interrupted him and finished the story. I remembered what happened. You guys told me I was just dreaming, but now I know the truth. I understand why you said it was a dream. I wouldn't want the cabin spoiled by people seeking miracles there either. I asked if we could bring Mom there, but Jon David explained the concept of divine contracts and how she must find her own way." His voice quivered. "I want to fly home and forgive my mother. I want to tell her that I'll always love her."

Colt's eyes brimmed with tears. "That would be a good thing to do, Danny. She might not take it well, but you saying those words to her will be healing for you."

"I know you tried with her, Dad. That's why I want you to marry Katie. You deserve to be loved."

All Colt could do was smile in reply. Katie kissed his cheek and held him close.

Danny continued. "Jon David spoke of how the answers we seek are within us. I'm going to wait on joining the Army until my heart speaks to me. If it's okay, I'd like to visit Portland and see if I might like it there. If I don't, may I stay with Nana and Grandpa and finish school here? I'd like it to be my choice."

Colt nodded. "The choice of what to do is yours to make. I propose this: You and Christa come back with me to California and help clear out the house. After that, we'll go to Portland, and you both can see if living there will appeal to you. My divorce won't be final for a few more months, so until then, I can't marry Katie or purchase a new home. If you want to live with us, we'll rent a house until we're able to buy."

"It sounds good, Dad. I promise I'll keep an open mind about Portland."

"Thanks, son."

"We want your input on starting a life together," said Katie. "I'm sure you'll have ideas we haven't considered. Danny, I say this contingent on your decision. I want you to know what you think matters to us."

He nodded.

"I'll tell Mom I love her when we're there, too," said Christa.

"I'm proud of you both for acknowledging your mother," said Colt. "Given all you two have been through, offering your mother such a gift speaks well of the goodness in your hearts." He stood and hugged his children.

"Well," said Pat. "If this family discussion is over, I propose ordering some pizza."

"I second the motion," Danny said with a smile, "especially if it's an Avalanche pizza from the Moose's Tooth."

44

A SECURITY GUARD CALLED Rachel at her office. "Hello, ma'am. I've got a Daniel Mercer here to see you. He says he's your son. Please come to the front desk."

A few minutes later, Rachel appeared, looking none too pleased. She ignored her son and focused on the guard. "Where do I sign for the visitor pass?"

"Right here, ma'am." She penned her name and firmly led her son by the arm to a quiet spot.

"What do you want, Danny? I'm busy. Are you in trouble again?" That she hadn't seen her son for months was irrelevant.

To her utter surprise, Danny hugged her. "Hello, Mom. No, I'm not in trouble. I flew down with Dad and Chris to help clear out the house. We were surprised to see you moved out when we got there."

"I found a duplex near here. It's small, so I couldn't take much from the house. Why are you here, Danny?"

"I've been doing a lot of thinking and believe I know what I want to do for a living. I wanted to tell you about it."

"Oh, I get it now," she said tersely. "You're here to get my permission to join the Army."

Danny didn't let her rudeness get to him. He took her hand in his. She flinched and tried to retract it, but he had a firm grip on her. "I want to become an astrophysicist like you. I remember how fun it was to look at the stars through our telescope when I was a kid. I think that's what I'd like to do. I'm here to ask you to give me a tour of the place."

What he said shocked his mother. She tried to dismiss him. "Danny, I'm sorry, but you don't mail in a few coupons, and back comes your college diploma. Let me assure you that getting a degree in my field is a challenging endeavor. It took years of schooling for me to get where I am. With your cavalier approach to school and life, you wouldn't last five minutes in a college class. Besides, you must be fluent in mathematics and physical sciences, and, as I recall, the words 'superior academic performance' have never been associated with you." She looked at her watch and frowned. "I'm sure there's some angle you're trying to work on me, but I'm not buying it. I'm sorry, but I have to go."

"Mom, look at me. There's no angle. I'm going to finish my senior year, and after that, I'll do everything necessary to prepare for college. I've changed, Mom. I'm ready to start my life."

She gazed deeply into his eyes, looking for the slightest hint of dishonesty. He held her gaze and didn't flinch.

"Okay, fine. I'll give you an hour." She led him through a labyrinth of hallways to her office, which was packed with years' worth of paperwork and boxes reaching for the ceiling. She didn't bother asking him to sit down. "The big news around here is the Dawn spacecraft is nearing the dwarf planet Ceres. If you promise to behave, I'll take you over and introduce you to the project team. If you act up or try to embarrass me, I'll have Security toss you out in a heartbeat. Am I clear?"

"Mom, I'm not here to embarrass you. What and where is the dwarf planet Ceres?"

She rustled through some photos. Here, look at this. This image of Ceres was taken a couple of weeks ago by Dawn from a distance of 46,000 kilometers."

He looked at the pock-marked orb. "There's not much to it. How far is it from Earth, and why are you interested in it?"

"The primary question that the Dawn spacecraft will address is the role of size and water in determining the evolution of the planets. Ceres is the perfect candidate to explore because it's the only dwarf planet within the inner reaches of our solar system. It lies between Mars and Jupiter, about 310 million miles from Earth, and is the largest object in the asteroid belt. It has a diameter of 950 kilometers and completes one full rotation in about nine hours. Look at these two bright spots. This has a lot of us excited around here. They could be caused by cryovolcanoes or, in laypeople's terms, ice volcanoes. If so, it raises the possibility that a life-giving ocean exists beneath the surface."

"So, is the planet composed mostly of ice?"

"It appears to be differentiated into a rocky core and an icy mantle. Its water, unlike Earth's, would be in the form of water ice and located in the mantle, which wraps around its solid core. Some of my colleagues speculate that Ceres may have more freshwater than Earth. As the spacecraft gets closer, we'll be able to get much sharper images of the surface." She paused a moment and looked at him. "If this bores you, we can stop. Or, if you want, I'll take you to meet some of the Dawn project team."

"It's fascinating, Mom. I'd love to meet them."

Rachel introduced Danny to her colleagues and was surprised at his poise and ability to ask articulate and relevant questions. The one hour turned into two. Back at her office, she showed him a myriad of high-definition pictures taken by MIRI of stars in distant galaxies that formed over 13.5 billion years ago. He peppered her with questions and, two hours later, showed no signs of losing steam. His interest, she concluded, appeared genuine. Then, a minor miracle occurred.

"Would you like to come home with me and have dinner?"

"I'd love to, Mom."

He followed her in his car to her new house.

Her place looked sparse and unadorned, a clear testament to her workaholic life. She heated a tray of frozen lasagna in the microwave. After dinner, Danny helped put the dishes in the dishwasher. Following that, his mom was ready to shoo him away.

"Well, I've got a lot of reports to read this evening. It was nice being with you. I wish you well with your father."

"Mom, I need to talk to you about something important. It won't take long."

"Oh, I see, here it comes. You must want something bad to be so attentive to me today."

Danny sighed. "No, Mom, I'm not here to ask for anything other than a few minutes of your time. I really need to talk to you. Please."

She softened ever so slightly.

"Have a seat on the couch. I mean it, though—I'm swamped."

He had to move a bunch of papers and binders to sit. He looked at his mother, who had sat at her desk. She swiveled the chair around to face him.

"Mom, I just got back from Alaska. While I was there, Uncle Jon David flew me out to the cabin. He told me about the miracle that happened to him." He looked at her a moment to emphasize what he had to say next. "He told me about the miracle that happened to me, too."

"Danny, please, I don't want to go there."

"Mom, give me five minutes. Please, just five more minutes."

She frowned and nodded.

"Jon David told me about my accident and how bad it was. He said you were by my side in total anguish. He spoke of how you blamed yourself for letting me come to Alaska for the summer. He told me how something inside of you snapped, and that fear soon replaced your joy of my healing. I remember you watching me like a hawk, afraid to let me out of your sight. Jon David said you feared me slipping back into a coma and that you begged Sara to give me a whole battery of tests to prove I was okay."

"Danny, you don't have to rehash this. I was there."

"Mom, I'm begging you to let me have three more minutes, then I'll leave."

"This is getting tiring, Danny. Okay, three minutes. That's it." She looked at her watch to emphasize the point.

Danny continued. "As the months passed, we all saw how your fears grew and how your only solace came when you were at work. It was as if you could keep your demons at bay there. As time passed, anger joined your fears, and together, fear and anger eclipsed your ability to love."

"Maybe you should go into psychiatry like my sister."

Danny ignored her comment. "Mom, the more you withdrew, the more I came to dislike you. That dislike grew into anger, and then the anger turned to hatred. I told this to Jon David. He said in wars, soldiers come back from combat with invisible wounds. It's called post-traumatic stress. Some soldiers never recover from these unseen wounds. He said he nearly committed suicide because of the wounds to his soul. He asked if I could accept post-traumatic stress as being a true mental affliction. I said, of course, I could. He then told me that anyone could suffer from post-traumatic stress, even kids. Even ... mothers. It was like a light bulb flashed in my head regarding you. Since my accident, you've had post-traumatic stress, and you've never recovered from your unseen wounds."

"Great, Danny. That's an excellent theory. It's time for you to leave."

"I'm not leaving until you hear the last of what I have to say."

"Oh, yes, you are!" She stood. "I know what's coming, and I'm not going to listen to you verbally pummeling me, saying how I screwed up your childhood."

"I'm not, Mom. That's not what I want to do at all."

"Danny, please, just leave."

He ignored her. "Before the accident, I remember what a wonderful mother you were, how you loved me, cared for me, and played with me. I thought I'd forgotten all that, but those memories came flooding back to me at the cabin. I won't forget them again. Christa was too young to remember, but I do. I remember, Mom. I loved you then. I'm here tonight to say that I now understand your invisible trauma and how you never recovered from it. I want to ask for your forgiveness for me being so angry with you when what you needed was my love and compassion. I love you, Mom. I will always love you."

A tear rolled down her cheek. "You need to go."

A tinge of sadness came to Danny's eyes. He stood. "Mom, there's one more thing. Dad and Katie are going to get married. I ask this of you: Please don't interfere. Please let Dad have another chance for love."

"You have nothing to worry about regarding that. I don't care what your dad does."

Danny wiped tears from his eyes. "Thank you for allowing me to say what I needed to say. And, I might surprise you one day, when I'm looking up at the heavens with a college diploma in my hand."

She didn't respond. He took a step to the front door, stopped, and faced her. "I know you still love me. I can feel it. The fear in you can't mask it anymore. I love you, Mom. I will love you forever." He smiled at her meekly and left.

Later that night, Christa called her mom to say she loved her and was moving to Portland with her dad. Rachel didn't reciprocate her daughter's statement of love, and the phone call lasted all of two minutes. It was yet another rebuff of her only daughter's affections.

The next day, Colt and the kids spent the morning sorting through what to keep, toss, or donate. Christa came out of his closet, holding a cylindrical leather bag. "What's in this, Dad?"

Colt took it from her and opened the bag with a sigh. "When I was traveling across North America on the Harley, Jekyll and I stayed with a Native family in British Columbia. They gave me this flute and taught me how to play it. This carving is called a fetish, and it's used to adjust the tonal quality. They carved it to look like Jekyll. See, it's missing an ear, like him."

"Why don't you ever play it, Dad?" asked Danny.

Colt hesitated before replying. Tears welled up in his eyes. "Whenever I played, Jekyll would howl along with me. Since he died, I can't bring myself to play without him."

"Well, Dad, maybe someday you could give it a try for Danny and me," said Christa. "We'd love to hear you play." Danny nodded in agreement.

"Maybe someday. I'll put it in the car to make sure we don't forget it. Do we have anything else that needs to be dotted?"

"Yeah," said Danny. "There are a few more things in the family room."

When they finished, their place was ablaze with colored dots. They took the blue-dot items out to the dumpster. Red dotted items, of which there were few, would be kept for Portland. Colt said it would be cheaper to buy new things there rather than hire a moving company to transport them. Besides, he said, getting rid of their stuff would signify a fresh start. The kids bought into the notion.

Packing the red-dot items didn't take long. They all fit into twenty boxes and mainly consisted of pictures, a few personal trinkets, an assortment of hand tools, and Danny's books. Danny's love of books was legendary, and it was the one thing he couldn't bear to part with. Colt said he'd forward the books to him if he later chose to live with his grandparents. The remaining items in their home, marked with green dots, would be donated to veterans.

They drove to the local UPS store and shipped the boxes to Katie. Another task done.

During the next two days, many veterans came and went, hauling away the family's belongings. Their profound gratitude touched Colt and the kids. By the end of the second day, the house was bare. They spent the night at a hotel and had the cleaning crew do their thing the next day. The entire process went remarkably fast. The house was ready for the new owners. A chapter of their lives had closed.

Six weeks later, the moving van pulled away from the house of their dreams. Inside, Katie was aflutter, moving from box to box, her face flushed but brimming with happiness. "Here's a box for you, Danny. I think it's your books since I can't budge it."

He laughed. "You look like you need to sit down, Aunt Katie. Do you want me to get you a glass of water?"

She smiled. "No, thanks. I'm having too much fun. I still can't believe we got this place, and you chose to live with us."

Colt came over. "Margie came through for us. A lease with an option to buy is perfect."

Katie wiped her brow. "You're good at naming things, Colt. What should we call our home?"

He thought for a moment and smiled. "How about we name it after the street? 'McNamee.' I think it has a certain ring to it."

She laughed. "I love it. There is something regal about the name. What do you think, kids?"

"I like it, too," said Christa as she lugged a box by. "I can't believe we have eighteen acres. I could get lost outside."

"I know," said Colt. "It'll take a while to get used to the quiet. I sure wish I could convert the barn into my writing studio, but until we buy the place, we'll have to wait to put our signature on it."

Danny lifted his box of books with a grunt and headed to his room. "McNamee is fine, but we could also call it 'Two Foxes' after seeing them run across our yard today."

"Are you talking about Katie and Christa?" Colt winked at the two ladies as he said it.

Danny laughed as he labored down the hall. "Yeah, Dad, they were the two foxes I saw."

They spent the rest of the day unpacking and sorting. Most of the stuff was Katie's belongings.

Dinner consisted of delivered pizza, which they ate on a makeshift cardboard-box table. In the weeks ahead, more furniture would need to be purchased. Christa and Katie decided that outfitting the house would be their task. Colt asked for the same type of decorating Katie had done at her condo. He liked her casual and inviting sense of style. Danny stressed the importance of having lots of comfortable recliners. They all looked happy.

That night, Katie came out of the bathroom, looking refreshed after showering. "It went well today, don't you think?"

"Yeah. The kids are excited. Portland will be a change for them, but they both seem motivated to make it work."

"I love them, Colt. It already feels like they've always been mine."

Colt kissed her. "It warms my heart to hear you say that."

The next morning, Danny rooted through a box of family photos. He found the one he was looking for and brought it to the others. "Do you mind hanging this picture in the living room? If you do, I'll put it in my room." He held up a picture of him and his mother. He was four years old and was planting an exaggerated kiss on his beaming mother's cheek. "Look at her, everyone. Wasn't she something? I've thought about this picture a lot lately. It helps make my sadness and anger go away. I'll love her forever because I'll remember the way she was before she changed."

Katie went over and hugged him. "I could think of nothing better than displaying it for all of us to see. She was something back then, wasn't she?" She took the picture and kissed her big sister.

45

Four months later ...

"I NOW PRONOUNCE YOU husband and wife. You may kiss the bride." Colt didn't need to be asked twice. He kissed his radiant bride with enthusiasm. He then shook the minister's hand and thanked him.

Christa and Danny, the bridesmaid and groomsman, planted kisses on the bride's cheeks. "Katie, Christa and I spent a lot of time talking about what wedding gift to give you. In the end, we kept coming back to the same thing. We'd be honored if you let us call you 'Mom.' Our gift to you is our hearts."

From the shock and then delight on her face, they knew they had given their new mother a worthy gift. She wrapped her arms around them, shedding the happiest tears of her life.

Annie came up and dabbed her daughter's eyes with a tissue. "The kids want to call me Mom." When seeing the pure joy on Katie's face, Annie joined her in tears. She looked at her grandchildren and beamed with pride at what they had done.

The wedding guests gathered around, offering the newlyweds congratulations. Scotty and Maggie were there, as well as Jon David and Sara. Several of Katie's friends from work hugged her, as did Jen, her childhood friend from Anchorage. The expansive patio of their home, with its extraordinary views, proved to be the ideal place to have the wedding. While their guests ate a catered dinner, Colt played his flute next to the fire pit. His haunting, beautiful songs touched them all. When he finished, they gave him a standing ovation.

Danny hugged his father. "I'm so glad you began playing your flute again. I had no idea you were so skilled at it. By the way, I still think you're nuts for wanting Chris and me to come on your honeymoon."

Katie heard him, came over, and kissed his cheek. "We could think of nothing better than sharing our joy with you and Chris. With you two soon going to college, we won't have many opportunities for vacations together. Danny, do me a favor since I'm so scattered—make sure to pack suntan lotion. Where we're going, I'll need a lot of it."

He laughed. "I will. Chris and I bought you a big, floppy sunhat, so everyone will know you're a tourist."

"Thanks. Where we're going, I'm sure I'll treasure it." She kissed her man. "My dear husband, will you play one more song just for me?"

He smiled at her saying 'husband.' It sounded good. The song he played for her reflected his happiness.

Four days later, the newly formed family was on a chartered catamaran slicing through azure-blue water, bound for Peter Island in the British Virgin Islands. The 45-foot-long vessel generated an adrenaline-inducing thrill ride. Colt, Katie, and Christa were lying on their bellies, clinging to the "trampettes," or netting, between the twin hulls, awed by the ocean whizzing by just a foot below. Drenched with ocean spray and bombarded with various sensations of weightlessness and dipsy-doodles from the waves, they squealed joyously. Under the captain's tutelage, Danny sailed the ship, hell-bent on keeping the mainsail taut for maximum speed. He yielded the ship's wheel to the captain and cupped his hands to his face. "Get ready; we're going to do some serious turns!"

The two-person catamaran crew had done well, tailoring the cruise itinerary to match their guests' desire for secluded islands to snorkel and scuba dive, plus a few incidental excursions ashore. They spent today, the third day of their week-long vacation, diving at Angelfish Reef, off Norman Island, where an incredible diversity of reef fish greeted them, along with Caribbean reef sharks, manta rays, and sea turtles. Tomorrow, they'd dive in the Black Forest at Peter Island. The captain spoke of a fantastic assortment of soft and hard corals there, including the endangered black coral for which the area was named.

After a casual dinner filled with laughter and lighthearted conversation, the family passed the evening on the deck, stargazing amid the moonlit waters. Even though shielded by what Colt called SPF two-million sunblock, Katie's fair skin succumbed to the tropical sun. Colt tried to tame her pain with a generous slathering of aloe lotion, but by mid-evening, she excused herself to soak her aching body in a cool-water bath. Later that night, before going to bed, Colt applied another liberal dose of lotion on her beet-red skin and marveled at how happy she was despite her discomfort. Wearing clothes hurt, so Katie opted to sleep naked on the queen-sized bed. With a sly smile, Colt agreed it was probably the best thing to do.

At 1 a.m., Colt woke with a start. A dream had visited him, leaving him troubled and conflicted. He looked at Katie, sleeping peacefully. He watched her bare chest rise and fall as she breathed and admired the curves and turns of her lithe body. She was a beautiful woman. He could spend the rest of his days observing her subtle head-to-toe dusting of freckles, and it wouldn't be a wasted life. So, on his honeymoon with Katie, why was he making passionate love to Rachel in his dream? *Dear God,* he thought. He then remembered the days of being madly in love with Rachel. The feelings for her were powerful in the dream, and the sex amazing. It felt so real—as if he were cheating on Katie. Guilt swept through him. He quietly got up, put on a swimsuit, and went to the deck.

The boat was anchored in a Peter Island cove with calm waters and a tropical air temperature requiring nothing more than his swimsuit. Colt plopped down on a trampette and looked at the stars. He thought about Katie. His love for her was powerful. She was a kind and considerate companion, a skilled lover, and there was no doubt that she loved him and his children. So, why was he having such intense feelings for Rachel? Was she the true love of his life? How could he be having these thoughts?

He looked at the heavens. "Mom and Dad, help me," he whispered. "I love them both." A moment later, a shooting star raced across the sky. When Colt was a kid, his dad would take him to Pronghorn Park in Prescott to view the heavens through a telescope. When they saw a shooting star, his dad would say, Colt, make a wish, and it will come true.

"Okay, Dad, I hear you. I'm supposed to make a wish." He thought for a few moments and looked upward. "I wish for the rest of my days to be with … *Katie*." He smiled when her name leaped forth. He now had no doubt Katie was the love of his life. "Thank you, my dear parents."

He sat up and pondered his life. He was two years shy of living a half-century, a notion that once seemed inconceivable. He mentally began calculating how many dark days he had endured. They started at seventeen when that drunk driver killed his parents. His war experiences and subsequent post-traumatic stress brought more sad days, as did the deaths of his soldier friends and the near-death of Danny. The passing of his faithful dog, Jekyll, added to the count. He thought of the barren years with Rachel. The total sadness amounted to nearly half of his adult life. He sighed.

Then, he turned his attention to the good. Childhood memories in Arizona with a home filled with love and laughter, dancing as a kid with Mom, rock-hounding in the Grand Canyon with Dad. Stargazing at night. Learning how to ride a—

"Colt, are you okay?" He nearly jumped out of his skin when Katie touched him. "I'm sorry I scared you. Not hearing your breathing woke me. Are you okay?"

He nodded. "I wasn't when I came out here, but now I am."

"Does it have something to do with Rachel?"

A soft gasp escaped him. "You're very perceptive."

"My love, when you've been married as long as I, you get to know what's troubling your man."

He smiled meekly at her humor and took her hand. "I talked to Mom and Dad. In a flash, they showed me you're the love of my life."

"You're not getting off that easy. Speak to me."

He shrugged his shoulders and sighed. "Okay ... I had a dream about Rachel being the 'pre-accident' version of herself, and it reawakened the passion I had for her. When we got married, I promised to love her for the rest of my days, so it made me wonder if I truly am a man of honor and integrity. I came out here and talked to my parents about my conflicted feelings. It only took a few minutes for them to set me straight. You are my love, Katie. The dream was only a dream, and Rachel released me from my promise to her when she said she wanted a divorce."

"Did I ever tell you how much I love your parents?"

"They love you, too." He gazed at her with sad eyes. "Just love me, Katie. Do that, and I will never disappoint you."

Katie responded with a tender kiss. "I intend to love you every day with my words, my touch, my kindness, and my deeds." She smiled. "C'mon, let's go back to bed and figure out a way to make love without touching my aching skin."

46

KATIE CAME OUT OF the house with a big tray of snacks. Their two golden retrievers, Mike and Ike, bounded after her. The Portland mist persisted throughout the day, so she hurried to their new pole barn to escape the rain. It was a simple open-air structure built on a 30-foot square concrete slab. Colt was with the kids, ranging in age from six to eight, teaching them a simplified version of tai chi involving twenty-four postures. Going through all the positions took eight minutes, which was within their attention span. From the laughter, it was clear they were having a good time. "How's it going?" she asked him.

"Apparently, they think my 'snake creeps down' move looks more like an injured duck." His happiness showed on his face. This was the fourth day-long retreat they had hosted in the last two months, and many of Katie's patients were already begging to come back again. For these abused children, their home was a safe harbor from the storm. Mike and Ike loved these get-togethers as much as the children.

"Hey, kids, let's have a snack before you go. Colt and I loved having you here today." One girl, Hailey, stayed close to the snack tray after the kids got what they wanted. She stuffed some food into her pocket when no one was looking. She looked around again and stuffed more into another pocket. From across the pole barn, Colt saw what she was doing. He motioned for Katie to join him. "Is Hailey getting enough to eat? She's cramming her pockets with food."

Katie sighed. "Her mother was a prostitute and heroin addict. When they found her, she was emaciated. The consequence of that is she hoards food. She's been in foster care for the last two years, and I've been seeing her for the past ten months. She's such a sweet little girl but so damaged on the inside. She finally started to talk to me, but progress has been slow. It breaks my heart to see children like her who've been so traumatized."

"Man, oh man," said Colt. He went over to her and knelt to be on her level. "I'm so glad you came to see us today, Hailey. You're really good at tai chi."

She hugged him. "Thank you, Mr. Colt. I love you."

"I love you, too, sweetheart. I hope to see you again."

He wiped a tear from his eye. Shortly after getting out of the Army, a neighbor's five-year-old daughter named Lilly befriended him and his dog, Jekyll. She always called him "Mr. Colt." It touched him then and now in the same way.

That night, Katie snuggled in next to him. "Today went well, don't you think?"

"I do. I'm so glad we built the pole barn. I love being outside, and having a roof over my head is perfect on days like today. Did you notice Mike and Ike working the crowd? They look forward to the retreats as much as the kids."

"I'm glad we got them. They're the perfect antidote for the loneliness I've felt since Christa left for college."

"There's nothing like a golden retriever to take your mind off being lonely." He kissed her. "I can't seem to get Hailey off my mind. What do you think her long-term prospects are?"

Katie sighed. "It's hard to say. I think stability in her life could work wonders. Her new foster parents are a nice young couple who are motivated to help her. Ideally, they'd adopt her since she's now a ward of the court. But, with kids like her, statistics aren't in their favor. My hope is she'll respond to their love and therapy sessions with me, but it's far from certain."

"Damn."

"I know. It's the reality of my profession."

"I don't see how you do it."

"One of the things drilled into us at med school was to keep an emotional detachment from your patients. Otherwise, you wouldn't last a year. I'm so glad we're able to host these retreats. It lets the kids know I care for them in ways I could never do at the office, and I love that."

"I'm glad we're able to do the retreats as well. Switching gears, Christa called saying she'll be coming home for Thanksgiving."

"Great! Let's invite Mom and Dad to fly down, too. We could have a family reunion."

"I'd like that. Danny and I can try cooking a turkey in our smoker."

"I'm so glad he's going to the community college here. At least we have one kid still living at home."

"He showed me his report card today. Man, he has caught fire academically."

Katie nodded. "Danny told me he wants to go to Cornell University next year. I'm okay with Christa being at Oregon State because it's just down the road, but Cornell is across the country."

"I know. Danny's changed so much since Jon David talked to him at the cabin. I love seeing the growth in him. He has turned into a fine young man."

"I agree. He talks a lot to Jon David. Do you know that?"

"Yeah. After chatting with JD, Danny comes to me to discuss what they talked about. I love how we're now able to talk like friends. He's hungry to learn more about living a spiritual life. Christa has been like a sponge, absorbing Danny's words about Spirit. They've become close, and I see her striving to live in Spirit, too. It's good to see. By the way, Jon David and Sara want us to come again next summer."

"We should reciprocate. Hey, do you want to invite the Lukes and Penny down for Thanksgiving, too?"

"Are you serious?"

"I am. We all get along famously, even the kids. I'm sure they'd love the chance to get out of the cold."

"You're right. How about tomorrow you call and invite your parents, and I'll call and invite the Lukes."

"Sure. This is exciting." She yawned. "Oh, man, the day has caught up to me. Goodnight, my love."

"Sweet dreams, sweet Katie."

"Who wants another piece of pecan pie?" No one took Colt up on his offer, so he placed the pie on the kitchen countertop loaded with the remains of the Thanksgiving meal.

Katie came in with a smile and kissed him. "If you and Danny clear off the table, Chris and I will do the dishes."

"Say yes, Dad," said Danny. "We're getting the better end of the deal."

Colt laughed. "Yeah, I agree. We're getting off easy."

Riley pitched in to help Danny and Colt clear the table. Sara, Penny, and Kelly then joined Katie and Christa in the kitchen to lend a helping hand. With everyone helping, the tedious task of cleanup happened quickly.

Colt stood back and gazed at everyone admiring the sunset through the living room windows. They all seemed so happy, he thought. Life was good.

Jon David saw him smiling and walked his way. "Thanks again for inviting us here, Colt. We're all having a great time. So, when are you going to show me your new writing gazebo?"

"Now is a good time. We can sneak away for a bit while everyone lets their meal settle." They walked out of the house with no one noticing.

Inside the octagon-shaped gazebo, Jon David looked around and whistled. "Man, this is something. I love how you left the rafters exposed to see the architectural details."

Colt beamed. "Yeah, it's nice. The Western red cedar holds up well to our rainy climate. I wanted to convert the barn that was here, but they said it would be more expensive to mess with it than to start from scratch. Don't even ask what it cost. I still shake my head at that, but it's a perfect place for writing. Mike and Ike love hanging out here with me when I'm working."

"They sure are friendly."

"Yeah, they are. Katie and I love them."

"So, what's your latest writing gig?"

"I'm going back to my roots with another kid's book."

"What's it about?"

"Let me show you the draft cover I just received from the designer." Colt handed him a printout of a distinguished-looking cartoon baboon crouching on his legs with both arms extending outward and palms facing upward.

Jon David smiled. *"barnaby b. baboon teaches tai chi.* I like the title."

"Thanks. He's in the 'repulse monkey' posture. I got the idea for this book from teaching a simplified version of tai chi to the kids at our retreats. They love learning it, so I think the book will do well. I plan on giving one to every kid who comes to our retreats."

"I envy your creativity. What you and Katie are doing with those children is inspiring."

"Thanks. Before Danny's accident, I did a lot of things to help veterans, but after his healing, I felt compelled to do more as my way of saying thanks to God. I've taught tai chi for years now to adults, but what a pleasure it's been teaching children to use it as a way of connecting to their divine essence."

"Sara would love having you in her holistic practice."

"How's that going with her?"

"She has more business than she can handle, but more importantly, Sara loves what she's doing. She suggested I join her to add a pediatric component to the business, but I still feel working at the Native hospital is right for me."

"Hey, if you move down here, Katie could be on the team, too."

"We'd love having Katie on the team, but our place is in Alaska. As you can see, Penny is slowing down, so any move would be hard on her."

"I'm sure Jamie would be happy at how well you and Sara care for her."

Jon David chuckled. "Penny's the one who takes care of us."

Colt turned serious. "I have another writing project after this one. A book for adults. I'm still working it out in my head."

"What's the basic drift of it?"

"I'd like to write a book about spirituality and living an authentic life—something to help others achieve a spiritual awakening. Talking to Danny about Spirit gave me the idea for this book."

"Man, a book like that might be more challenging to write than you think. So, what do you think you've learned that could fill a book?"

"That's a good question. Don't laugh, but I think I'd begin with the spiritual lessons taught to me by the dogs who've graced my life."

Jon David looked dubious. "You'll have to enlighten me on that angle because I don't picture dogs as spiritual teachers."

Colt smiled. "Dogs are the best spiritual teachers on the planet. For example, they taught me to live in the now moment because life exists there and nowhere else. They don't fret over the past or worry about the future."

"Yeah, I'll admit they're masters of living in the 'now' moment. It took years for me to embrace and practice that concept, but until you do, you'll never be at peace."

Colt nodded. "Dogs also demonstrate the power of unconditional love, which includes the ability to forgive. Jekyll loved me and listened to me in my darkest of times without judgment. He forgave my many failings and didn't dwell on all my wrongs. Compared to the enormity of what he gave to me, he asked for so little in return. His love healed my wounded heart and taught me that loving and forgiving others is a spiritual endeavor."

Colt motioned for Jon David to take a seat. He swiveled his desk chair around to face his friend and sat. "Mike and Ike are as skilled as any psychotherapist. You should see how their love affects the mistreated children we see here at our retreats. It's as if they look directly into the souls of these battered and abused kids. A dog knows how to listen in such a pure way. Unlike humans, they never butt in or offer unwelcomed advice. I see something deeply spiritual in this."

Colt paused a few moments before continuing. "What I'm about to say is tough to adequately articulate."

"Go on. Just say what's on your mind."

"I've observed these beaten down kids a lot, and sadly, I see how they consider themselves to be irrelevant as human beings. I don't know, maybe it's because of the trauma my soul has experienced, but I can spot a broken spirit in an instant. Then I see Mike or Ike going up to one of them, being so happy to see them—you know—being over-the-top excited about the kid paying them some attention, and, well, it makes the kid think that they're important, that somebody really wants what they have to offer. I see the profound joy on their faces when the awareness that they matter dawns on them. And it's not just that. Mike or Ike will put their head on a kid's lap or bark excitedly when the kid invites them to play—they have so many ways of saying I love you and that you matter. To me, they are consummate spiritual healers. On my spiritual path, I try to emulate what they teach. Does this make any sense?"

"It does. It makes a lot of sense. It's like when Jesus healed the wretched people that society discarded. Those people mattered to him. Your dogs are doing the same kind of holy work. I see what you're saying about their spirituality. It seems as if you've got the first part of the book conceptualized, but what comes after that?"

Colt grinned. "I think I've got that covered. I'll describe how spirituality and happiness go together by offering the words of a few insightful people." He rifled through the papers on his desk and found the one he wanted. "Here, read these four quotes—I can build a good portion of the book around them."

Jon David took the paper and read the words aloud:

"He who knows others is wise; he who knows himself is enlightened. — Lao Tzu

I now see how owning our story and loving ourselves through that process is the bravest thing that we will ever do. — Brené Brown

Life will give you whatever experience is most helpful for the evolution of your consciousness. — Eckhart Tolle

Every time you don't follow your inner guidance, you feel a loss of energy, loss of power, a sense of spiritual deadness. — Shakti Gawain"

Jon David looked at Colt. "Wow. I see what you mean."

"Yep. You've spoken to me many times about universal truths, and one of them is to 'know thyself.' To me, it's the basic premise for leading a spiritual life. I mean, who knows more about you than you? It's pretty hard to hide secrets from yourself. My spiritual journey began with self-forgiveness and making peace with myself. In other words, I became friends with myself, and through meditation, I found the incredible light that shines within me. When I discovered the still, small voice within me, my ego-self gave way to my authentic self—my true self—where my soul guides and comforts me. As I came to know and love myself and the Spirit residing within me, that's when I found my way, and true happiness entered my life."

"You've come far in your understanding of this truth. Buddha said, 'You, yourself, as much as anybody in the entire universe, deserve your love and affection.'"

"Thanks. For years, I was my own worst enemy and was miserable. Now, I accept myself and have even come to celebrate my imperfections and flaws. I think that's also what spirituality is all about. Rasheed Ogunlaru said it best: 'Live your life, sing your song. Not full of expectations. Not for the ovations. But for the joy of it.' Even if I'm the worst singer in the world, if my imperfect voice brings joy to my heart, I celebrate it. I also love this quote by Mark Twain: 'Sing like no one is listening, love like you've never been hurt, dance like nobody is watching, and live like it's heaven on earth.' I guess what I'm trying to say is while we're here on Earth, we all need to take the time to rejoice in the wonder of being here."

Jon David chuckled. "You'd have strong competition from me in a bad singer contest. I agree with what you just said, but so far, you've spoken in broad strokes regarding happiness. What else would you discuss to achieve happiness?"

"Well, I'd talk about free will and the power to choose; how we can opt to let our ego run our life or choose to have God communicate with our internal self to help guide and direct us. Hold on a second. I want to read something to you, which I think is the 'spiritual glue' that binds the universe together." He retrieved a book from his bookcase. "The apostle Paul wrote these biblical verses:

If I speak with the languages of men and of angels, but don't have love, I have become sounding brass, or a clanging cymbal.

If I have the gift of prophecy, and know all mysteries and all knowledge; and if I have all faith, so as to remove mountains, but don't have love, I am nothing. If I give away all my goods to feed the poor, and if I give my body to be burned, but don't have love, it profits me nothing.

Love is patient and is kind; love doesn't envy. Love doesn't brag, is not proud, doesn't behave itself inappropriately, doesn't seek its own way, is not provoked, takes no account of evil; doesn't rejoice in unrighteousness, but rejoices with the truth; bears all things, believes all things, hopes all things, endures all things. Love never fails ...

When I was a child, I spoke as a child, I felt as a child, I thought as a child. Now that I have become a man, I have put away childish things. For now we see in a mirror, dimly, but then face to face. Now I know in part, but then I will know fully, even as I was also fully known. But now faith, hope, and love remain—these three. The greatest of these is love."

Colt closed the book and looked at his friend. "That, to me, is one of the most insightful passages ever written. For so many years, I *'saw in the mirror, dimly,'* but with meditation, I see clearly now. Living in Spirit is living in love. I love what George Vaillant says about there being two pillars of happiness: *'One is love. The other is finding a way of coping with life that does not push love away.'* How true his words are. So, to answer your question on what steps to take to achieve happiness, I'd begin with knowing and loving yourself, forgiving yourself and others, and, through meditation, cultivating a conversation with God."

"You're on the right path with all this, but I suppose I'd want a more nuts-and-bolts guide for finding happiness. *'Show me,'* as they say in Missouri."

Colt glanced at his watch. "I could talk all night about specifics, but let me cover a few points before they send out a search party for us. I'd focus on practicing gratitude. Here's an example. I'd ask, how many red cars did you see on your way home from work today? Most people would say they didn't notice any. Then, I'd say, tomorrow, I'll pay you a dollar for every red car you see. The next day, I'd bet they'd spot a whole lot of red cars. After paying them, I'd say, what if red cars were like blessings. How many blessings do you pass each day without noticing?"

"I love it. It's a good analogy."

"Thanks. Then, I'd speak of cultivating kindness and the joy that comes from giving a piece of your heart to others. Volunteering to work at a Habitat for Humanity event, tutoring kids, adult literacy—the list is endless. I would talk about living in simplicity, where you seek a life filled with simple pleasures that keep Spirit at the center of all you do. I'd focus on the joy that comes from expressing yourself by doing activities such as dancing, singing, gardening, or tai chi.

"From there, I'd transition to how happiness is linked to taking care of your body and exercising and the joys of being out in nature. Oh. I'd stress the importance of camaraderie—you know—being with friends who're on a similar path as you, and I'd cover things that detract from happiness, such as worry, negative thinking, and judging others. Lastly, I'd talk about the power of prayer and being a light where God's grace shines on others through you."

"Wow. Write the book, Colt."

"I'd like to talk to you during the writing process to bounce things off you like I'm doing now. Danny said he'd offer his talents to the project as well. That alone makes me want to write the book."

"Count me in. Working with Danny will bring you two even closer. Do you have a working title yet?"

"No. It's still in the embryonic stage."

"I know we need to head back, but I have one more thing to say. Right after Danny's healing, do you remember when you asked me what you should do, and I said I'm not your guru?"

"Yeah. You gave me sound advice by saying I should listen to the still, small voice within me."

"Well, my friend, you're doing just that. I saw at dinner how you and Katie glow when you look at each other. It's easy to see God's light shining on the two of you. I'm so honored to have witnessed your spiritual awakening, and it warms my heart how you've found a loving wife who lives in Spirit with you. You've come far, pilgrim."

"Thanks. I'm so blessed to have Katie. I tell her we have a quantum entanglement. It sounds better than saying we're soul mates."

Jon David laughed. "A 'quantum entanglement.' I love it. I'm going to use that on Sara."

"Hey, let's go to my firewood stash and bring some wood to the fire pit on the patio. After Thanksgiving dinner, there's no better way to spend an evening than sitting in front of a fire."

"I'll help if you agree to play your flute next to that fire."

Colt smiled. "I could do that."

47

Several years later …

AT FIVE P.M., THE University Marshal led a procession of Ph.D. candidates, faculty, trustees, and the university president to the Barton Hall stage at Cornell University. Danny grinned as he marched with his fellow candidates. He waved to his family and blew a kiss to his beaming birthmother. During the ceremony, the dean placed a doctoral hood on Danny, signifying his success in completing the rigorous program. He was now an astrophysicist, just like his mother.

At the reception following the graduation ceremony, Annie hugged her handsome grandson. "So, tell me again the title of your dissertation."

Danny laughed. "Three-dimensional magneto-hydrodynamic simulations of turbulence, wave-particle interactions, and the astrophysical plasma of solar wind acceleration."

Pat shook his head. "I'd need a degree in linguistics just to say it."

Rachel walked up with her partner Lori. "Danny, we're both so proud of you. Congratulations on landing the postdoc research position at JPL. We'll soon be able to have lunches together."

"I'm looking forward to it, Mom."

She handed a camera to her father. "Dad, will you take a picture of the three of us?"

"Sure. After that, I'd like to get a family picture outside before the sun sets."

After Pat took their picture, Danny spotted friends in the crowd and waved frantically. "Jon David and Sara!" He looked at his mom. "Pardon me for a moment; I need to say hello to them." He sprinted over, his graduation robe flowing as he ran. Danny greeted his 'uncle' with a robust hug. "Thanks for coming." He then hugged Sara, lifting her off her feet. "I love you two." They looked as proud as his parents.

"Riley and Kelly wish they could be here," said Jon David. "He's buried in his residency. In another year, he'll be a bona fide cardiothoracic surgeon. Kelly's in the field, conducting a geological survey in the Mackenzie Delta for Shell Canada. Penny gives her regards. She'd love to be here, but she's too frail to travel."

"Please tell them I say hello. As soon as I get a place in Pasadena, I'll invite Riley to spend some time with me."

"He'd like that," said Sara.

Colt and Katie joined them. She kissed her son on the cheek. "Hello, Dr. Daniel Patrick Mercer. You look ultra-handsome today in your graduation garb. I'm so proud of you."

"Thanks, Mom. Thanks for everything you've done for me."

"You're welcome." She put her arm around her husband. "I've had to keep a firm hand on your papa today. He's practically walking on air from being so happy."

Colt beamed. "Danny, I'm proud of you, too."

"Thanks, Dad. This degree did take some effort."

"It's not just the degree, son. I'm proud of you for what you've become. You're a fine man, and you've overcome a lot to get where you are. As your father, I have boundless love and respect for you."

Danny hugged him. "Thanks, Dad. I feel the same about you. We've both come far in our lives. I'm so glad you found Katie; I hope I'll find someone like her someday."

"Me, too." He kissed his wife. "But be careful if she, like Katie, knows martial arts."

Katie laughed. "Hey, it can't all be milk and cookies." She touched Colt's cheek and lovingly looked into his eyes. "You don't look like you're suffering too much." He winked and nodded.

Danny smiled at their playful exchange. "Grandpa wants to take a family picture outside. Jon David and Sara, I'd be honored if you join us. You're family, too."

"The honor will be ours," he replied.

Pat hustled over. "C'mon, everyone; we need to hurry before the sun sets." He looked across the room, cupped his hands to his face, and yelled. "Scott and Maggie, let's go outside for a family picture." Scotty gave a 'thumbs up' in reply.

The family gathered in a grassy area near the reception hall. "Do you want me to take the picture, sir?" Scott asked.

"Oh, hell no. You and Maggie join us. You're family." He looked at Rachel and Lori, who were standing a respectful distance away. "Ladies, quit dawdling and get over here." They smiled and joined them.

Pat flagged down another graduate's father and asked him to take their picture. The extended family formed two rows, with Danny front and center. He had his arm around his smiling sister. Pat requested several photos to make sure one would turn out. Their impromptu photographer was patient and had them cracking up with his pre-snap antics.

After the picture taking, Rachel walked to a quiet area. Colt noticed her leaving. When he saw her wiping away tears, he gestured to Katie that he was going to be with her. She nodded for him to go.

"Hey, are you okay?"

"Hi, Colt. Yes. Thanks for asking. I'm so proud of Danny. He's become a fine person despite me." She looked at him. "You've been a good father, and I thank you for that."

Colt nodded. "Danny loves you, Rachel. You know that, right?"

"Yes, but I don't know why."

"I still love you. I hope you know that, too."

She wiped her eyes again. "I find that hard to believe. I treated you so terribly. I've been in therapy and now understand how my fears and anger consumed me. You bore the brunt of my anger, and for that, I'm truly sorry. I hope you're happy with Katie."

"I am."

"That's good to hear. Katie's a good person, and I'm glad you're with her."

"Thanks. How about you and Lori? Are you happy?"

"I am. She saved me. I finally listened to her urgings and sought counseling. It's been hard, but I've stuck to it. I learned how wrong I was about my anger. For the longest time, I thought it protected me from getting hurt again. It became my best friend. I thought I possessed it, but I was wrong. It ended up possessing me. The world looks so much better without anger. I hope you've also released the anger in you, what you called your inner rage."

"I have. My healing didn't begin until I was able to forgive myself. With all my heart, I hope you'll find a way to forgive yourself, too."

"I'm working on it."

"By the way, I don't know if you noticed Christa on the phone all day. She's found love, too. His name is Christopher, which makes me smile. Chris and Chris. It sounds redundant. She met him at Oregon State. I think we'll soon have two veterinarians in the family."

"I'll give her my congratulations before we leave."

"You're welcome to attend her wedding if and when it happens. Rachel, you're still part of this family. Lori, too. Katie still hopes you and her will reconcile. She loves you so much."

"Thanks. I've been working up the courage to write Katie a letter saying she's been a wonderful stepmother to our kids and that it's time to be sisters again. Well, we better get back." She hesitated a moment and put her hand on his. "I remember our time together before the accident. I loved you then. I just wanted you to know."

"I loved you, too, Rachel. It was one of the happiest times of my life. We produced some exceptional children. They'll always be a shining testimony to what we had." He hugged her. She returned his hug and held him a little longer than necessary. At that moment, they made their peace.

Back with the others, Colt smiled at Katie to let her know everything was fine. Pat walked up with a big grin on his face. "I wish you two would join us on our trip. We'd have a blast." He and

Annie were leaving for a two-week trip to Ireland in the morning. Pat wanted to explore the towns and counties of his ancestors. This would be their first vacation since he retired. After the vacation, they were moving to Oregon with plans to build a house on an acre Colt and Katie had given to them at McNamee.

"I wish we could," said Colt, "but we have kid retreats booked for the next four weekends. Summer is our busy time. Drink a pint or two of that fine Irish ale for me when you're there."

"I will. So, what's up with our grandchildren?"

"Well, Danny said he's heading to California with Rachel and Lori in a week or so. They want to see New England, and he offered to be their tour guide. He'll be starting his new job at JPL a month from now. Christa leaves in the morning to go back to Corvallis. She's been missing her man. I think it's serious between the two of them."

Pat shook his head. "They're all grown up now. We're getting old, aren't we? It's mindboggling to think that one day, in the not-so-distant future, I could be a great-grandfather."

"I know. I can't imagine being called Grandpa."

"You'll love it, trust me."

That night, Jon David and Colt planned on doing a late-evening swim in their hotel's indoor pool. When Colt knocked on Jon David's room door, he was surprised to see his friend on crutches with his stump exposed. Most of the time, he forgot Jon David even had a disability.

After doing a few laps with just the two of them in the pool, they took a break and stood in the water.

"I'm glad it's just you and me here."

"Me, too, Colt. It's good to spend some one-on-one time with you. Wasn't Danny something today? He was so gracious, ensuring everyone got some of his attention, even though it was his special day. Rachel looked happy, too, which was good to see."

Colt nodded. "I talked to her after the family photo. She told me she's in therapy now. I think Lori's been good for her. Rachel complimented me on being a good father and even mentioned remembering how we loved each other before the accident."

"Hearing that must've warmed your heart."

"It did." Colt turned serious. "Jon David, all of this today was because of you. You saved my family. I can't begin to imagine the darkness I would've faced if not for you. I've wracked my brain for the proper words to express my gratitude to you and Sara, but those words don't exist. I hope you understand what I'm trying to say. From the bottom of my heart, I thank you for all you've done. I'm so honored to call you my friend."

Jon David smiled. "Thanks. And I'm honored to call you my friend as well. Now you know how I feel about Jamie. He was the one who made this possible for you and me." He looked upward. "Thank you, my dear friend."

Colt looked up, too. "Thank you, Jamie. Thank you for all you've done."

EPILOGUE

Many years later ...

CHRISTMAS MORNING ARRIVED AT McNamee. Colt woke before the sun and lingered a while in bed before stirring. For years, he and Katie slept with the window cracked open, even in winter, and they loved snuggling under their down comforter. He turned on his side and gazed at his wife sleeping peacefully with her face bathed in moonlight. After all their years together, he never tired of looking at her. Her winsome shock of red hair had long ago faded, and a wrinkle here and there had staked a claim on her face. He smiled. She was still as beautiful as ever. He mouthed "I love you" to her and slipped out of their warm cocoon. The cool night air nipped at him as he walked to the bathroom, where he put on his bathrobe and slippers and then tiptoed out of their bedroom.

Though the house was dark, he didn't turn on a light. A hand gliding over the hallway wall was all he needed to confirm the route etched into his memory. Quiet as a mouse, Colt exited his home and headed across the dew-laced grass to his writing retreat. As he walked, his exhaled breaths formed clouds in the frosty air.

He glanced at Pat and Annie's former home to see if Jon David and Sara had stirred. No lights were on in their home. Four years ago, they lost Annie to a stroke, and two years later, Pat followed her, eager to be with his true love again in heaven. Jon David and Sara bought their home last year after the harsh winters in Alaska became too much to endure. Having their dear friends so near brought much joy to Colt and Katie.

In the heated gazebo, Colt eased into his well-worn leather desk chair. He and Jon David spent a lot of time here enjoying each other's company—talking, laughing, and reminiscing. Their bond, which began with Danny's healing, had developed into a deep friendship.

As Colt sat in reflective silence, the years of his life paraded before him. When the first rays of sunshine graced the day, he got a pen and paper from the desk drawer and started writing.

Dear God:

Today, we celebrate Christmas with our home filled with love and good cheer. Our children and grandchildren are here. A rarity this is, given how we've scattered to the winds. I thank you for this reunion, and I thank you for your many blessings. I woke this morning filled with gratitude. Meister Eckhart said, "If the only prayer you ever say is 'thank you,' it will be more than enough." I'm writing this letter to say those words to you.

Emerson said, "The years teach what the days will never know." How true his words are. In retrospect, it took all the years of my life to become who I am. Many times in my adulthood, I have looked to the heavens and shook my fist at you, wondering why you had forsaken me. Mine has not been an easy life, but as the years have passed, I now have the wisdom of hindsight. This quote from an unknown author articulates my hard-won wisdom: "Bless this pain, for it will reveal its perfect gift to me at the proper moment."

I see clearly now how the pain in my life spurred me to change and grow, and how the dark times have made the good times so much sweeter. Everything I am, everything I have, and all those whom I hold dear have come to me due to pain. As a young man, I could never have imagined thanking you for my hardships and challenges, but here I am, an old man, thanking you now.

I thank you for those who have graced my life: My wonderful parents, my Army friends, my dog Jekyll, the Brennans, the Moreys, the Lukes, Mike and Ike, and my children and grandchildren. Rachel, and then Katie. Sweet Katie.

Thank you for my wonderful experiences—my mother's love and infectious smile, rafting down the Colorado River with my father, the brotherhood of Rangers, riding the Harley across North America with Jekyll, the joy I felt from writing, playing my flute, and sharing my life with my family and friends.

He stopped writing for a moment and closed his eyes. Years of reflections—both good and bad—flooded his thinking. He took a deep breath and smiled, though his face revealed a hint of melancholy. This was the fabric of his life. He continued writing.

I thank you for healing my son and the spiritual awakening it fostered in me. I thank you for the wisdom you give me when I close my eyes and listen to your voice within me. Living in Spirit fills my days with peace and joy.

I thank you for my children and for living long enough to see them blossom into exceptional human beings walking in your light. My grandchildren melt my heart, and for that, I am profoundly grateful.

I thank you for my wife. After all our years together, Katie still finds new ways to love me with her words, her touch, her deeds, and her soothing smile. Her love is the measure of what is good in my life. I love her so.

I thank you for Jekyll. I have no doubt he was your emissary, healing my wounded heart with his tender, unconditional love. And I will never forget Mike and Ike, who loved the many mistreated children we invited to our home.

I thank you for Jon David ...

He tapped his pen on the desktop while thinking of what to say.

How can I thank you enough for bringing this man into my life? Without him and the courage of his convictions, how different my son's life and my life would've been. I love him. I love Sara. Thank you.

I thank you for the sages whose writings have inspired me on my journey. As I write this, two come to mind: Lao Tzu said, "If I am depressed, I am living in the past. If I am anxious, I am living in the future. If I am at peace, I am living in the present." And in the present moment, in the stillness, I hear your loving words. And how I love the whimsical wisdom of Pema Chödrön: "You are the sky. Everything else—it's just the weather." This passage taught me that no matter how dark or troubling a storm may be, the sky—like Spirit—is still there.

I thank you for the wild places, which are like cathedrals to my soul. In those places, I've learned to knock on the sky and listen to the sound.

I'll close by saying that in the twilight of my life, I feel blessed, I feel happy, I feel loved. For the gift of my life and what you have taught me, I thank you. I love you. Colt

ACKNOWLEDGMENTS

I am indebted to many individuals who enthusiastically gave their time, wisdom, and talents to make this book sparkle and shine. My heartfelt thanks to Kathleen Watson and Wanda Oldham for their superb editing and the people at Damonza for the book's cover design. To my German-born wife, Carmen, thank you for your continued love, patience, and support. Du bist meine größte Liebe (you are my greatest love).

And lastly, special thanks to you, the reader. May the light of God shine always on your path.

ABOUT THE AUTHOR

James Randall Miller was born in Germany and has traveled and lived throughout the world. After thirty years in Alaska, he now lives near the White Tank Mountains in Arizona. Other books by James include *Julius*, an illustrated children's story, and the inspirational novels *Howling Across Bridges, After the Purple Heart, Gus and Billy, Untangling Claire,* and *Because of You.*

Hearing from his readers always delights James. You can reach him at JamesMillerBooks@gmail.com

FINAL THOUGHTS

There is a candle in your heart, ready to be kindled. There is a void in your soul, ready to be filled. You feel it, don't you? — JELALUDDIN RUMI

You have to grow from the inside out. None can teach you, none can make you spiritual. There is no other teacher but your own soul.
— SWAMI VIVEKANANDA

Truth is one; the sages call it by many names. — HINDU SAYING

Prayer is when you talk to God; meditation is when you listen to God.
— DIANA ROBINSON

Find your silence. The answers are there. — JAMES RANDALL MILLER

I wish I could show you when you are lonely or in darkness the astonishing light of your own being. — HAFIZ OF PERSIA

We can experience nothing but the present moment, live in no other second of time, and to understand this is as close as we can get to eternal life.
— P. D. JAMES

Every moment is a fresh beginning. — T. S. ELIOT

There are years that ask questions and years that answer.
— ZORA NEALE HURSTON

When I let go of what I am, I become what I might be. — LAO TZU

If you realized how powerful your thoughts are, you would never think a negative thought. — PEACE PILGRIM

For everything there is a season, and a time for every purpose under heaven:
  a time to be born, and a time to die;
  a time to plant, and a time to pluck up that which is planted;
  a time to kill, and a time to heal;
  a time to break down, and a time to build up;
  a time to weep, and a time to laugh;
  a time to mourn, and a time to dance;
  a time to cast away stones, and a time to gather stones together;
  a time to embrace, and a time to refrain from embracing;
  a time to seek, and a time to lose;
  a time to keep, and a time to cast away;
  a time to tear, and a time to sew;
  a time to keep silence, and a time to speak;
  a time to love, and a time to hate;
  a time for war, and a time for peace.
                          — ECCLESIASTES 3:1-8

We have two lives, and the second begins when we realize we only have one.
                          — CONFUCIUS

Awakening is not changing who you are, but discarding who you are not.
                          — DEEPAK CHOPRA

Speak your heart. If they don't understand, the message was never meant for them anyway. *—* YASMIN MOGAHED

The smallest act of kindness is worth more than the greatest intention.
                          — KAHLIL GIBRAN

As soon as healing takes place, go out and heal somebody else.
                          — MAYA ANGELOU

Goodbye? Oh no, please. Can't we just go back to page one and start all over again? *—* WINNIE THE POOH

www.ingramcontent.com/pod-product-compliance
Lightning Source LLC
Chambersburg PA
CBHW050014180626
46810CB00002B/406